Acknowledgments
I would like to humbly thank David & Heather Doyle,
Brian & Lisa McCabe, Betty Clayton, and a host of other generous
friends without whom this project would not have been possible.
Thank you.

Dedication
To my wife, kids, mom, and
You-Know-Who for You-Know-What.

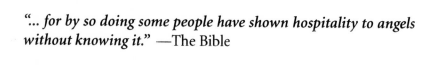

"... for by so doing some people have shown hospitality to angels without knowing it." —The Bible

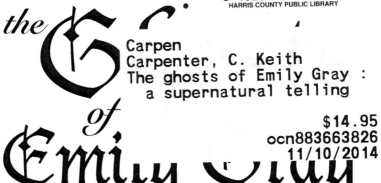

the Ghosts of Emily Gray

A Supernatural Telling

C. KEITH CARPENTER

HOLLOW HORSE PUBLISHING

The Ghosts Of Emily Gray: A Supernatural Telling

For information, address Hollow Horse Publishing, 3217 Rippling Falls Ln., Dickinson, TX 77539.

Book cover and interior design by
C. Keith Carpenter

ISBN: 978-0-615-92022-1

Published by Hollow Horse Publishing

Printed in the U.S.A.

Prelude — The Legacy

VICTORIAN AMERICA WAS A TIME of immense turmoil and destruction. Untold numbers had lost family members to the slaughter of civil war or to the ravages of childhood diseases or both. Some, especially prominent members of society interested in the new religious movement of Spiritualism that migrated from the Midwest, turned to attending or hosting "circles," in which people gathered to receive messages from shades of the departed with the aid of entranced spirit mediums.

One evening in 1863, such a circle was about to begin. The lady of the house had everything prepared in her favorite parlor. The handsome, spacious room contained rich furniture decorated with crimson satin and gold damask. The grand piano stood under a life-size portrait hanging from one of the towering walls clothed in red satin. Ancient vases and other works of antiquity were proudly displayed on the finest furniture handcrafted of carved and finished woods appointed with decorative gilt hardware.

Outside, swirling gusts of wind kicked up dry fallen leaves and rattled windows in nearby streets bare of mortal citizens.

"Where is my husband?" the woman barked. "He is never punctual, and I, for one, find it rude!"

The "hellcat," as some called her behind her back, made sure everyone within earshot knew her feelings. Dressed in the most expensive of plush evening gowns cinched tightly about her not-too-thin waist, she bustled out the door and down the hall, heels angrily clip-clopping on the wood floor. "I swear this man is going to drive me to the insane asylum!"

The steps came to an abrupt stop. Those waiting in the parlor could overhear the conversation echo from a distant chamber. "I am so embarrassed. We are ready to commence, and you have everyone waiting. What is keeping you? Why must you continually exhibit this untoward social behavior? Why?" She frowned up at him, rubbing her temples.

"Molly, please try to contain yourself. I have some important business to which I must attend." He clutched documents and maps in his melanoid, leathery hands. "I'm sure they understand, and I shall attend in a moment, but—"

"Do not tell me to contain myself! You know I have been anticipating this for quite some time. You know of its import to me." Her voice cracked as manipulative tears welled up in her sagging puppy-dog eyes. "Don't you?"

"Dear, yes. I do know what it means to you, but—"

"But what? William was your son, too. Don't you want to speak with him again? Discover how he's doing on the other side?"

"Of course I do, but—"

"And you persistently violating his coffin confirms that the child has indeed succumbed to his woeful affliction?"

"Yes, dear."

"Splendid," she interrupted as her countenance quickly changed to business mode. "Now come with me."

Grabbing his bony rail of an arm, she quickly forced him up the hallway. His papers lay strewn across the floor, awaiting his return. As the couple rounded the corner into the parlor and stepped onto its ornate red carpet, the small crowd, consisting mostly of prominent members of government and their spouses, immediately stood to receive them and respectfully bowed.

Almost in unison, they all greeted the tall, lanky gentleman. "Mr. President."

Lincoln, standing six feet four inches tall and wearing his usual black attire, responded with a bow of his own. "I thank you all for coming." He smiled nervously, fearing they might have heard the cross words spoken in the war room. "I do apologize for my overdue arrival. Please, be seated."

"Now you sit here, Abraham," ordered his wife, her temper now abated, as she led him to his assigned chair. "Tonight," Mary continued while standing behind a woman seated at the round table, "we have the privilege of the estimable Mrs. Cranston Laurie from Georgetown as our deep-trance medium. She is well known and very respected in her field."

The small group responded with light applause.

"Ever since our poor young son, Willie, passed on last year from the fever, the sight of his face, so pale and thin on the satin pillow of his coffin, haunts me. His spirit comes to me almost every night and stands at the foot of my bed with the same sweet, adorable smile he always had. But I now desire to reach beyond the veil and communicate with him; that is why I invited you, and Mrs. Laurie, here tonight. And with that, I direct your undivided attention to the prophetess. Please do exactly as she says."

"Thank you, Mrs. Lincoln." The lady scanned the room. "Before we proceed, I need the lights dimmed, please."

With a directorial nod from the First Lady, the White House maids slowly turned down the lights and lit surrounding candles. A blood-amber ambiance washed The Red Room, as it is called, as deep, dark shadows cast by the flickering candle flames erratically danced among those present.

President Lincoln noticed in a bureau mirror across the room a double reflection of his gaunt face, one paler than the other. The two marbles he had been nervously twirling in his hand stopped orbiting one another. He stared at the unsettling vision with a sallow expression, unsuccessfully seeking answers as to its significance in memorized stories of one of his favorite authors, Edgar Allan Poe.

"I see you've spied your doppelganger in the looking glass, Mr. President, and it troubles your thoughts," said Mrs. Laurie. "Do you know its meaning?"

He sat staring at it with no response, but he had an ominous feeling as to its implication.

"It means, sir, that you shall be fortunate enough to be re-elected to a second term. However, you will not live through it."

Her dark prediction elicited gasps followed by faint murmuring.

After that, with the framed likeness of founding father George Washington looking on from his position above the piano, the Lincolns held their séance. By all accounts it was a success. Mary conversed with her dead son through the entranced Mrs. Laurie and learned that he was happy and content. The information gleaned that night was more than she had dreamed of, and it spawned many more circles in the White House thereafter.

TWELVE YEARS LATER, in the early morning twilight just before sunrise, a black carriage made its way through a town on the outskirts of Chicago, the resonance of hooves clip-clopping down the cobblestone street. Distant rumbling thunder made the horses skittish. After the carriage pulled up to 333 South Jefferson Street, its door slowly creaked open. Two large men waited outside under the an arched sign above the courtyard's entrance: Bellevue Place. They approached the carriage, and one grabbed the horses' reins to steady them. The other methodically yet forcibly extracted from within the plain-clothed woman, who violently kicked and scratched in defiance.

"I am not insane! Do you hear me?" she screamed, her hair a rat's nest from the struggle. "Let go of me! Do you know who I am?"

Ignoring her pleas, they overpowered the insubordinate woman and tried to whisk her inside. Through pure determination fueled with beastlike adrenaline, she stopped the two white-uniformed brutes abducting her in their tracks. She turned to the sullen man still seated in the carriage, peering at her through its window. "Oh, Robert, to think that my son would ever do this to me. I will never forgive you."

On May 20, 1875, Mary Todd Lincoln, widow and former First Lady, was committed to an insane asylum.

SOME WORLDS SHOULD NEVER come into contact. But theirs are colliding—polar forces converging, meshing, head-on in a steady, irreversible impact with life-altering consequences.

Over a century after the widow Lincoln was institutionalized, Erin and Brad lived two lives co-existing yet never connecting—like parallel universes running side by side, each without a clue as to the other's existence…until recently.

THE CEMETERY ON THIS BRISK AUTUMN LATE AFTER-
NOON is uninhabited except for the buried, some ancient oaks,
and a family of three. Toward the back of the property, on the east
side, a frail 13-year-old girl sits on a park bench, seemingly unin-
terested and bored. Intermittently coughing and patting her nose
with tissue, she fidgets, hoping to depart soon. Leaning against the
family car is her 17-year-old sister, Erin, patiently waiting with head
down and hands tucked inside her coat pockets. Kneeling on the
ground, clutching the base of a life-size winged angel statue rigidly
standing watch over a grave is the girls' weeping mother, Rose.

The epitaph:
Emily Gray
Beloved Daughter and Sister
Unjustly Taken Away at Age 16

No birth or death date is inscribed.
 "I hate you, God!" Rose cries out. She hugs even tighter the
cold cement guardian peering down at her with unsympathetic eyes
void of pupils. "I will never forgive you! Never! What right did you
have to take away my baby?"
 She slumps over, crying, moaning, sobbing. Rose has never really buried Emily, not in her heart or mind.
 "I promise you this." She looks up with tears streaming down
her cheeks from bloodshot eyes and clenching a fist defiantly toward heaven. "I will reunite with her. Do you hear me? I will contact
her, someway, somehow. You will not keep me from her! You *cannot*

keep me from her!"

Erin, Emily's surviving identical twin, dislodges herself from the side of the Buick and slowly makes her way toward her mother. The sun is all but gone, and the ambient glow from streetlights above illuminates a fine foggy mist slowly drifting downward. "Mom, we need to go now. The cemetery's closing."

An audience of grackles in trees nearby takes off all at once, as if on cue. The large, dark swarm of several hundred fowl flies in unison past the entrance and toward the town square. As Erin stoops down, grabbing her mom's shoulders, Rose gathers herself and stands. The fresh-cut bouquet provides a warm burst of life-giving color against the dreary backdrop of the cold gray tombstone. Rose slips one of the flowers out and lays it on the grave next to Emily's.

Erin is already on her way back to the car.

Sliding behind the steering wheel of the sedan, Rose checks her rearview mirror to make sure her youngest daughter, Queenie, is there. Erin takes her place up front in the passenger seat.

"All right, girls." Rose dabs her face with tissue. "We're going into town. I have an appointment."

"Aw, can't we just go home?" whines Queenie from the back seat. "I got stuff to do."

"You can tend to your pigs later. Besides, I think you'll be interested in where we're going."

Rose starts the vehicle and puts it in gear. As the car meanders down the winding pebble driveway toward the gated entrance, Erin stares out her window as small rocks crackle and pop beneath the tires. All is deathly quiet inside, though, with no radio or talking. Reflections of tombstones and trees scroll across the window. Mrs. Gray lights up a cigarette.

Passing through the oldest part of the graveyard, Erin fixes her eyes on the rusted wrought-iron fences around some of the graves. They are not high enough to really keep anyone from hopping over. So why the short fences topped by pointy, spear-like spindles? They seem to her more like symbolic jails erected in a feeble attempt to keep unseen entities from escaping.

Erin's phone buzzes with a new text message: *Practice over. Tomorrow's the big day. I'm a little nervous, but ready to get it over with.—Brad.* She flips the phone shut and closes her eyes, wondering if *she* is ready.

Twenty minutes later they pull into a parking space in front of a storefront window with PSYCHIC boldly painted across. Underneath the arched title is an open-palmed hand with an eye smack-dab in the middle and Madame Zelda! proudly scribed below. Next to the door is listed Books, Charms & Novelties. The shop is sandwiched between a liquor store and tattoo parlor.

"Really, mom?" asks Erin. "You have an appointment with *her?*"

"Yes I do, as a matter of fact." Rose rummages through her large, deep purse. "And besides, I would think that *you*, of all people, would approve of such…practices."

Erin rolls her eyes and sighs. The threesome gets out and enters the store, with the elder daughter reluctantly strolling in last. The girl looks as if she would be comfortably at home in such an establishment. She is dressed in all black, but unlike her mother, who is darkly outfitted only to express her mourning, Erin is what some of the townspeople have come to understand as Goth.

Over the past year Erin has toned down her look, but is still unmistakably Gothic, especially with her dyed jet-black hair, dark eyeliner, and aniline wardrobe. But the extremely pale makeup, death-obsessed fashion, and body piercings have been laid to rest.

Their entrance into the occult bookstore is announced by the clanking of zodiac-shaped wind chimes and a couple of small cowbells hanging from the top of the glass door. After a frozen false start, the gray shop cat darts behind a counter just slow enough for its tail to be spotted disappearing.

"Just a minnnnnnute," sings out a response from the back room. "I'll be right therrrrrrre."

The dimly lit and earth-tone colored establishment is contrasted by the many vibrant fragrances of past burnt incense and candles. The one currently smoldering is either vanilla or tonka bean. Walls painted with a deep golden parchment texture are overlaid with large, black, Olde English and Latin phrases of magick. Thick, floor-length, blood-red velvet curtains hang from the ceiling at each end of the large storefront window. In the back on an accent wall, a large painted portrait of Aleister Crowley ominously stares down with his piercing eyes at any who dare enter. Lit candles in strategic areas enhance the mysticism.

In other words, the interior designer did a splendid job.

Emerging from the back room through hanging doorway beads is the store's proprietor and self-described psychic extraordinaire. She is a short pudgy woman proudly standing five feet tall with cropped curly blonde hair and sporting the latest in seventies chic women's hippie muumuu fashion. Today it looks as if she has succeeded in hanging more hardware around her neck than on the front door. In her arms she carries her baby, Aleister, a two-foot-long orange male iguana.

"Rose Gray?" She extends her right hand while struggling to hold up Aleister with the other.

"Yes. Um…does that thing bite?" Rose fails to return the offer of a handshake.

"Aleister? Oh no, he's a pussycat." She places the miniature dragon on her counter. "But our precious feline, who must be hiding around here somewhere, will. So it's best you leave her alone." Then Zelda whispers loudly, so as not to hurt the cat's feelings, "Ashen's old and cranky."

Aleister spots the cat below and hisses at her. Ashen responds with a crouching escape into the back room.

"Well, Miss Zelda, I hope I'm not too late."

"Oh no, you're right on time, Mrs. Gray." Then Erin catches her eye. "Hey there, aren't you…Yes, you're that young lady who used to come in here with Lucus. You look a little different now, though. A bit…plain. Well, I have plenty of makeup and fashion items if you need some. They're on sale."

Erin, standing defiantly with arms crossed, does not respond, but thinks, *If only you knew how much of the overpriced cheaply-made imported junk I swiped from you when your back was turned.*

"Oh," Madame Zelda continues, "would you tell Lucus the books he ordered are in? That would save me a phone call. Thanks, sweetheart. Help yourself to a mint." She gestures toward the counter, where Aleister is already rooting around in the crystal bowl full of breath-freshening confectionaries.

As Erin turns to leave, Queenie is already perusing the book aisles. She has never been in this store, and not quite sure what she is looking for, but will know when she finds it.

Madame Zelda escorts Rose into the back room, where the first sitting is to take place.

Erin walks back to the car, her mind preoccupied with myriad concerns. Madame Zelda is at best an inept medium who doesn't quite know what she's doing. Erin has both sat in with Zelda and also taken part in rituals with real practitioners who produced tangible results. One thing is for sure, though; Madame Zelda is quite the showman and salesperson.

Erin opens the car door and sits inside, eyes closed, thoughts turning to her relationship with Brad. Tomorrow is the "big day" in which their romantic bond will be made public at school. They would have waited longer had that photo of them together at the movies not been shared all over the Internet, forcing them into the open.

Tomorrow's big reveal comes on the heels of last night, when they both walked into the student center of Brad's church for Wednesday night Bible study. They did not drive there together. She met him in the parking lot. And they did not hold hands, so their status as a couple remained somewhat ambiguous. Although the youth pastor was warm and welcoming, the students were distant. In all honesty, she knew it would have been a fairy tale for those kids to accept her unconditionally, like Brad has.

Were they just too shocked to see her, a "bad" girl, with the town's popular sports hero, a straight-laced Christian? Or was it the likes of her walking into a church at all that seemed too incredible? Nevertheless, if those who are supposed to be accepting and loving reacted that way, how will those in the real world respond? It is a consistent, troubling thought for her.

The music by the mediocre student band didn't seem all that great, so Erin wasn't sure why some of the other kids were so into it. She and Brad had parked themselves on the back row of chairs. Although Erin does not see herself going back there, one thing sticks with her: the biblical text from which Mike, the student minister, taught.

Jesus encountered a man possessed by many demons, who

called themselves Legion. The deranged man mutilated himself and had superhuman strength no mortal could bind, even with chains. Yet the Son of God spoke, and immediately the evil spirits departed and entered a herd of swine that charged down into the sea and violently drowned. She is fascinated that a man, that Jesus, could wield so much power with just his words. As far as she's concerned, the pigs got what they deserved because she is, for good reason, fearful of the creatures.

Lost in the lesson, she forgot about those around her. For once she was not socially uncomfortable around "normal" people. Captivated, Erin hung on every word. Mike was eloquent and obviously had a passion for teaching. It was almost enough to make her want to crack open a Bible on her own. Almost.

Brad? He is the exact opposite. She knows he has a lot of Bible knowledge. He has probably read that old book from cover to cover. Unlike her, he grew up in a home where that is encouraged. However, Brad never really talks to her about spiritual matters. Sure, they discuss important and deeply personal issues, but topics like heaven and hell or Jesus' resurrection never seem to materialize.

But that's okay with Erin. She is happy to just be with him and does not want any conflict to jeopardize their relationship. He really seems to accept her for who she is, which is a miracle since he knows all about her. Well, he knows *a lot* about her, but he does not really know *everything*. What will happen when he finds out all she has done? Will he leave? Will he look at her the way the kids did at the church? These haunting questions keep running through her mind.

A large chorus of birds, harshly calling outside the car, snap her out of her thoughts. The grackles from the cemetery. The flock is numerous and loud. Ever since their town became an official bird sanctuary, the fowl population in the area has risen to incredibly annoying proportions.

Erin pulls her knees in and hugs herself for warmth as the temperature drops, producing foggy bursts from her mouth with every exhale. Her mind drifts back to Brad, how happy and complete he makes her feel, yet how unsure she is that they can stay together. The thought of losing him burdens her heart.

Leaning toward the window, she blows her steamy breath, fogging the glass, and draws a face. First a large circle, then two dots for eyes. As she starts to draw the mouth, she pauses with her finger still on the glass. How should she make it? A smile? A worried squiggle? A sad look? She cannot decide.

A jingling at the shop door alerts Erin that her mom and sister are headed for the car.

"Goodbye, Mrs. Gray. See you tomorrow night," belts Madame Zelda.

Erin erases the expressionless face from the window with a single swipe of her sleeve. Both driver's side doors open, and in plops Mom with an earth-friendly canvas bag of paraphernalia and Queenie with a voluminous book.

"So, how'd it go?" Erin asks.

"Pretty good. No contact, but Madame Zelda said she got some good vibes. She says we need to hold a séance at our house, preferably in Emily's room."

"I see she sold you plenty of stuff." Erin rummages through the tote between them.

"Yeah, it wasn't cheap, but a good investment."

Erin sighs.

Thirty minutes later, after detouring through a fast-food drive-thru, they pull onto the long dirt driveway of their two-story farmhouse, which sits toward the back of the premises next to a tree line. Nestled on a few acres of land, it is out in the middle of nowhere down a rarely used stretch of farm road.

Queenie, book in hand, bolts out the door and around the back of the house toward the barn. Erin and her mom are greeted on the front porch by Emily's dog, Shep. A gentle, loving dog, he clutches a pair of leather work gloves in his mouth. Shep is part husky and part border collie with the most exotic ice-blue eyes you have ever seen. They almost appear to be lit up from the inside. He had worked on a farm until a bull's kick to his pelvis ended Shep's herding career. Emily had adopted him from those who would otherwise have had him euthanized. She paid his medical expenses and nursed him back to health. He couldn't run anymore and walked with a limp, but he made a fine, loyal companion. He and Emily had been best friends.

"I'm going to set things up in Emily's room." Rose ascends the creaky wooden staircase. "I can't wait for tomorrow night."

"Good night, Mom." Erin knows her mother won't come out until morning, because she has taken up the habit of sleeping in Emily's bed in hopes of feeling her presence, or better yet, catching a glimpse of her spirit.

After grabbing a glass of milk from the kitchen, Erin goes upstairs and makes her way past Emily's and Queenie's rooms, past her own, to the very end of the hallway. She approaches quietly, puts her ear up to the closed door, and taps lightly. A chilled draft slips underneath from the other side and streams past her feet. She looks down. No light beaming through.

"Dad?" she asks in a hushed tone.

"Yes, Erin. I'm here."

"How are you feeling?"

"Oh"—he coughs—"about the same. I still don't feel well enough to get out of bed. How was your visit to Emily's resting place?"

"It was nice, I suppose." Erin leans her head against the hard wooden door and rests her hand on its cold antique brass handle.

"Sorry I couldn't make it, but I was there in spirit. I sure miss her."

"I do too, Daddy. Is there anything I can get you?"

"I don't think so. Are you going to bed now?"

"Yeah, today's been a bit draining, and I'm pretty tired."

"Okay darlin', sweet dreams. I love you."

"I love you, too."

HIGH SCHOOL CAFETERIAS ARE PRIME LOCATIONS to suffer sensory overload, unless you are one of the hyperactive teenagers contributing to the mayhem. Throngs of kids packed into a single room finally get their chance to let off pent-up energy. There are no rules governing chatter here, like in classrooms or libraries where one might find oneself on the receiving end of a "Shush!" administered by an overly strict adult—and the students take full advantage of this freedom while inhaling large quantities of salty and sugary food products.

The usual topic of conversation: gossip.

The occasional dropped food tray elicits outbursts of applause, cheers, and jeers. One can go crazy trying to filter out all the noise bouncing off the painted cinderblock walls and cement floor.

Except for today.

Erin and Brad are seated together, alone, on an outer aisle. Holding hands underneath the table, they endure the other students murmuring and staring wide-eyed in disbelief. The girls at the cheerleader table have not closed their gaping mouths since the school's newest couple strolled in together, hand-in-hand, about ten minutes ago, that weirdo Goth girl wearing the star quarterback's prized letterman jacket. Erin and Brad make small talk while he eats his lunch. She has no appetite, and has yet to look up.

"Wow, you would think they're all staring at a couple of ghosts." Brad cuts into his burrito and glances around.

"Well, you can't really blame them, can you? I mean, look at us. We are very, VERY different from one another."

"They do say that opposites attract," Brad replies lightheartedly.

Erin does not reciprocate with a smile.

"But seriously, other than in appearance, I don't think we're all that different. Otherwise, how could we hang out and talk for hours like we do?"

"Brad, we come from two totally different families. Yours is upper-middle-class; mine is from the other side of the tracks, the scraps of society. You're a Christian; I'm a...well...I'm not quite sure what I am, but definitely not a Christian. You're the most popular person on campus; I'm one of the outcasts. I can definitely see how our little 'shock and awe' campaign here today would cause such a reaction. I was expecting it."

"Erin, you know we're both independent thinkers; that's one of the things I like about you. Even though I'm so-called 'popular,' I've never followed the crowd. I may be well known, but I don't care about that. I really don't concern myself with what they think. I don't have many friends; just a couple of close ones. And I've never dated seriously, until now."

Brad is mature beyond his years because of a strong family upbringing. His words are few and well thought out. He knows that being a Christian means being different from prevalent society; that it means striving for righteousness and practicing self-denial.

Not that he's perfect. Personal Bible study and quiet time with God have taken a back seat to academics and athletics. Too much time is required to maintain his straight-A average, and if he is going to play college ball—and some scouts have already been looking at him—he needs to take full advantage of extra time for practice and conditioning.

Throwing Erin into this mix further taxes his schedule.

As for relationships with the opposite sex, advice from his father has guided him through the maze of his teen years: *Brad, son, let me tell you this from experience. The best memories you will have at this point in your life will be with your closest friends. The worst memories will be with so-called girlfriends. My advice is to wait until after high school, or maybe even after college, to date seriously.*

Then along came Erin with those eyes, those green eyes, and all that was blown out of the water with the force of a thermonuclear bomb. But she is worth it. No, the girl is not a Christian, but she is real, not like all the other awestruck girls continually swooning over him. He knows with them it is just superficial attraction, that they don't really know him.

However, when Erin speaks to him he knows it is genuine and not empty flattery or attempted manipulation. Even now, in the wake of today's revelation, each cheerleader is strategizing how to tear apart Brad's new relationship. But Erin is reflecting on Brad's opinion of her. He has conveyed all of this before. And whatever she has told him about her *has* been the truth. She just has not revealed *all* the ugly details of her past life—not yet.

"That still doesn't make you an outcast like me," she says.

"I am now, thanks to you." He lightly bumps her shoulder with his.

She finally grins but still does not look up.

The noise level has almost returned to its normal volume, with everyone conversing as usual. That is, except for the cheerleaders who are still stunned at what is before them. The squad had a running bet as to which of them would first snag the school's most eligible bachelor (and his letterman jacket). The shell-shocked group scurries in tandem toward the bathroom to console one another in private. As they exit through the double doors of the cafeteria, they pass someone forcefully entering.

The tall, ominous figure, wearing all black, walks in with his small gang of followers close behind. It is Lucus. As students notice his presence, the cafeteria steadily comes to a complete silence once again. They all return their attention to the new couple.

Erin squeezes Brad's hand tighter. "He's here, isn't he?" Without having to look up, she knows full well the answer.

"Who, Lucus? Yeah, he's here. So what? You have nothing to be afraid of."

Erin does not share Brad's naïve confidence.

Lucus dresses to intimidate and gets away with it at school, partly because he never overtly causes any trouble and makes decent grades. He is polite to faculty and staff, quiet until addressed first. He flies under the radar. More importantly, his father, who owns several car dealerships in the area (as well as other anonymous business interests), is a big-time school contributor with hefty donations, especially to the sports programs. Lucus lacks for no material possessions, another draw for those who associate with him. He is generous with others, but not out of the kindness of his heart; favors are expected in return.

However, he was not always the confident foreboding presence he is today. Attending a Marilyn Manson concert during junior high changed his life. He became "born again," so to speak. One might even say that is who he's trying to emulate. In fact, that is what those who are not intimidated by him, mostly the upper-class jocks, call him irreverently.

Before then he had been a total nerd. With absolutely no coordination, he could not make any of the sports teams. He tried out for every one, but each attempt resulted in humiliating failure. His lack of social skills, scrawny frame, and buckteeth made him a prime target for bullying. Throughout his sophomore year in high school, Lucus was still getting harassed on a semiregular basis. But he did not fail to make mental notes on a checklist he called *the account*.

The summer before eleventh grade, Lucus's body shot up to nearly six feet tall, while his voice lowered to a deep bass tone. The first day of that new school year was the beginning of the rest of his life. He then got attention for all the right reasons: tall, cool, mysterious, and a bad reputation. Even the girls, some of them anyway, had started to flirt and vie for his attention. Lucus was no longer the weak pushover, but an intimidator who was not afraid to stand up for himself anymore.

Though he rarely showed it on the outside, he was full of boiling rage on the inside, and this rage fueled the quest for power he pursued by delving into the dark arts. One day he would have his revenge. One day they would respect and fear him. He was making plans and forging alliances with demonic forces that would eventually do his bidding. And there would be no remorse for whoever had crossed or betrayed him.

He is also Erin's ex-boyfriend.

Lucus stands in the cafeteria with fists clenched by his side, scanning the room. Students anxiously wait, anticipating what will happen next. Then he spots them, Erin and Brad, together. So the rumor is true. It is embarrassing. Humiliating. Lucus breathes even deeper and more rapidly through his flaring nostrils. Heart racing. Adrenalin pumping. The angry, jilted lover peers at Brad, his hands squeezing tighter. Brad stares back in what appears to be a contest of wills. Erin still has not looked up.

"What are you staring at, Marilyn?" comes a challenging voice from Lucus's side. It is John, better known as "Big John," Brad's best friend, the team's fullback and strongside linebacker. Lucus has three inches on him in height, but John packs about fifty pounds more of solid muscle. The faint outline of a cross pendant dangling from a gold necklace is seen underneath his tight-fitting T-shirt.

Big John, chest bowed out, positions himself in front of Lucus. "You got a problem, freak?"

Lucus looks around; everyone is staring. No, he's not going to back down. Instinctively, his hand clutches his umbrella tighter and pulls it up a little, preparing for what may happen next. John, noticing the move, smirks.

"What, you think that thing could do any damage? You can't be serious."

The towering figure peers down at his enemy with an expression of confidence, itching to show him and everyone else just exactly what he is capable of. Out of the corner of his eye he catches a teacher approaching quickly in hopes of averting a physical altercation. Knowing there's a time and place for everything, he leans down uncomfortably close to John's face. "Be careful tonight on the football field," he warns. "Don't underestimate your rival, no matter how nonthreatening he may appear to be."

"What?!" John asks, confused and irritated. "What is that supposed to mean?"

Lucus stares a moment longer to show he's not afraid, that *he's* in control, then slowly turns and leaves.

Freak, John thinks. He turns to Brad across the room and gives him a *Do-you-now-see-what-you've-gotten-yourself-into?* look. Ever since Brad started spending time with Erin, his friendship with John, who does not approve, has been strained. John is the only person who knew about Brad and Erin's relationship before today. Brad had confided in him, knowing his best friend would keep their secret. But as best friends should, John frankly let him know he didn't like her and warned that she was bad news.

"I feel sick to my stomach. I need to leave," Erin says.

"But you haven't eaten anything."

"Please, can we just get out of here?"

"Okay, sure."

They get up and walk toward the exit. All is still deathly quiet, except for their footsteps, which to Erin sound like cannons booming with each step on the tile floor. Finally, after what seems an eternity, the couple is out. As soon as they depart through the doors, everyone grabs their cell phones and starts rapidly texting to the other half of the school, who is currently in class, about what just went down.

The pep squad returns to the cafeteria, which is all abuzz with fingers tapping furiously and mouths jabbering in frenzied excitement. One of the puzzled cheerleaders looks around and asks, "Like, did we miss something?"

OUTSIDE, SPORADIC FLUFFY CLOUDS LAZILY DRIFT along unseen pathways in the wide-open expanse of blue sky above. Erin and Brad have found a semiprivate area around the side of the school building so they can be alone for what is left of their lunch break.

Erin releases a long, deep breath. "It's good to be out of there." She and Brad embrace while he leans his back against the wall, her head resting on his chest.

His heartbeat is strong. Consistent. Predictable. Assuring.

After a long silence savoring their precious solitude, Brad makes a prediction. "By Monday this won't be a big deal to anyone anymore."

"I hope so," she responds, eyes closed, enjoying the breeze kissing her face. The bell will ring any moment, and Erin wants to hold onto every precious second with him. She squeezes his waist a little tighter. It is nice to be alone.

Two giggling freshmen girls pop around the corner, and one snaps a photo of them with her cell phone. Brad notices but says nothing. As quickly as the girls had arrived, they vanish with their digital memento.

The fragrance of Erin's hair is wonderful, intoxicating. Constant humming of car tires from the busy, not-too-distant highway has a soothing, hypnotic effect. It's almost time to go. The moment is quiet and peaceful. Brad slowly brings his hands up, caressing her back, toward her shoulders.

Erin's eyes pop open. "What are you doing?" She screeches, breaking his embrace, retreating quickly.

"I'm sorry! I'm, sorry! I totally forgot!" He raises his hands.

"I told you to never touch me there!" Erin hugs herself, cringing.

She cannot stand contact with the area around her shoulder blades, especially from him. Lower back, arms, holding hands are all acceptable, but not up there—ever.

Brad does not know why but has always complied, until now. "I'm so sorry. It was careless of me. I wasn't thinking."

She stands there with eyes tightly shut, trying to regain her composure. After a deep breath she looks at him. "I know you didn't mean to." She approaches and hugs her remorseful boyfriend. "I know you don't understand. Thank you for putting up with my…weirdness."

Brad holds his hands out just beyond Erin's shoulders, afraid of touching her. "You're…you're trembling."

Rrrrrrriiiiiiiing!

"Oh, there's the bell. Time for History," she laments.

"Are you going to be okay, Erin?"

"Yeah, I'm fine. I'm over it."

"You sure?"

"Yes. I'm okay." She removes his jacket.

"Wh—what are you doing?" Brad asks nervously.

"You're going to need this for the pep rally this afternoon. We can't have you going in there without your 'colors.' Everyone would freak."

"No, I don't need it. I want you to wear it."

"It doesn't mean I'm breaking up with you, silly." She smiles. "Look, I'll get it back when you come over tomorrow. You are still planning on coming, aren't you?"

"Oh, yeah. And I'm bringing us lunch."

"Well, good luck tonight. You guys gonna win?"

"We should, easily. They've only won half their games, and none in district. You think you'll ever make it to a game? Next week's is the last one of the season before playoffs."

"I'm not sure. It's a bit violent for my taste."

"I understand. Well, we better get going."

"Mm, you sure do look good in this jacket," she confesses while grasping the opening with both hands.

Brad smiles, staring into her emerald eyes. "Well...I gotta go this way." He nods to the right.

"History class is this way." Erin nods in the opposite direction.

Walking away, Erin hears, "Hey!" As she spins around, Brad's jacket comes flying at her, and she instinctively catches it.

"Oops," he says sarcastically. "You wouldn't want them to think they got to us, would you?"

Knowing what he means, and agreeing he is right, she slips it on once again.

The two part ways. They won't see each other again today, except for briefly passing in the hallways on the way to other classes. Immediately after school, Brad will head for the field house to prepare for tonight's matchup. Later the team will board a bus for the opponent's stadium about an hour away.

Erin could go to the pep rally, but she won't. There were already enough eyes stabbing at her during lunch. And with the entire student body in the gym this afternoon, the potential for judgmental gawking is far too great. Besides, she is afraid that the negative attention might cause a distraction for Brad. She attends the rest of her classes, then hangs in the library during assembly.

SCHOOL IS OUT. This emotionally draining day is finally over. Erin cannot wait to go spend the evening at home vegging and keeping herself superficially occupied until Brad visits tomorrow. Like a rabbit escaping the death grip of a boa constrictor, she bolts from the school grounds. Reflecting on the day's events, she drives out of the parking lot when an incoming text surprises her.

i need to see you—Luc

It was only a matter of time, but this was way sooner than she expected—Lucus is typically more calculating.

She replies, *no*, hanging a left onto the highway, steering with one hand.

cmon you owe it to me baby

I owe you nothing and I am NOT your baby

She's not paying attention to the road. Her car drifts onto the shoulder. She corrects.

PLEASE

Please? Please? Was this *the* Lucus actually using the word *please*? This concept was *not* in his thinking; the "most fit" never succumbs to groveling. Or did someone steal his phone to play some sick practical joke? Most likely, though, it is his attempt at manipulating her…again.

no way stop texting me

i have something u want

what on earth could u hav that I would want

His reply shocks her.

Em's necklace

Erin pauses. Can he really have it? Or is it another one of his lies? When authorities found her mangled body, Emily's cross neck-lace was unaccounted for. While walking this planet, she was always seen with the large sterling silver pendant dangling from her neck. It had never been located and was presumed lost in the brush some-where between the location of the impact and where her remains were found.

how did u get it?

that nite before the accident she gave it to me

theres no way she would hav just given it to u

do u want it or not?

He knew she did.

Erin does not know what to believe. It would not be beneath Lucus to lie about the whole thing just for a chance to meet up with her. But for what reason? Would he try to kidnap her? Attack her? *Kill* her? All these scenarios race through her mind; none of them out of the realm of possibility as far as she is concerned. But it is plausible that he indeed does have the necklace, and she would love to get it. She *needs* to get it. It was the last thing Emily was wearing while alive that is probably not blood-soaked or ripped apart from being dragged across the asphalt for over a hundred feet.

how do I know I can trust u?

what do u mean?

u know what i mean

ok lets meet in public

where?

in front of the shop in 20 min

She knows he means Madame Zelda's; it was "their place" back in the day. Meeting Lucus alone terrifies her. On the other hand, though, it will be in public, and in broad daylight. But this still doesn't mean any guarantees.

Lucus texts again: *it will be the last time i ask u to meet me i promise*

In her experience, Lucus's word was as good as a guarantee from a slick-haired used car salesman with a comb-over, or worse yet, a politician sporting a thick luscious mane. She also knows he will keep hounding her and hounding her nonstop. Almost every-thing inside tells the girl to decline the jeopardous liaison, but if there is a chance the necklace is in his possession, and if there is a possibility that afterwards he will be out of her and Brad's lives, she will chance it.

ok ill be there but u only got 5 min then im gone

perfect see you there, Lucus replies.

Fifteen minutes later, Erin pulls up in front of Madame Zelda's. Through her storefront glass, the pseudopsychic is seen busily rearranging products inside her shop to help boost sales. Aleister again is trapped on the countertop looking for a way to get down, while a curled-up Ashen peacefully naps in a corner.

With half the community already en route to the away football game, downtown is somewhat of a ghost town, and Lucus knows it. Too nervous to sit, and wanting to just get this over with, Erin gets out of her car and briskly paces the sidewalk. Brad's large jacket wrapped around her body gives the anxious girl a sense of security. Five minutes pass and no Lucus. Another ten minutes go by, and she's still alone—except for Ashen who has awakened and inquisitively stares up at her.

Finally, after a few more ticks of the clock, his black BMW pulls into a parking space with booming yet muffled industrial-style music thumping inside. After the car shuts off, its rhythmic noise dies and the driver-side door opens. A leather umbrella emerges and the canopy pops open with a fwoomp. Lucus exits; he is alone and snacking on chocolate-covered raisins.

Lucus is an intimidating figure, standing well over six feet tall with long, straight ebony hair. As the undisputed leader of the subculture outcasts at school, he has two distinctive trademarks: his custom-made umbrella, or parasol (he doesn't care what people call it), and his stingray boots.

The oversized black umbrella is crafted from leather with a stitched spider-web pattern, and the image of a black widow wrapping its prey is embroidered near the edge, which Lucus likes to make sure is facing anyone he's talking to. Its handle, adorned with a menacing skull, minus the lower jawbone, is carved out of illegally acquired African ivory, supposedly crafted by a witch doctor in Haiti who presided over numerous human sacrifices. A medical release for his epidermal condition allows Lucus to carry it on school campus, claiming that his extremely pale, unnatural-looking skin tone is the result of a rare genetic condition, and the parasol is needed to protect it from sunlight.

He is not an albino with light eyes, but rather, has cold, soulless piercing dark ones lurking behind opaque sunglasses. All of his shirts are long sleeved, again to help with UV protection, it is claimed. In public he never has any skin showing except his face. Even his hands are always covered in tight-fitting leather gloves.

His boots are fashioned out of stingray leather. They have a unique texture: small bumps with a semi-gloss sheen. The most noticeable characteristic is the vertically elongated white diamond shapes, one on each foot, centered above the toes. They are reminiscent of the pupils on a viper that is poised to instantly, and without mercy, strike at any moment.

Body piercings round out the look that is Lucus. A deep, powerful voice echoes from his diaphragm when he chooses to speak. His appetites for sugar and power are unquenchable. He approaches. Ashen scurries back into hiding somewhere in the back of the shop. Erin finds herself in the shadow of his umbrella, which eclipses the slanting afternoon sunlight.

"Hello, my sweet."

"You're late," she scolds. Though she puts up a front of bravery, her heart is pounding with fear.

"I had a matter of urgent business that needed my…motivation. What, no proper greeting?" Lucus asks holding out his hands knowing there's not a chance in hell that she will embrace him.

Two figures hide in the shadows of an alleyway across the street, watching events unfold.

"Hold still, you're shaking too much!" barks one in a hushed tone.

"Stop yanking on my shoulder trying to see, and I might be able to!" retorts the other.

"Where is it?" Erin demands.

Lucus ignores the question. "How are you holding up? Today must have been hard on you."

"If I don't see it right now, I'm outta here." She knows he does not care how she is doing emotionally. He's just trying to finesse her.

Lucus sighs and pops another sugary treat past his black lips as Erin resolutely stares at her own reflection in his dark sunglasses, pretending she can actually see his eyes. He slowly lifts it out of his trench coat pocket.

That's it! He actually has Emily's cross pendant. She makes a grab. Lucus jerks it away.

"Eh, eh, eh…" Lucus taunts. "Can't you say *please*?"

"Look, that does not belong to you. She—"

"She gave it to *me*, that night, *not* you."

"Listen, I am not going to stand here all evening and play games; *your* games."

"I don't want to play games, Rin. I just want to spend some time with you. I miss you so much."

"Please, don't patronize me. Exactly why are you doing this?"

After a short hesitation and deep breath, Lucus's demeanor changes. He now seems vulnerable, fragile.

"I'm…" his voice cracks a little. "I'm just afraid that as soon as this is in your hands you'll be out of my life…forever."

Erin stands there stunned. This is new territory, bizarre territory. Though trying, she is unable to wrap her mind around his last statement.

"There's now a void in my soul. I know it sounds ridiculous coming from me, but it's true. When I saw you two today it was the lowest point in my life. You have to believe me."

A small pause gives Erin a chance to try gathering her thoughts, which is impossible at the moment. Lucus just stands there silently peering down at her. She slowly raises her hand and lifts his sunglasses. A tear crawls down his gaunt face, another first for Lucus (as long as Erin has known him, anyway). Sad, bloodshot eyes stare back down at her.

"What are you on right now?" Erin pulls her hand away, letting his shades drop down. "This is not like you." She steps back with arms crossed.

"I'm clean," he answers. "I swear. A lot has changed with me over the last year. Why can't you believe me?"

Because I know you, she thinks. But this is a side of him she has never seen a hint of before, or even thought possible. She keeps studying his face, trying to read him.

"Look," he continues, "I know we can never go back to the way things were. And I've come to the realization that you're with Brad Ross now, as much as it pains me to admit it. But I just can't go on knowing how you feel about me. I need you to forgive me, Erin."

His deep, steady voice has a way of penetrating the soul, especially hers.

Forgiveness? First *please* and now *forgiveness*? It is starting to gradually sink in now. Something must have really changed within him, especially judging by the look in his eyes. Was it some sort of religious conversion? Or psychotherapy? An alien encounter of the third kind, perhaps? But it doesn't matter enough for her to inquire about now. She's having a hard enough time wrestling with the concept of granting forgiveness, especially to Lucus.

They had been through a lot together, and he hurt her deeply. Supposedly forgiveness is what God wants, but it is so hard. Why forgiveness? It's just not how the world operates. She sighs and decides to reluctantly grant it, at least outwardly, if only just barely on the inside. And it should put to rest her relationship with Lucus so she and Brad can get on with their lives together.

"Okay."

"Okay? Really?"

"Yes, really."

"Oh Erin, what a heavy burden you've lifted off my shoulders. Thank you." Lucus extends his arms again, open umbrella in one hand and necklace in the other, indicating one last goodbye hug is needed. "I'll be leaving now. Thank you again *so* much."

Erin cautiously approaches and wraps her arms around Lucus's waist. His hands come up her back and over Brad's name stitched across the upper part of the jacket. Erin winces but does not let on that she feels vulnerable in that area. As they embrace, the umbrella slowly tips over, blocking surveillance from across the street. The two hiding over there are perplexed.

"What's he doing? Now we can't see anything."

"It doesn't matter, keep steady."

After a few moments Erin lets go so she can leave, but Lucus does not reciprocate. She places her hand on his back and pats a couple of times, indicating that the hug is over. Lucus continues clinging to her.

"What are you doing?" Erin asks.

No response. She attempts to push him off with all her might, but he is too strong.

"Let go of me." Panic starts to set in.

Lucus squeezes tighter. His mouth next to her ear, she can vividly hear his accelerated deep breathing and feel each balmy exhale cling down her neck. His cold facial piercings burrow into her flesh.

"I said let go!" She struggles but cannot free herself.

He repositions himself to forcibly press his lips against her mouth, but this weakens his grip and, with a well-placed knee to his inner thigh and one last shove, the victim frees herself just as a large delivery truck passes by. The two separate and his umbrella goes vertical again. During the struggle Lucus's sunglasses had fallen to the ground, revealing the rage and hatred in his eyes.

"What was that?" She caresses the side of her head where his facial hardware left painful indentions in her soft skin.

"I *hate* you," he growls deeply. "How *could* you?"

"How could I *what?*" Perplexed, she continues massaging the pain away.

"How could you hook up with that!" He points at Brad's jacket. "I mean, who do you think you are, now?"

"I should have known better," she responds. "Why did I let myself—"

Lucus grabs the white sleeve of her jacket. "I suppose you're going to join the cheerleading squad now? Change your name to…*Brittany?*"

"You have no idea who I am, Lucus! You never did!" Erin yanks her arm from his grip.

"Oh, *don't* I," he responds. "I know *this* isn't you! Church-boy's jacket won't cover your past sins—disguise who you really are. Have you told Brad *everything?*"

Erin just glares at him.

"Have you?!"

She still does not answer.

"So, you haven't, eh? Well, it appears I know more about you than your new boyfriend does. Well, I can fix that!"

"You don't miss me. You've just got a bruised ego. You know, I believed you just now." Anger fuels her newfound courage. "When you just said you were hurt and needed my forgiveness, I really accepted it. You wanna know why? Because I believed your *eyes*. They say the eyes are the windows to the soul, Lucus. Well, I've looked inside and now I see you have no soul. You were a liar from the beginning, and you are a liar now!"

"*You* are the liar!" Lucus points at her with the hand gripping Emily's necklace. The dangling cross erratically dances with every violent jerk of his arm. "*You're* the one trying to pretend you're something you're not! *You're* the one keeping secrets! Tell Brad! Tell him all about yourself, about us. Confess *all* your sins, then see if he sticks with you!"

She stands still, breathing heavily, not knowing how to respond.

"I may be a liar," Lucus continues, "but you're more. Oh *so* much more! You are not only a liar, you *are* the *lie*! Tell Brad! Tell him everything or I will, you hypocrite!"

Impulsively, Erin snatches the necklace out of his hand and quickly jumps into her car and locks it. After nervously fumbling the keys then starting up, she backs out and speeds away while Lucus keeps yelling, "*You* are the lie! *You* are the lie! I *hate* you! Do you hear me? I *hate* you!" He stands there fuming and watches her disappear around the corner with a small screech.

After a few moments he stares across the street and motions with an index finger across his neck like a knife slitting his throat. The emotionally charged Lucus is still hyperventilating when a *tap-tap-tap* comes from behind. Madame Zelda is knocking on the window to get his attention. Lucus turns around to see her, wide-eyed and smiling, motioning with her hands connected, palms facing upward, like a book opening. The clairvoyant is clueless as to what just occurred outside her own store.

"YOUR ORDER IS IN!" she yells, with overly exaggerated mouth movements in case he cannot hear through the glass pane and has difficulty reading lips. He can hear her just fine as she keeps shouting and making that silly book-opening gesture.

Lucus raises his hand and nods. Zelda then belts, "COME ON IN!" with a giant wave of her arm over her head as she spins around and heads to the counter.

ERIN RACES HOME DOWN THE HIGHWAY. Both sorrowful and angry, she continually wipes tears streaming down her face. Frequent glances behind confirm that he is not in pursuit, at least not yet. A litter of thoughts whirl around inside her head like debris from an F5 tornado. A quick tap on the radio instigates a burst of aggressive techno music.

"Why?" she bitterly asks, talking out loud to herself. "Why did I fall for that? Why did I let my guard down? I *knew* better!" She pounds on the steering wheel with her fist and moans out a somewhat stifled roar.

And what about Lucus threatening to tell Brad everything? Will he actually do it? If so, would Brad believe him? It does not matter, because she will not lie and would have to come clean if Lucus does indeed tell him—which she is still not yet ready to do.

"*Am* I a hypocrite? *Am* I the lie?"

In her mind, Erin was previously comfortable with what she had and had not shared with Brad about her past. She *was* going to eventually reveal everything in due time. Or was she?

"Why did I let him get into my head like that? *Why*?" She bangs on the steering wheel again. "Rrrrrr!" The girl cranks her music louder and presses the gas pedal down farther. Lucus is still nowhere in sight. Gaining some composure with a deep, sustained breath, she glances to the passenger seat and picks up Emily's necklace. At least she has this, finally, in her hands. It brings back a flood of memories, both good and bad. Her eyes well up again, clouding her vision. "Oh, Emily…I miss you *so* much. I wish you were still here."

Emily—exactly one year ago—was struck on the side of the highway by a drunk driver late that night. The man, over twice the legal limit, momentarily passed out and veered onto the shoulder where the girl was walking. Miles and miles of stretched highway, seemingly innumerable places to blindly detour, yet it happened at that exact point in space and time. It was almost as if the horrific accident was predestined.

Hooooonnnnnk!

Erin looks up, wiping her eyes. She has drifted onto the other side of the road. An oncoming car speeds right at her.

She screams. Jerks the wheel back to the right. Narrowly avoids a head-on collision. Tires screeching, her car overadjusts onto the right shoulder, but she regains control and gets back squarely in her lane. Erin spots in her rearview mirror the other car hastily pulling a fast U-turn in the middle of the road with its red-and-blues flashing. That all-too-familiar siren wail informs her she's in trouble with the law…again.

And, as if her day couldn't get any worse, it is Sheriff Knox.

WHILE ERIN IS QUIETLY PULLED OVER on the side of the highway nervously waiting for Sheriff Knox to exit his vehicle and approach, a testosterone-filled bus of high school gridiron warriors rambles toward the rival's field of battle. The jovial team, confident in tonight's sure victory over a much inferior opponent, kills time by hazing underclassmen and giving obnoxious impromptu karaoke performances of the latest pop singles.

The revelry and noise are exponentially more intense toward the back of the rolling yellow tin can. This is why Brad, the quintessential perfectionist, is seated alone up front, one row behind the coaches, with his head buried in the playbook.

Big John, who just finished leading the guys in an awful rendition of the latest musical hit (with thunderous applause and high-fives afterward), saunters up front and plops down next to Brad. He tilts up his curled, worn-out straw cowboy hat and, with his T-shirt, wipes perspiration from his brow.

"Whew! I'm gonna wear myself out before the game, not that it matters tonight, hee hee."

"You're sweating, too," Brad responds without looking over.

"You know you love it." John rubs his face on Brad's shoulder.

He finally reacts with a grin.

"Dude, why are you reading that thing again? I bet you could rewrite it from memory." No response from Brad. John continues, "Blindfolded… with your hands tied behind your back…in a coma…" His attempt to elicit a response fails, and Brad's eyes remain focused downward.

"Here, gimme that." Big John grabs the playbook and tosses it to the back of the bus with a loud shout of "Incoming!"

"Ow!" shouts the unlucky recipient.

"Why did you do that?" asks Brad.

"Because you, my friend, need to loosen up. Tonight's game is in the bag, so relax and have some fun."

"Your overconfidence will be your downfall, if you're not careful."

"*Your overconfidence will be your downfall, if you're not careful,*" John repeats in a sarcastic, overly serious tone. "Honestly, Brad, we'll be pouring a bucket of ice water on coach by the end of the first quarter. I'm even thinking of running a few plays with my eyes closed."

"Would we be able to tell the difference?"

"Ooh, burn! Very funny. You know you're talking to an all-state fullback, don't you?"

"I know, I know, but you might end up being an all-state *fool* back if you're not careful."

"With two hundred and forty pounds of pure muscle and guns like these"—flexing his large biceps—"I doubt it."

"They say the bigger you are, the harder you fall," Brad warns his Herculean friend.

"Yeah, but if you never fall it doesn't matter, does it?" John gives a big, teeth-baring smile.

Brad bursts out laughing. "Oh man, how did we ever become best friends? We are *so* different."

"Maybe it has something to do with our dads being best friends? I'm just guessing."

"Speaking of dads, is yours going to be able to make it to the game tonight?"

"Oh yeah, nothing could keep him away…unless some major crime goes down that needs his expert sheriffing skills. Sheriffing is a word, isn't it?"

"I'm thinking…no."

"Or unless some crazy female driver not paying attention recklessly forces him off the road."

"Hey, I heard that!" barks a rough and almost feminine smoker's voice from the driver's seat.

"Oh, sorry, ma'am," John responds, as two beady eyes with

prominent crow's-feet scowl at him through the vibrating rearview mirror. John and Brad snicker at each other.

"Um, Brad…" John takes advantage of the pause. "Speaking of being different…"

"Yeah?"

"About Erin. I thought you would have come to your senses by now."

"What do you mean?"

"You know her reputation, like everyone else does. You know the crowd she hangs with."

"*Used* to hang with."

"Yeah, supposedly. But what about the partying and the drugs, and all the other stuff?"

"Erin's admitted all that to me and promises she turned from that way of life, and I believe her."

"You do? Really?"

"Yes, unless I see evidence otherwise. Look, I'm not stupid—"

"I didn't say you were."

"Then what are you saying?"

"Well…you're, maybe, a little naïve."

"Naïve?"

"Yeah. And it's your first real, ahem, girlfriend. I'm just saying your vision may be clouded at the moment. I gotta be honest, the whole relationship looks very bizarre from the outside. And I'm not the only one who thinks so."

"John, who's the most level-headed person you know?"

"Well, *you*, I suppose."

"That's right. Who's the one who got caught filling the principal's office with live chickens?"

"Um, me," John sheepishly admits.

"That's right. Who got busted hooking up a giant bra made of bed sheets on the town's water tower?"

John snickers and raises his hand, "Guilty."

"And who's known throughout the school as 'Captain Burrito Pants?'"

"Okay, okay," he concedes raising his hands in surrender. "You made your point."

"John, you should be able to trust my judgment by now. And *you*, you with your crazy pranks, who knows where you'd be by now if your dad wasn't sheriff. And I'm supposed to trust *your* discernment?"

"You're right."

"Besides, you said it looks bizarre from the *outside*. Well I'm on the inside, and it's not bizarre, it…feels right. Erin is totally honest with me. She's real—a bit eccentric, okay—but her genuineness is refreshing. You'd like her if you got to know her."

That is what happened with Brad after Erin's sister died—he got to know her. Prompted by his youth pastor's plea for other students to reach out to her after the accident, he reluctantly called Erin two weeks later to express his condolences.

Apparently, Brad was the only one who did.

She was shocked to get a call from Brad Ross. He was nothing like she thought he would be; he was friendly and sympathetic. They spent two hours talking on the phone that night. Erin originally was his "project," so to speak. Like he had been taught in church, Brad became her friend in order to "earn the right" to share Jesus with her.

But he finally realized that their friendship was developing into more than a platonic relationship. Sustained glances and smiles in the school's hallways led to secretly dropping notes into each other's locker, as well as frequent text messages throughout the day. At first he struggled with his feelings, but discovered he could not suppress them no matter how hard he tried.

She was witty and smart, not weird. Her poetry was beautiful (as far as he could judge poetry). Erin was unlike the other girls who fawned all over the school's most popular guy (who did not want to be some bimbo's arm trophy); and she was very straightforward with him, even as far as once telling him that his left eye was ever so slightly larger than his right.

Her eyes, though, were perfect. The heavy black frames of eyeliner could not possibly eclipse her hypnotic emerald gaze. For Brad, all that makeup did not mask her natural beauty. Her wide, captivating smile made his heart soar and plunge simultaneously. And how he loved to make her smile. The more Brad got to know the girl, the more spellbound he became. The more Erin fell for him, the more she shed her dark, gloomy appearance. Little by little, Erin had devolved further and further from her unapproachable Goth persona.

IN MANY WAYS SHE IS more mature than the other girls, but with a sense of burden and vulnerability mixed in. And right now those gorgeous green eyes are watching, in the side view mirror, Big John's father, Sheriff Knox, walking up to her car window, which has already been rolled down in anticipation of the conversation about to transpire. Erin once again finds herself staring up at her own reflection in another dominant male's sunglasses.

"You okay, miss?" The stoic sheriff asks robotically. He is just being formal calling her "miss," because he knows full well who she is. It is all just part of his intimidation tactics.

"Yes."

"Well you don't look it. Your eyes are bloodshot. Have you been drinking?"

"No."

"Drugs?"

"No."

"Then what gives?"

"I was crying?"

"Crying? What for?"

After a short pause, "I'm a girl. It's what we do."

"Hmm, I suppose so. I'm going to need to see your driver's license."

Erin hands it over. She had already pulled the I.D. out of her purse, which is now snapped closed on the seat beside her. Originally she was going to place her bag on the passenger side floorboard, but that would have looked too suspicious and she did not want to unnecessarily draw any attention to it.

"You know you almost killed us both back there?"

"I'm aware of that."

"And now I'm probably going to be late for kickoff."

"That's just horrible," she responds in a dry sarcastic tone.

After a short pause with no response, she looks up into his sunglasses. Suddenly a different reflection appears in his right lens. It looks like Erin in full-blown Goth mode. Or is it Emily? Yes, it is Emily! Erin gasps and immediately turns away.

"What's wrong?" the lawman asks. She does not respond, but Knox notices her breathing is much heavier and accelerated now. This girl is definitely nervous about something. He places a hand on his pistol.

"Okay, I'm going to need you to shut off the engine and step out of the car right now."

She swallows a big gulp then complies, dreading what is probably going to happen next.

"Look at me," he directs to her, as she stands there avoiding eye contact. Erin slowly pans up and, to her relief, sees only *her* image now reflected in both lenses. But the heart palpitations continue.

"Why are you so nervous all of a sudden?"

"Um, mood swing. One of those female things again."

"Really?" Knox asks suspiciously.

But she is not swaying back and forth. Pupils are not dilated. Speech is not slurred. However, the colloidal artery in her neck is pounding violently. The experienced officer can tell, though, that she is not on anything…at least not at the moment. He glances in her car, then looks at his watch, worried he will not make it to the start of the game.

"You stand back here," Knox directs as he grabs the girl's arm and leads her to the back of her car. "Stay put until I return." He then heads to his vehicle and gets in to run a license number check to determine if she has any outstanding warrants elsewhere.

Erin leans against her trunk with arms crossed, anxiously awaiting her fate. Mulling the possibilities, she is surprised when a moth unexpectedly lands on her chest over her heart. The exquisite light-colored creature has an otherworldly look to it, with a prominent triangular shape and bulging fuzzy legs. It just clings there, peacefully opening and closing its wings. For some reason she finds this unusual event comforting. Its undulating wings induce her breathing into the same slow rhythmic pattern, calming her nerves. After a few seconds, Erin reaches over, attempting to perch it on her finger, but the moth takes off and flutters past her head. She spins and watches it fly straight up into the dimming sky of twilight.

Sheriff Knox, just finishing a citation for "failure to control vehicle," looks up and sees the jacket. His eyes go wide. Plastered across the back is "Ross." It is Brad's letterman jacket. What in the world? Why is *she* wearing it? Erin stands there looking up while Knox quickly digs out his cell phone and places a call.

The moth has disappeared by now, but she keeps gazing heavenward, hoping to catch another glimpse of the ascending creature. Following his phone conversation, Knox disconnects and rips up the ticket. He notices Erin standing motionless looking straight up, and pulls forward in his seat to observe what is so interesting up there. Nothing.

"That girl sure is a strange one. Always has been," the befuddled officer says out loud to himself in the car. He then exits and approaches her while extracting his handcuffs from their holster.

"Okay—"

"Whoa!" Erin exclaims turning around quickly with her hand over her heart. "You startled me."

"Yeah. Um, anyway, I'm going to let you go this time with a verbal warning." Then, holding up the cuffs he says, "But if I catch you driving reckless again, I'm hauling you in. Is that clear?"

"Yes, sir. Thank you. It won't happen again, I swear."

"It better not. Now get going and drive safe."

"Drive safe*ly*," she responds.

He stares a moment, hands back her driver's license, and heads toward his vehicle at a brisk pace. He will surely be exceeding the speed limit to make it in time for kickoff.

Erin gets in the car, clasps her hands together, and looks up. "Thank you, thank you! I finally got a break!"

Five

AT LAST, ERIN IS HOME safe and sound. She leans back in the seat of her parked car with eyes closed, relishing the peace and quiet. What to do now? It is Friday night, not much good on TV, and her present for Brad is finished. There *is* that incomplete jigsaw puzzle of cherubs in the den. Yeah, that's the perfect way to keep occupied for the evening; that and some hot chocolate, with marshmallows of course.

She gets out and meanders up the steps. On the porch she finds Shep asleep, but not completely still. Lying on his side whimpering in R.E.M. stage, the dreaming animal moves his feet back and forth as if paddling in water. This is a recurring nightmare for Shep that Erin is now used to. She kneels down and gently pets him.

"Shep? Shep?"

He comes to, lifting his head high as if struggling to gulp for air with eyes rolled back. Erin continues stroking and speaks softly.

"It's okay, boy. You're all right."

The waking dog realizes where he is and reaches over to clasp the leather gloves with his teeth. Now calm, he looks up directly at Erin.

"Welcome back to the real world, my friend. Looks like your day hasn't been much better than mine."

The dog's tail drifts side to one side as he savors being massaged behind his ears.

"Hey, where's your collar? I don't think I've ever seen you without it. Hmmm, that's odd." Erin briefly looks around for it, and then gives up. "You want to go in?" She heads toward the door. Shep gives a hefty yawn tapering to a faint whimper and slowly returns to his favorite napping spot on the porch. Judging from his response, the answer is no. She places her hand on the doorknob to go in and, at the same time, notices a gecko gripping the doorframe just beside it.

"Ew!" Her hand retracts instinctively.

The squatty, large-headed lizard scurries halfway up the wall and freezes. These tan, wart-covered, squirmy creatures give Erin the creeps, but this should be the last one around before winter sets in. Too bad it's not winter here all year long for that very reason. She enters through the weather-crackled door and notices her mom and Queenie sitting in the den. Rose is looking at a sheet of paper with a puzzled expression while her sister sports a wide grin. Erin approaches, digging into her purse.

"Mom, great news. I got Em—"

"Are you crazy?" Rose jumps out of the chair.

"What?"

"Have you lost your ever-loving mind?"

"What do you mean, Mom?"

"This." She draws near and flips the paper around so her daughter can see the picture displayed on it: the photo of her and Brad embracing outside the school building. The pic has been spreading like wildfire since noon.

Rose continues, "*Please* tell me this is isn't true. *Please* tell me I'm seeing things. *Please* tell me there's something else going on here."

"Mom," Queenie interjects from the couch pointing with her eyes, "her jacket."

In her fervor Rose hadn't noticed it yet. She grabs Erin's arm and spins the girl around. Yes, it is *his* jacket. "I don't believe it." She lets go. "How long has this been going on?"

"Yes, Mom. Brad Ross and I are together. So what? What's the big deal?"

"I said, how long?"

"A little less than a year now. Why? What is your problem?"

"Do I really have to spell it out for you?"

"Look, Mom, today has really been—"

"Erin, he and his kind are *not* to be trusted."

"His *kind*?"

"Yeah, you know: rich, snobbish, holier-than-though religious hypocrites. Shall I go on?"

"You know nothing about Brad. He's not anything like that at all."

"Are you really that naïve?"

"Naïve?"

"Yes. People like that don't associate with people like us. He must be setting you up for some big practical joke."

"For almost a year, Mom? That's some elaborate setup!"

"Look at him. He's staring right into the camera while your eyes are closed. Did *you* know about this picture?"

"Mom, you're being ridiculously paranoid." However, she indeed did not know about the photo.

"He'll have his fun with you and then discard you like a piece of trash."

"Mom, we haven't even kissed yet."

"Well, something ain't right. You're forbidden from seeing him." Rose lights up a cigarette.

"You just…" Erin pauses with her hands up to keep her composure, "…need to trust my judgment."

"Yeah, well, I'd have to say your judgment in boys hasn't been all that stellar. Yours *or* Emily's for that matter."

Erin stands there frozen. She cannot believe what just spewed out of her mother's mouth. Rose takes another deep drag and slowly exhales, staring. She realizes it was the wrong thing to say in the heat of the moment, but pride keeps her from recanting.

"How dare you!" Erin says pointing. "How *dare* you!"

She spins and bolts out the door, leaving it wide open. Shep springs up and whimpers again. Gunning for her car, Erin launches from the porch to the ground without touching a step. Rose runs out a moment later.

"Erin! Erin! I'm sorry! I didn't mean for it to come out that way! Let me explain!"

But her daughter has grown ears of stone and is intently focused on getting as far away as possible, with no destination in mind. She jumps in, starts the car, hits the pedal, and speeds down the long winding driveway, leaving a trail of dust plumes snaking behind.

"Can this day possibly get any worse?" Erin cries to herself.

She will soon have her answer.

MEANWHILE, BRAD AND HIS TEAMMATES ARE having a great night on the field. Late in the third quarter they are up forty-nine to nothing. Stadium lights illuminate a clear, brisk night, while fans on the visiting side celebrate exuberantly. The home bleachers, conversely, are dead except for the cheerleaders executing their routine in obligatory, yet perky, fashion.

Following an injury time-out for the opposing team's player, Brad trots to the huddle from the sideline, bringing in the coach's play for his offense in these final seconds of the quarter. "All right, guys, this is the last play for us. Coach will be substituting second string for the remainder of the game to keep us healthy for next week and the playoffs."

"Too bad, I'm having way too much fun. We need to make this one count guys, we have to break fifty." says Big John.

"John," responds Brad, "don't get greedy. We've thoroughly crushed these guys. They're completely demoralized. Just look at 'em."

John glances over. Yes, they are beat up, bruised, dirty, and ready to go home. "Hey," says John, "look at the scrawny pipsqueak they put in at defensive end. I bet he doesn't even weigh a hundred pounds. Is he even in high school?"

The guys laugh in response. Brad calls the play. "Okay, we're running seventy-nine end around."

"Yes!" Big John pumps a clenched fist. He'll get the ball tossed to him and will run right past, nay, over, the small kid on the outside. "Okay Danny," he says to the left tackle, "don't worry about blocking the tiny tot in front of you. Go past him and head for the linebacker. I'll trample the fresh meat and, if you block the linebacker, I've got a sure sixty yards for the touch and we'll go over fifty points."

The huddle reacts jovially with the slapping of hands, except Brad, who interjects, "Okay guys, on two. Ready…" And with a simultaneous single clap they all yell, "Break!"

BACK NEAR THEIR HOMETOWN, in an abandoned manufacturing plant isolated on a wide-open tract of land littered with tall dead grass, weeds, and rocks, a small group gathers. Inside the dark, empty ghost factory, whispers fill the air. "Pull him up. Careful. Higher. Slowly."

The clanking of chains echoes throughout the spacious metal room. Five large lit candles set in an equidistant placement around a red painted circle faintly reveal a large metal tree-like structure that disappears into the ascending darkness.

"He's bleeding," blurts a female voice as crimson drops from above spatter on the cement floor.

"It's okay, that's normal. He's locked in. Everyone assume your position."

Hooded figures kneel in front of each candle. The individual leading this somber quintet, with long blonde ringlets flowing out from her oversized hood, opens a large leather-bound volume and begins to chant phrases in Latin while the others repeat each line in unison.

Their cryptic ceremony progresses this way for half an hour, until the prescribed incantations have been fulfilled. The participants obediently remain still and silent, not daring to look up. Then a faint moan comes from the pitch above. Rats instinctively scurry for safety from their hiding places, frantically racing along walls, making their way to any exit they can find, fighting each other to get out.

The deep moaning becomes louder, filling the cavernous space with dreadful, unearthly sounds, while his kneeling worshippers remain lifeless, frozen in position, praying to their god. Almost undetectably, the wailing morphs into chanting, chanting like that of old Indian shamans beckoning the spirit world. It steadily becomes more intense, heading toward a state of climactic anarchy.

The hanging chains start to violently rattle and shake. Like a fish trying to free itself from an angler's hook, that which is on the other end above fiercely thrusts itself to and fro. Animalistic howling and gurgling eerily broadcasts from overhead.

It is too much to bear. One of the worshippers, a newcomer—this is her inaugural baptism into a ceremony so deep and secret—defies orders and looks up to spy what is happening. A beam of moonlight filtering in from a rusted breach in the roof spotlights the bizarre ordeal. Her hands spring to her face and she screams a bloodcurdling cry in reaction to the horror filling her eyes.

The golden-locked leader immediately looks over. "Shhh! Quiet! Look down!"

Then, all is silent. The chains slowly come to a quiet, static resting position.

"Now you've done it," she informs the shaking offender. "The ritual was not yet finished."

A crumpled piece of paper falls from above and lands on the floor. It slowly unfolds revealing an image, a photo of Big John.

"Let me down from here!" bursts an angry demand from on high, echoing throughout the chamber. The chains clatter. "Did you hear me? I said let me down, NOW!"

"DON'T LET ME DOWN, NOW," Big John says, patting his powerful legs lovingly. "Just sixty yards from glory, guys." He calls his legs "guys" because they have been affectionately named; one Zeus, the other Apollo. At times he also refers to them as his "golden calves."

Big John and his teammates have lined up for the final play of the quarter. Brad is under center. "Blue, 42. Blue, 42. Set…Hut Hut!" He takes the snap, pivots left, and pitches the ball to John, who catches it in stride and heads around the end. As planned, the left tackle ignores the small player in front of him and makes a beeline for the larger linebacker. Watching events unfold downfield, John merely takes note of the unintimidating pawn in his path through his peripheral vision. What he expects to be just a speed bump on his way to six points turns out to be a disastrous stumbling block.

A roar of pain tears across the field. "My knee!" John lies on the ground, the "pipsqueak" on top. Before getting off, the runt gives a low-pitched growl, staring down with eyes housing pupils dilated to unnatural proportions. John rolls around, writhing and moaning in pain, clutching his knee. "I think it's broken! Ow! I think it's broken!"

He is fortunate. It was supposed to be his spine that snapped.

ERIN IS RACING TO NOWHERE, subconsciously drawn to a place where she will confront suppressed fears. In her mind, though, she is merely placing as much distance as possible between herself and her so-called home; a house that right now is receiving an invited guest pulling up the driveway.

Madame Zelda has come to direct tonight's séance. This second attempt to contact Emily will take place in one of two locations with the best chance of succeeding: her bedroom. According to Zelda, the very best site would be exactly where Emily departed this life, but Rose could not bring herself to go there. She has never visited the accident scene, where a white roadside cross has been placed in honor of her daughter. In fact, she has not even been down that road since Emily's demise.

The robust psychic spills out of her small car into a drizzling rain. She walks around then pops open the hatchback. She grabs several bags, almost too much for her to carry, and waddles up the porch steps, nearly slipping once. Shep raises his head to investigate.

"Oh, aren't you a handsome boy." Zelda presses the doorbell button.

Shep responds with a whimper, struggles to his feet, and walks away with gloves in tow.

"Humph." She is a little offended, but cats are superior to dogs anyway, so it's not worth getting all disjointed about.

The door opens. "Hello, Madame Zelda." Rose gleefully gives the clairvoyant a big hug. "Please, come in. Come in."

The two enter, and Zelda gives the place a quick scan, noticing the staircase. "What a beautiful place you have here. It has a…an *ancestral* feel to it."

"Why, thank you. It dates back to colonial times, though it's not as quaint as you might find on a Christmas card."

"Hmmm." Zelda glances at the staircase again. She closes her eyes tightly, inhales deeply through her nostrils, and speaks mysteriously. "I can feel her. Yes"—nodding—"she's here. Upstairs, maybe."

"Yes!" answers Rose, with hopeful surprise in her voice. "That's where Emily's bedroom is!"

The psychic's eyes, heavily outlined with deep purple shadow, pop wide open in dramatic fashion, pupils contracting. "Then that's where we shall go. Hurry, we've not a moment to lose!" Rose quickly ascends the staircase, all the while describing where Emily's room is and how it has been fully prepped to the given specifications. Reaching the top, she turns around to observe that Madame Zelda has not yet made it up one-third of the way. Her chubby, cylindrical legs show no distinction between calf and ankle.

"Do you need help?"

"No," the proud woman struggles to say between puffs, "I'm…good."

Zelda labors to lift her right leg to an upper step, then her left one on the same tread in this manner: Knee, shin, cankle, foot. Knee, shin, cankle, foot.

Creak, creak…creak, creak…creak, creak …

"Please, let me take a bag for you."

"No, no. I need the exercise, anyway."

So Rose stands there impatiently waiting, tapping her foot and gnawing a fingernail, as the plump woman slowly tackles each stair like she's dangerously scaling the cliffs of Mount Everest, firmly grasping the banister as if it is her lifeline (which it probably is). Distinct tick-tocking of the grandfather clock below makes the whole ordeal seem as if it is taking that much longer. Rose lights up a cigarette. Finally, though, Zelda reaches the summit as deep chimes from the grand old timekeeper ring out, almost as if the clock is celebrating her hard-fought monumental achievement.

With her agitation starting to seep out, Madame makes small talk so she can stand still and catch her breath for a moment, "Those stairs…aren't to code…are they?"

"I'm sorry?"

"They're not constructed to current builders' code. Otherwise, I would have made it up quicker."

"I think…they're to code. But they are pretty old, so I suppose—"

"Well, remind me to give you my brother's card. He's a contractor."

"Um, okay."

"Now, whew, where is Emily's room?"

"This way."

The two make their way down the hallway, Madame Zelda's heels clip-clopping on the wood floor beneath her in a brisk pace dictated by the short stride of her stumpy legs. They come to the first door on the right and enter. A small round table inhabits the center of the floor in an already cramped space. Three chairs are set around it in equidistant placement.

"This will do nicely," says Zelda.

The look and feel of Emily's room are conducive to a supernatural experience. The aged yellowish walls, constructed of horizontal slats, exhibit lighter rectangles of differing sizes where picture frames and posters once hung, giving the room a macabre, ghostly art gallery look to it. Removing the posters was the only thing Rose changed after Emily's death, because they reflected the girl's dark alternative lifestyle. And that is not how she chooses to remember her daughter.

"Thank you," replies Rose. "I followed your instructions exactly."

"I see. Candles in place, incense ready to burn, and something precious that belonged to your daughter in her chair. Well done."

That something she speaks of is Shep's collar. Of course, Rose wasn't going to be able to persuade the large dog to stay in a chair too small for him anyway, so she got the next best thing. Emily's cross necklace was her first choice, because it is spiritual in nature and was always with her, but that has been long lost (or so she thinks).

Underneath the collar are several faded newspaper clippings about the twins' birth.

Madame Zelda unloads her bags onto the bed and begins to pull out paraphernalia, mostly electronics. Not only is she a psychic, she also fancies herself a ghost hunter (actually, a "paranormal investigator," she would say), inspired by popular reality TV shows. First, there are two tripods, one for each video camera. She sets them up behind her chair and Rose's, pointed directly at the third seat.

"What are the cameras?" asks Rose.

"That one has night vision, and this one uses infrared. Now, I didn't have a chance to charge the batteries, so is there an outlet where I can plug these in?"

"Of course." Rose reaches behind a table and unplugs a vintage radio that once belonged to her father. She wraps the cord around it and places it on the bed behind their chairs to get it out of the way.

"Perfect." Zelda plugs in the video equipment. Next she pulls out several handheld devices. "This one," she says, holding it up, "is a digital thermometer. Fluctuations in room temperature may indicate a paranormal presence. And this is an ion meter."

"What's that do?"

"Well, it measures ions. I'm not sure what ions are, but there are two theories on how they relate to paranormal activity. First, a spirit might generate large quantities of ions because they emit high amounts of electromagnetic discharges. Or, they may simply disrupt the normal balance of ions in an area when they are passing through it."

"Oh," replies Rose, not really understanding.

"This is a digital audio recorder. It should pick up any EVPs"

"EVPs?"

"Yes, electronic voice phenomena. It's for any auditory sounds or noises that we might miss. Back in the past they used what were called spirit trumpets. They were horn-shaped speaking tubes that magnified the faint utterances of disembodied spirits. People would stick them into their ears and listen. But the digital audio recorders are much more sensitive."

"Okay."

"And *this*…" she announces proudly, "this is my electromagnetic field scanner."

"An electromagnetic field scanner?"

"Yes, EFD for short. It measures the electromagnetic field in a surrounding area. Now, man-made electromagnetic fields generally create a low, steady reading. But when there's a sudden spike—see these colored lights here?" Zelda points to the top of the instrument.

"Yes."

"Well, when it spikes from the green here on the left all the way to the red on the other end, *that* indicates probable paranormal activity."

"You mean spirits?"

"Exactly. This is pretty much the modern-day Ouija board. Also in the past, they used to try and have the spirits knock to communicate. However, it has been surmised that it's very difficult and exhausting for them to accomplish, while some may not even be strong enough to do it at all. But with this, we can ask Emily questions and direct her to spike once for no and twice for yes, and it will be much easier for her to accomplish."

"Really? We can directly communicate with Emily?"

"Yep," Zelda answers with a big grin. "But don't get your hopes up." Her tone turns sober. "It very rarely happens, and never on the first attempt. But I'll have it on just in case."

"Okay, can we get started? Please?"

"Sure thing, honey. You light the incense and candles while I turn everything on."

After these things are done, the lights are killed, and the bedroom door shut, the two women sit at the table amid dancing candlelight shadows. Zelda instructs Rose. "Now you hold my hand and stretch yours across the table toward the other chair with palm up as if you are going to hold that person's hand. I will do the same."

Rose complies.

"Good," continues Zelda, "Now close your eyes tightly and concentrate hard. You must have faith that it will work. You *must* believe."

"Oh, I do."

"Okay. Now be very still and quiet."

Rose can only hear her heart thumping with anticipation. The medium begins to breathe heavily through her nostrils, preparing to contact her own spirit guide. After a few moments, she speaks. "Spirit world…I now summon from the other side the soul of Mrs. Cranston Laurie, great spirit guide while here on earth and hereafter, to be with us. Come forth. Come forth now and make your presence known."

Zelda peeks with one eye to see if the lights on the EFD spike.

They do not. She quickly glances over at Rose, whose head is still bowed. The psychic shuts her eye and continues in a louder and more forceful tone. "Oh, teacher of wisdom, I hereby summon you to our presence. Come forth. Come forth now and make your presence known."

Still nothing. This goes on for some time without any results. At one point, Rose slightly adjusts her posture to get comfortable and clears her throat. Zelda whispers, "Be still and listen." The two sit, holding hands for a while. The clairvoyant, realizing her client is getting antsy and worried that tonight, like last time at the shop, there will be no contact, glances at the hopeful mother, turns her open palm down and taps the table with her lengthy solid plastic fingernail.

Tap-tap-tap

She quickly faces her palm back up.

Rose's eyes open immediately. "Did you hear that?!"

"Shush, Mrs. Gray" responds Zelda in a hushed tone. "You'll scare them off."

"Oh," she whispers. "Did that thingy's lights go off?"

"Yes, they did."

No, they didn't. That was a lie.

"Now close your eyes and concentrate even harder, Mrs. Gray. I'm really starting to feel it."

"Yes, of course."

Zelda starts to sway with a low, almost inaudible, hum. "Oh spirit guide, we ask that you lead Emily Gray to our presence." More humming. "Bring Emily to us, now." Hum, hum. Zelda stops swaying and gives Rose's hand a small squeeze, indicating that she can open her eyes now. In a hushed tone she says, "Okay, honey, call out to your daughter but in a whisper, not too loud. You have a better chance at eliciting a response from her than I. And keep your eyes focused on those lights."

"So I just start talking?"

"That's right, go ahead."

"Um…Emily? It's Mom. Can you hear me?"

Rose pauses and stares at the electromagnetic field scanner for a short while.

Nothing.

"Do I maybe need to hum?" Rose asks.

"No, no. That's my job. Go on, call out to her again, I can feel her presence.

The women fail to notice shadows of two feet now protruding into the room underneath the door to their right. Someone is out there.

"Okay. Ahem. Emily, it's Mom. We need you to give us a sign. Please let us know you're here. Can you make these lights go on?"

Rose has not noticed that Madame Zelda's other hand is no longer on the table, but down at her side. In her grasp is a remote control, used covertly to cause the lights to spike on command.

Now, Madame Zelda is not a charlatan in the classic sense of the word. She is a true believer in the paranormal, and trusts that ghosts can affect physical surroundings, but this does not always happen, for whatever reason. So as a public service, in order that seekers not become dissuaded because some uncooperative spirit chooses not to make contact at a certain time, she has devised this backup plan in which she makes the lights pop when the button is pushed.

This is all for very ethical reasons, of course. It would be a travesty for someone to become a skeptic of paranormal occurrences due to a one-time bout of inactivity. Given enough attempts, the departed *will* make their presence known.

And it has absolutely nothing to do with generating repeat business to make more money—another lie she has even sold to herself.

Rose takes a deep breath and makes an impassioned plea. "Emily. *Emily.* I need to hear from you. I need this more than anything in the world. Please, do whatever you can to give me a sign. *Please.*"

They pause again, waiting in silence. Zelda's finger, touching the remote's button, starts to press it when—

Kkkkkzzzzzkkkkkk.

Noise, from behind. It is static, static from the old radio lying on the bed. They both spin around.

"That thing's unplugged…isn't it?" asks Zelda.

"Yeah, that's the cord wrapped around it."

"And it doesn't run on batteries?"

"No."

The transmission continues…

Kkkkkzzzzzkkkkkk—"Mmmmmmommy?"—Kkkkkzzzzzk-kkkkk.

It was a voice. Her voice. Emily's voice.

Zelda pops to her feet as the device in her hand hits the floor, like her jaw is almost doing. The impact of the remote activates a spike in the lights on the EFD behind them, a reaction that goes unnoticed.

"Emily?" asks Rose, not really believing what she's hearing.

The voice undulates in a stronger and weaker volume amidst white noise.

"Mommy. It's me, Em."

Rose reservedly slides off her chair and kneels next to the bed, extending her shaking hands toward the radio, not knowing whether or not to grasp it.

"Baby!" Rose starts crying. "Is it really you?"

"Yes, Mom. I found you! I really found you!"

Zelda is frozen in place with a deadpan expression. This has never happened before—ever.

"Yes, baby," Rose continues. "You found me! You found me!"

"Oh, Mom, I miss you so much."

It is too much to bear. Rose breaks down sobbing, her face and hands buried in the mattress.

"Oh no," the voice announces. "They're coming."

Rose lifts her head. "Who, baby? Who's coming?"

"I have to go now."

"No. Please, please don't go."

"I love you, Mom. Bye."

The radio goes dead.

"No. No. Emily? *Emily?*"

Nothing. The event has passed. Both ladies are fixed in position, still absorbing what just happened. Suddenly, Rose spins around, still on her knees, and hugs the psychic. "Oh, Madame Zelda. You did it! I have to admit, I was starting to have my doubts. But you really did it. You made contact with Emily."

Zelda is still somewhat in shock and not responding.

"I'll never doubt you again. Never—Hey, what's this?" She picks the remote off the floor and holds it up.

Zelda gazes down and starts to come back out of it. "Oh. That. It's, um, nothing; part of my equipment. Here, give it to me."

Out in the hallway, with her ear up against the door, Queenie has heard everything. Outside, booming thunder echoes in the distance. A storm approaches.

ERIN FINDS HERSELF LOST in a sea of emotions while racing down the highway. The hum of her car's engine, the clicking of the wipers on their lowest intermittent setting, and the passing of time help to clear the distraught girl's mind. Realizing where she's come to, Erin now knows where she must go. It is up ahead a couple of miles or so.

Two minutes later, she pulls off onto the shoulder and directs her headlights to illuminate Emily's roadside memorial. Sitting and staring at it, she rests in the peacefulness of the moment. Then, almost without thinking, Erin reaches over, pulls the necklace out of her purse, and slips the leather strap over her head and around her neck. Clutching the silver cross with her right hand, she stares forward with unblinking eyes. Erin decides to get out, even though it's sprinkling harder now. Not wanting to soil Brad's jacket, she leaves it in the car, wearing only a flannel shirt to protect her from the cold, wet weather.

Rolling thunder draws nearer.

On the small, white wooden cross, where the two bars intersect, is a red placard with white engraved letters. Erin reads it, again, for what seems to be the millionth time:

In Loving Memory of Emily Gray
Beloved Daughter and Sister
Rest in Peace

She still can't fathom that her sister is forever gone. It's been a whole year, but time has not healed the wound of her loss. Two words keep pounding inside her head. *What if.*

What if Erin hadn't driven them both there that night?

What if they had not fought?

What if she had not angrily taken off, leaving Emily abandoned?

What if…?

Erin drops to her knees crying, again. "I'm so sorry, Em. It's my fault. I should have driven you home. I shouldn't have left you alone. I shouldn't have let him get between us. I'm so sorry." She slumps over the cross; leaning on its support and melting into a puddle of tears. It seems there could not possibly be any more energy or bodily fluid left for crying, but her tears keep flowing. The burden of guilt weighs heavily on Erin's shoulders. She laments decisions made and their irreversible consequences. Nothing will bring her sister back. Nothing.

"Erin," calls a voice.

She stops weeping with a series of rapid short inhales and listens without raising her head. Who was that? It was a crystal clear whisper in the distance.

"Erin."

There it is again. She looks up.

"Erin."

The voice's location is now evident; it is coming from the woods directly ahead behind the cross. She peers past her headlight's illumination and into the darkness.

"Erin, it's me."

Sounds like Emily. No, it can't be.

"It's me, Em."

Erin springs to her feet, stepping back a few paces. Her sister's voice indeed beckons from the wilderness.

"I'm here."

Here? Here where? In the woods? No, that's absurd.

Erin starts talking to herself. "I know it's been a crazy couple of days, but now I think I'm really losing it. Come on, Erin, get your act together." She takes a deep breath and wipes the precipitation off her face.

The voice continues, "Erin, please. I need to show you something, something important."

What? What's so important? Is it some sort of clue to shed more light on what happened that night? To find out, Erin will have to go in there, into the woods. But that's where Emily's body was found, about thirty yards in. Erin has never been back there.

On the night of the accident, after impact, the drunk driver, upon realizing what he had just done, panicked. With no one else on the road, no witnesses, he dragged the victim's bloody body through the trees and left it there. It was a hit-and-run that the alcoholic might have gotten away with, except that he passed out again about a mile down the road, and his dented, bloody car was found partially embedded into some brush by a passing trooper the next morning. The vehicle was still idling, its radio crackling out vintage country and western classics.

The coroner later determined that if the girl had been found and treated in time, she quite possibly could have been saved— though horribly disfigured.

"No, no, Erin," she continues to reason with herself out loud. "No one is talking to you. It's all in your mind." She looks up and down the road to see if anyone is coming.

"*Erin, please. You owe it to me. Hurry, in here.*" The voice hits success playing on Erin's guilt.

"Okay, I'll do it," she says. "Just to prove to myself that it's all my imagination." But in her soul she really is not sure.

Erin makes her way to the tree line and peers in. The beams from her car light up the path just far enough to where she needs to go, except where her elongated shadow is cast. The hesitant girl slowly enters, brushing aside branches at face level. Dead twigs crack beneath her feet, and thorny vines snag her clothing as she carefully zigzags her way in deeper. A carpet of wet fallen leaves makes for slippery footing on the descending grade.

Twenty yards in, the light is starting to fade, but it's just barely bright enough for her to make out ethereal shapes. Five more yards and Erin finds herself in a clearing. She stands still, waiting for her eyes to adjust. As pupils dilate, a round shape unveils itself in front of her. It is the hole, the hole where Emily's remains were dumped. Six feet deep and about thirteen across, it is some sort of sinkhole that, as far as anyone can tell, happened naturally. Erin looks away from it, thinking about her sister being discarded like a piece of trash. But it does not matter; it is too dark to see down in there anyway (except in her mind's eye).

She waits a few moments, listening for the voice. Thunderclaps come louder and more frequently as wind gusts intensify. Other than that, nothing is happening here.

"I knew it. It was all just my imagination."

A noise off to the side catches her attention. Now it is moving, encircling her. Is there someone out there? It sounds like something rustling about in the shadows, an animal perhaps. Now it is behind her. She spins but sees nothing. It stops. Her heart races. She has an eerie feeling that she is being observed, but not from ground level. Up. That is where her attention is being drawn. In the trees, *what are those?* It is the birds, the grackles. They perch high in branches surrounding the clearing, as if to watch what is going down. When did they get there? Have they been here all along? The winged creatures are not making any sound or moving, they all just sit completely still, peering down.

"Erin."

The voice comes from the hole. Erin turns around and gently approaches. She gazes down into what appears to be an abyss, its black nothingness having the illusion of being solid.

More sounds now, but from above. The birds—they all flap frantically. Not screeching, not taking off, just beating their wings as if to announce the arrival of something, something important.

Squeeeeeeeee. The sound comes from behind.

Erin turns. Exploding from the shadows is a boar: a black wild hog with thick hair bristles spiking along the ridge of its back. The almost prehistoric-sized beast is huge, easily over five hundred pounds, maybe six hundred, charging straight at her with a blood-curdling squeal.

Two large protruding tusks distinctly flash in what little light there is. Erin has no time to react. It bumps her ferociously. She falls in with a thud.

Looking up through squinting eyes, she sees the boar snort down at her: a blasting spray of mucus from its nostrils followed by clouds of warm steam that billow upward. Then all goes dark.

AFTER A WHILE, ERIN COMES BACK into consciousness, sort of. She is missing one of her senses—sight. All is black, pitch black. The kind of solid darkness that would make a claustrophobic hyperventilate in terror. She waves a hand in front of her face, but detects nothing. And the temperature is a piercing, bitter cold. Goose bumps on her arms are prominent as she rubs them for warmth.

Adding to the misery of her shaking body is frigid water randomly trickling down on it from above. Erin's mouth feels as if it is full of cotton, with a swollen leathery tongue. Her craving for water is insatiable, as if she is dehydrated from being stranded in the desert for many sweltering days. Desperate for relief, she catches the falling water in cupped hands, opens her dry, parched mouth and pours it in. But the liquid is bitter, bitter like a toxic chemical that she immediately spits out, coughing and gagging.

The pungent stench of sulfur stings as it scratches its way into her nostrils.

Ow, my back, she thinks. It must have been punctured on some rocks or something else lying at the bottom of the pit. *What's that noise?* There are sounds all around, reminiscent of something industrial, a factory of some kind perhaps. The rattling of chains, squeaking of metal and loud bursts of steam exhaust echo all about. Now the temperature is starting to warm up a little. It is welcomed relief, though the water continues to douse her. A steady breeze hits the confused girl head on. Her eyes must be adjusting because shapes begin to appear while a deep red glow materializes ahead. Suddenly comes a jolt accompanied by the clanking of chains.

Erin screams. "My back!" Sharp pain instantly branches out through her nervous system as a fiery throbbing spans her shoulder blades. She hears a different sound, like someone else, or something else, screaming. *What's that figure in front of me?*

Another jolt, another wail. The pain is excruciating. Erin now realizes that her body is jerking up and down in slight undulations, feeling the sensation of forward movement. The other distressful wails become more distinct.

Squeeeeeeeee, squeeeeeeeee.

It is the squealing of pigs. Many of them. And there is one right in front of her. The diffused reddish glow now illuminates her surroundings. The large pink creature in front hangs with its back facing her. Four very large thick hooks, connected to chains suspended from above, pierce the flesh across its upper back. The swine squeals and struggles violently to free itself, only adding to the pain and flowing of blood from the puncture wounds. In all honesty, if the barbs ripped through its flesh and the hog fell to its death, it would be compassionate.

With her eyes, Erin follows the chains up and sees that they are connected to some sort of conveyor system. She and the swine are being transported, but to where? An elaborate grid of steel beams forms the support and structure of this massive complex. Erin looks down and realizes that she must be in the air at least twenty stories or more.

What is this place, and who built it?

The squeals become louder, almost intolerable. Erin struggles to turn her head around and look back. Out of the corner of her eye she sees what appears to be an endless line of suspended pigs, all struggling in futile attempts to free themselves. She turns back around, takes her hand and slowly, painfully, reaches over behind her shoulder. Feeling a solid sharp point, her fingers run down a little and meet flesh. The returning of her shaking, bloody hand confirms her fear—she is hanging, hooks pierced through her back, just like the pigs!

No longer able to squeal, the one in front of her starts gagging. An instant later, it becomes apparent why. Streams of geckos come flooding out of the distraught creature's mouth. They frantically scurry about looking for an escape, but there is not one. Soon, the pig's body is covered in a massive swarming blanket of lizards. Her eyes widen in disbelief. Prayers for blinding darkness go unanswered. She is surely going into shock now. But it feels too warm for that. In fact, it is becoming hot, real hot. The ambient roar of raging fire draws near.

Up ahead is some sort of platform. On it, there appears to be large furnace with a dark figure beside it pacing back and forth on all fours like a caged lion anxious for his overdue meal. The pigs ahead—the conveyer system is pulling them all into the furnace one by one. They thrash violently as it forces them into the engulfing flames. Squeals of unspeakable horror tell the story of what they are going through inside the blazing inferno.

Erin is almost there. The dark figure stops pacing, stands up on its two hind legs, and stares directly at her, as if what he has been waiting for has finally arrived. He stoops over and picks up a rod-like object.

A grackle swoops in from nowhere and lands on the head of the pig in front of her. Rapidly cocking its head back and forth, it stairs at Erin a few moments, emits a sharp, shrill screech, plucks a gecko into its beak and flies off as quickly as it arrived.

She looks around for a way to escape, but it is hopeless. Efforts to grab the chains above result in unbearable pain, as does any movement at all. So she hangs there, limp, arms at her side, awaiting her fate in fear. The pig in front of her slowly enters the consuming fire. One by one the geckos, no longer able to stand the heat and hold on, begin to drop off its body. Rather quickly they fall in waves until none are left.

As the rickety system carries Erin to the platform just in front of the furnace, all movement comes to an abrupt halt with a loud metallic screech. The dark figure takes his hand off a lever. Erin's dangling body painfully swings back and forth from the jolting force of the sudden stop.

The pig in the furnace is now being scorched alive. It struggles in a vain effort to fend off the flames that now melt the skin off its body like wax slowly cascading down a candle.

Out from concealing shadows, the entity approaches. Erin knows what it is now. It is not a man. It is not an animal. The threatening creature bears the face of both a human and a goat. Where humanoid characteristics end and animalistic features begin is hard to distinguish, but the crooked horns spiraling out from the top of its skull are unmistakable. A shiny jet-black coating of skin encases his hairless body.

She reaches up to grab Emily's cross hanging from her neck, but the necklace is not there.

The dark beast comes closer, hooves clanking on the grated metal platform, and stands in front of her. Even with Erin hanging several feet above the platform, he still towers over her. His cooling shadow brings temporary relief from the waves of intense heat. A slow, deliberate turn of the creature's head reveals a yellow eye encompassing a black vertical diamond-shaped pupil with jagged edges.

"Well hello, my sweet. Enjoy the ride?"

His throaty voice resonates deeply with such a quality that it penetrates directly into her mind, her soul. Hanging there with head turned and eyes clenched tightly shut, Erin does not answer.

"Some claim it's a…religious experience. What say you?"

Still refusing to respond.

"You can't make me disappear or change your fate by ignoring me, my precious Erin. You might as well open your eyes and face the truth."

Even though the presence of this evil one is far greater and more intimidating than she has ever experienced, she summons the strength to faintly mumble an inaudible response.

"What's that, my dear? I didn't quite hear you."

She speaks again with a very shaky, cracking voice. "I…I know I'm not perfect, but I don't deserve to be tortured, hanging here like this."

"Oh, don't tell me you've forgotten. Surely you recall. You hung yourself up here. Remember?"

"No. No"—shaking her head, eyes still closed.

"Well, let me see if I can remind you."

Erin slowly cracks one eye. In front of her face the creature holds a branding iron topped with an encircled pentagram. To her horror it automatically heats up, going from cold black steel to a red-hot glow as she watches.

"Think this will do the trick?" he asks in a condescending tone.

Erin turns her head. "No, please." She knows what is coming. He steps aside and walks behind her. The sudden burst of heat and light from the furnace startles her and she squints tighter, sweat pouring down her face. The roasting pig is still frantically wailing in agony, which does not make sense. Its body should have been completely consumed by now, but is not, because that would be merciful, and in this dark place, from which no one may return, there is no mercy or relief.

Erin screams.

The piercing sting of the blistering red-hot iron presses against her back with a distinct sizzle. The smell of burning flesh escapes with rising smoke. The beast closes his eyes and deeply inhales the intoxicating aroma. After a few moments, he pulls it away and walks back around.

"Ring a bell?"

She cannot answer. Her body shakes uncontrollably to try and cope with the unbearable pain.

"You are *mine*, now." The beast walks back to the lever, smiles at Erin, and pulls it down. With a jolt, the conveyer starts pulling her toward the furnace.

It's too much to take. The heat. The pain. The terror. The hopelessness. Before she reaches the flames, Erin's mind shuts down, and all goes black again.

COUGHING AND GAGGING, ERIN wakes up suddenly, struggling for breath. A booming clap of thunder too close for comfort still echoes throughout the forest. She finds herself drowning at the bottom of the pit, as a torrential downpour fills the depression with streams of runoff. Luckily the water is only about a foot deep, so Erin sits up, and her lungs violently expel the remaining water and phlegm. Gathering her bearings, she notices the glow above from her car's headlights.

I must be in the hole off the side of the highway. Her memory begins to gradually return.

Splashing the mucky water, Erin staggers to her feet and feels around for a way to escape. She happens upon a root system protruding from the earthen wall, like a hand reaching down to rescue her. Erin grabs a hold of it and begins to pull herself out. After a few moments of struggling with feet slipping up the muddy embankment, she emerges from the grave and lies on the ground, fatigued with the memory of her dream (or vision) still fresh in her mind.

Being out in the open exposes her to wind blowing with great force. Amidst howling gusts and rain driven almost horizontal, Erin slowly gets to her feet and stumbles to the car. Once inside, she cranks the engine and rests, waiting for it to warm up. With teeth chattering and body shivering, she glances at Brad's jacket, thankful it did not get soiled. And luckily, the rain has washed most of the mud off of her own clothes. Finally blowing, heated air brings soothing relief, warming her bones. Still quivering, she places the car in drive and heads home.

ABOUT HALF AN HOUR LATER she turns off her car and races onto the porch. While she jostles her keys at the door, several geckos scurry off, radiating out from around the porch light. Shep greets her as she enters. He is the only one still up, as it is now late and everyone else is fast asleep.

Erin makes her way up the stairs, with Shep trailing, and comes to Emily's room. On the bed, Rose is curled up hugging the old radio. Erin pauses for a moment to do a double take. *That's weird.* She makes her way past Queenie's bedroom, noting that no light shines from beneath the closed door. At the end of the hallway, Erin listens at Dad's door and hears him sawing logs.

"His snoring could wake the dead," she whispers to Shep, who looks up at her with a cocked head. Erin gives him a quick rub behind the ears and heads to her bedroom.

While she dries off and changes into fresh clothes, her stomach rumbles with hunger pangs. She has not eaten since lunch. But she's too exhausted to go back downstairs to get something to eat, or even to take a shower. Erin immediately sinks down into her soft bed with Shep struggling up to join her. He curls next to her legs, bringing welcome warmth and comfort. She is quickly in a deep sleep.

THE DOOR TO THE BEDROOM QUIETLY CRACKS OPEN while the sore, unsuspecting victim gingerly rolls over in bed, sleeping off the previous night's exhaustion. It is exactly eight o'clock in the morning, and a small gathering looks into the bedroom with one thing on their mind—*attack!*

One in the group looks to the leader and mutely asks, *Now?* After an affirmative nod, the "assassin" stealthily creeps in, stops bedside, and looks back, awaiting the go-ahead signal. The leader once again tips his head, and the intruder, with clenched fists and slightly bent knees, springs forward through the air with a scream.

"Happy Birthday, Brad!" belts his family from the hallway, as his six-year-old sister pounces on him and starts tickling. "Happy birthday, brother—hee hee hee."

Brad wakes up with a startle and, after a second to catch his thoughts, grabs his sibling and returns the favor. "You little rascal. I bet you couldn't wait to do that, could you, Jess?"

"Ha, ha, ha," Jessica cries out uncontrollably as her brother attacks her sensitive sides and knees. "Okay, okay, let me go. I've had enough!"

Brad releases her, and she crawls off his bed, struggling to catch her breath. "Good morning, guys," he says, looking at his family camped in the doorway.

"Rise and shine," says Mom.

His grandmother follows with, "Now get out of bed; you can't sleep all day, you know. The day is already half gone."

"Yes ma'am, Granna."

His father adds, "Now son, we'll give you about thirty minutes to get ready. We're all going out for breakfast. All right?"

"I can't wait for you to see your present." Jessica gleefully claps, jumping up and down.

"Really? I get more than your tickle attack? Nothing could be better than that."

"All right, Jess," their dad says, "let's go so Brad can get ready."

"Okay, Daddy."

About half an hour later, Brad makes his way down the curving staircase of their professionally decorated upper-middle-class home. Upon seeing him, Jessica bolts from the bottom of the stairs heading for the kitchen yelling, "He's coming! He's coming!"

The scooting of chairs can be heard as his family breaks away from the table, where they've been drinking coffee, to meet him in the living room.

Mom is the first to approach and hug the boy. "Happy birthday, baby." She reaches up and gives him a kiss on the cheek. "How does it feel to be eighteen?"

"Oh, about the same so far, I guess."

They all chuckle.

Dad embraces him. "Happy birthday, son."

"Thanks, Dad."

"Good game last night. You sore?"

"A little," he says, with a big grin. "I don't think I got touched once. The offensive line did a great job. Have you heard anything new about John's leg?"

"Not yet. I'm sure his dad will call me sometime today and let us know."

"Now you all stop talking football and let me through." Brad's grandmother wobbles forward with the aid of a cane. She's a small woman but has a big spirit. The matriarch of the family, Granna keeps everyone in line with her straightforward demeanor and extensive knowledge of proper etiquette and God's word. She is known for speaking in short, authoritative bursts. Though Eleanor's body is running down, her mind is sharp as a tack (except for an increasingly challenged short-term memory).

"Good morning, Granna." Brad bends over to hug her gently enough so as not to break her.

"Is that all you got, football boy? Give me a *real* hug."

He tightens his grip a little. "Yes ma'am."

"Now that's more like it. Did you say your prayers this morning?"

"Well…not yet. I was hurrying down here. I didn't want to keep you guys waiting."

"I am not a guy, and you will say grace for breakfast this morning at the restaurant."

Brad's parents look at each other, suppressing snickers with hands over their mouths.

"Yes ma'am. I would be honored to."

"Good, let's get going. I'm famished."

"The present! The present!" Jessica jumps up and down, clapping.

"Oh, that's right." Dad, feigning forgetfulness, pats his pockets. "His present. Now where did I put it?"

"Dad!" Jessica knows it's too big and special to misplace. "We need to blindfold him, remember?"

"Blindfold me?"

"Yes," answers his mom. "Jessica wants to cover your eyes and lead you to where it is."

"Well, if that's what Jess wants then that's what we'll do." He smiles down at her.

"Okay, squat down so I can wrap this around your eyes." She holds up a bandana. Brad complies, and his sister places the blindfold with the precision of a brain surgeon or bomb technician, making sure there is absolutely, positively no way he can peek out. "Now, grab my hand and I'll lead you."

"Okay." He stands back up.

His sister points and mouths silently (because he can't have any clues as to where they are going), *Open the door.* Mom walks over and opens it. "Now come on, big brother, right this way." She proudly leads him outside. They stop on the brick landing of the steps leading down to the circular driveway that gracefully slices through their immaculately manicured front lawn. "Now, we're going to have to step down," his sister warns, "so lean on me."

On the other side, Brad's father grabs underneath his arm to help stabilize him.

Jessica announces with each pace downward, "Step…step… step…" After five steps they come to a halt and she blurts, "Open your eyes!"

Brad slowly removes the bandana, and his jaw drops. Sitting before him is a 1965 Corvette coupe. It is coated with a fresh, shiny, apple-red paint job and has twin black leather seats. The classic has been fully restored and is ready for its new driver.

"No way!" Brad stares at his dad.

"Yes way." His father holds up the keys.

Brad looks back at his mom. "Are you guys serious?"

"Your mother is not a guy," says Granna.

"Son," his father continues, "your mom and I, all of us, are so proud of you. You're a great young man with high standards and a drive for excellence. You study hard and make near-perfect grades. You work hard and excel in sports—and anything else you set your mind to, for that matter. Your morals are beyond reproach. You have a kind, loving heart. You give to anyone in need. It's obvious you love the Lord and people, and we think an attitude and track record such as yours deserves to be rewarded. So here you go." He holds up the keys in front of his son's bewildered face.

Brad does not grab the keys but immediately hugs his dad, then bounds up the steps to embrace his mom. "Thank you! Thank you so much! I love it, and I'll take good care of it."

"We know you will, son," his mom responds. "We know you will."

"Well, before anything," Granna interjects, "we need to cover the Chevette in prayer."

"Corvette, Mother," Brad's mom responds. "It's a Corvette."

"Well, whatever it is, we need to lay hands on it and ask the Lord for Brad's protection. This thing looks fast and dangerous."

So the whole family encircles the car, placing their hands on it, and prays along silently while Brad's father leads them out loud. After about a minute and an "amen," the group ends its intercessory prayer.

"Let's go eat; daylight's a burnin'," belts Granna.

"All right, everyone," says Mr. Ross, "you all go in the van. I'm going to ride with Brad in the Vette."

"Aw," Jessica whines, "I wanted to ride in it."

"You can ride in it back from the restaurant. How's that sound?"

"Yay!" Jessica claps, satisfied with the compromise.

Brad and his father sink into the low-profile sports car while everyone else walks to the garage. It starts up with a vroom.

"Be careful, son. This thing does have a lot of power for such a small vehicle."

"Yes, sir." He puts it in first and slowly exits the driveway, hanging a right.

"How's it feel?" asks his dad.

"Awesome. Simply awesome." The classic purrs down the road like a proud lion.

"Now you need to know the antenna is broken and won't retract like it should, but it still works as far as doing what antennas do. Anyway, it would have to be in the shop today to be fixed, and your mother and I really wanted to give the car to you this morning. The dealer said to bring it in next Saturday, and they'll take care of it in a jiffy."

"That's fine dad, no big deal. I would love the car even if it didn't have an antenna, or even a radio, for that matter."

"Thanks for understanding, son. Oh, turn left up here; let's take the scenic route." Jack Ross actually wants extra time to talk to him about some troubling news. "Where's your jacket, son? Why aren't you wearing it?"

This catches Brad completely off guard. "Well...I...uh..."

"Look," his dad saves Brad from any more awkward attempts at pausing. "John called me last night and said he pulled over a girl wearing your letterman jacket."

"Pulled her over?"

"Yeah, said she nearly ran him off the road. Care to tell me what's going on?"

"Well, I was gonna tell you and Mom today. Honest. Erin and I have sorta been seeing each other."

"How long has this been going on?"

"About a year. Not that we've been serious for a year. But it took that long for...y'know...our feelings for each other to grow stronger. We only made our relationship public yesterday at school."

"How serious are you two?"

"Pretty serious, I guess."

"Hmm," Dad responds.

"Hmm? Hmm, what?" Brad asks.

"How much do you know about this Erin girl?"

"Dad, I think I know where you're going. I know she's had a troubled past, but she's changed. Is changing. And I think God is using me to be a good influence on her."

"Hmm," Dad responds again.

"Hmm, what?"

"Well, it's just that John told me a lot about her past, about her…acquaintances."

"Dad, she put that all behind her. I wouldn't be with Erin if I wasn't sure."

"Then why all the secrecy?"

"Because I knew it was going to be a big deal, and I wasn't sure how everyone would react. As for you and Mom, I wanted to be sure enough about the relationship before I announced I had a girlfriend. It's uncharted territory for us as a family, and I knew my first relationship would be important to you two."

"It is, son. Very important. Most of all, I'm worried about your well-being. How serious are you two?"

"Don't worry. I've made sure we're never in tempting situations. We haven't even kissed; she knows my rule about that."

"And she's okay with it?"

"Absolutely, Erin has accepted my boundaries. As a matter of fact, I think she respects them, given her experiences with other guys."

"And you're sure you two are serious?"

"Yes, sir. Why do you keep asking me that?"

"Well, there's something I need to disclose to you."

"What's that?"

"Her mother, Rose. She and I…sort of have a past together."

"What? What are you talking about?"

Jack pauses to collect his thoughts and emotions then begins to recount a tale of deceit and cruelty. "When I was your age, a senior in high school, there were three of us who were very close friends. In fact, we were known as the Three Amigos. Our trio consisted of me and John—"

"Yes, Sheriff Knox. I knew you and he were best friends, but I've never heard about this other guy."

"That's for good reason. Jason Riley grew up in this town as well. We were all three the best of friends since I could remember. We played Little League ball together, went to the same school, and our families even attended the same church."

"Wow, you guys were practically brothers."

"That's right. That is, until Jason started getting into the wrong crowd. He began drinking, and maybe even drugs as well. It was a girl, Brad. It was a girl who Jason thought he was in love with, and her friends who influenced him down the wrong path."

"Okay, but how does this connect you and Mrs. Gray?"

"Well, about a week before homecoming Jason and his girlfriend had a huge argument at school and broke up. It was a big scene in the cafeteria during lunch. The next day Jason asked Rose to the dance, and she accepted. Now, Rose was a bit of a loner, which was why she didn't already have a date, so I guess she was excited about going with Jason, who was one of the popular kids. She bought a nice dress, even though her family was poor. John and I agreed to let Jason and Rose ride with us in our limousine to the dance. At first we weren't going to, because of his last girlfriend and their behavior, but we changed our minds because he promised us he had changed after the breakup. And besides, we each then only had to share a third of the cost of the ride instead of half.

"That Saturday we arrived at the gym and all got out of the limo. It was a grand entrance, to say the least. We were the only ones to arrive like that, and everyone noticed. All six of us entered together, and Rose was beaming with joy. I noticed Jason's ex-girlfriend was there without a date. I didn't think it peculiar at the time. As the evening wore on, Jason acted normal and seemed to be having fun. He danced with Rose exclusively, giving her devoted attention—didn't interact with his ex at all.

"At one point, Jason had her sit against the wall in a specific chair that, we discovered later, had a small X marked with tape underneath it on the floor. He went to get refreshments and, upon returning, handed Rose some punch and cake. He didn't sit next to her and a small crowd, including Jason's ex, gathered. John and I went over to investigate. Just as we got there, Jason made a toast to the most special girl at the dance—the belle of the ball. Then they all raised their glasses high."

"That's strange. I have a feeling something bad happened next."

"You're right, son. In an instant, there was mayhem. From overhead, a dead possum fell on her."

"What!"

"It had been suspended with fishing line near the ceiling behind a banner. The raising of glasses was the signal. Someone cut the line, and the carcass fell into Rose's lap. She sat there, frozen, trying to process what was going on, while everyone, including Jason and his ex—now in each other's arms—stood there pointing and laughing."

"How cruel. What was the deal with his ex?"

"Well, the big fight at school earlier in the week was totally fake. It was all planned—they never really broke up."

"Why did they do it?"

"Jason's girlfriend hated Rose for some reason, I'm not really sure why. Maybe because Rose was different, dressing in black with strange hair and listening to unpopular music. But who knows really why people do such cruel things to other human beings."

"What happened to Rose?"

"After the initial shock, realizing what had happened, she bolted out of the gym screaming. A teacher followed her. Some others and I went as well, but the assistant principal wouldn't let us talk to her, and she was driven home."

"What happened to Jason?"

"John and I severed all ties with him after that. He was expelled and continued down the wrong path. Eventually he moved out of state and hasn't been back. As for Rose, she's never really forgiven me, or Sheriff Knox. She still believes we were in on it. Repeated attempts to convince her otherwise have fallen on deaf ears."

"That's heavy."

"Yes, and that's why I wanted to talk to you, to warn you of what you might be getting into. She knows you're my son, and dating her daughter is not going to be well received. I'm just saying you need to proceed with caution."

"I will, Dad. Thanks for the—"

"Stop!" Jack yells, placing his arm across Brad's chest.

Brad slams the brakes. The car screeches to a halt at the intersection. A black sports car roars through the intersection in front of them at breakneck speed, completely running the stop sign. Had Mr. Ross not seen it coming out of the corner of his eye, they both would have been crushed in a fatal collision. Hearts racing, father and son sit for a moment, collecting their thoughts, then look at each other.

"That was close," says Brad.

Jack looks to see if there is a police pursuit. There is not. "It's amazing," he says, turning back to Brad, "how some people completely ignore the law. The consequences here would have been devastating, and for more than just the two of us."

"Yeah, and what if Jess had been with me instead of you?"

"I don't even want to think about that, Brad. In fact, let's not mention any of this to the ladies. They don't need to know; it would just upset them. Did you get a good look at the car?"

"No sir, it happened all too fast."

"Yeah, same here. No point filing a report with the police, I guess."

The small line of cars gathered behind them begins honking. Brad proceeds through the intersection cautiously and heads for the restaurant. Their near-death experience that day would remain a secret between them.

ROSE GRAY IS HAPPY, TRULY HAPPY, for the first time since before she received that horrific call a year ago. Thrilled with what happened last night and finally optimistic for the future, she scurries about cleaning the house like a mom preparing for her "baby" to come home and visit after being far away at college for an extended period of time. There is a spring in her step and a tune in her heart as she whistles melodically while dusting here and there.

A jaw-dropped Queenie sits on the couch with a clasped glass of iced tea resting on her knee, staring at her mom with a *Who is this strange woman?* expression on her face.

Curtains that are accustomed to being permanently closed are now drawn back, allowing a flood of light to illuminate layers of dust that have collected everywhere. But now is the perfect time to prepare for a visit because Madame Zelda is returning tonight to make contact again, and the house needs to be in perfect condition to welcome Emily home. Though winter approaches, it's more like springtime to Rose, who finally feels some joy once again.

There is a knock at the front door; an unexpected visitor. Rose makes her way to the entrance, humming and gently brushing objects with her feather duster en route. Normally unannounced company or solicitors would not be welcome here, but she is in a great mood today and ready for whoever might be on the other side. Queenie sips her drink, watching events unfold as if viewing a matinee drama at the local movie theater. A gleeful Rose swings open her door with a pleasant, "Yes?"

"Hello ma'am, I'm—"

"I know who you are," Rose's tone is short and irritated. Her face drops as quickly as her mood.

"Yes ma'am. Well I'm here to—"

"I know why you're here." She stands with arms crossed and eyes squinting. "And don't think I don't know *exactly* why you're here."

"I'm sorry. I don't know what you mean."

"Oh, don't you? Why else would someone like *you* be slumming around here?" She eyes his red sports car parked back a ways just off the dirt driveway.

"Um, Erin asked me to meet her here for lunch." Brad holds up a paper bag in one hand and a drink holder with two sodas in the other. "But if it's not a good time, I can—"

"Mom!"

Erin whisks past Rose and grabs her boyfriend by the arm to lead him away as quickly as possible. As Brad is dragged down the porch steps by an embarrassed daughter, he, in his ever-persistent polite demeanor, looks back at the woman staring at him with a deathly cold glare and tells her, "It was nice to meet you, ma'am."

As they round the corner of the house, a slam of the front door follows Brad's kind words. In the den, Queenie immediately plants her glass on the coffee table and bounds upstairs. The second floor is perfect for spying, because much of the property can be seen from the windows.

"I'm so sorry about my mom, Brad. What did she say to you?" Erin asks as they come to a stop on the side of the house.

"It wasn't that bad," he replies.

Erin looks at him as if waiting for an honest answer.

"No, really, it could have gone a lot worse." He reflects on what his dad told him. "Chicken sandwich?" He smiles and holds up the bag.

Erin reciprocates with a grin, but her eyes draw upward, beyond the boy's six-foot frame, and the unexpected sight of her mother standing in the window scowling down at them startles her. With a sigh of irritation, she grabs Brad and once again leads him away to find some real privacy. As they depart the side of the house, Queenie can now see them clearly from Erin's room. She is wrapped in Brad's letterman jacket. As it swallows her lanky preteen body, she longingly stares down at its handsome owner, intermittently coughing.

"Where's my jacket?" asks Brad.

"Oh." Erin briskly rubs her arms. "When I heard you and Mom talking I grabbed the nearest thing to put on—this hoodie—and rushed down to keep Mom from running you off. She's really freaking out about us."

Brad, unsure whether Erin knows the history between her mom and his dad, decides to shelve that topic for now. "Well, I'm sure she'll eventually warm up to the idea."

"Hopefully, before she drives me crazy. What did *your* parents say?"

"They were surprised, but they're not against my having a girlfriend. They just want to make sure I don't rush into anything."

"That sounds reasonably sane, I guess."

"Do you look forward to meeting them, Erin?"

"Yes…and no. I'm nervous about what they'll think of me."

"You have absolutely nothing to be nervous about, I promise." Something catches his eye. "Hey, is that a '56 Ford?"

Brad and Erin walk to the back of the property and discover a classic pickup truck that appears to have been sitting there for quite some time. Tall grass borders the edges where the riding lawnmower is unable to reach. Metal skin diseased with rust and blistered, peeling paint. Both headlights busted. Tires completely dry-rotted. A worn, thick towrope is still tightly cinched around its front axle.

In the bed of the truck, up next to its back window, lies a barely recognizable deteriorated baby stroller, a double-seater, that has fallen victim to years of rain and radiation from the unrelenting sun pounding on it. What is left of its deteriorated, flaky fabric is bleached to a colorless hue, and the wheels have frozen stiff over time.

"Yeah. I guess. I don't know. It's just an old truck as far as I know."

Brad pops opened the hood and snoops around the engine. "Does it run?"

"No, it's deader than a doornail. But Dad plans on resurrecting it someday, after he gets better."

"Oh, um…sure." Brad replies in a somber tone. Looking down, he is unsure what to say next but Erin chimes in, breaking the brief, awkward silence.

"I'm starving. Let's eat."

Erin grabs the bag out of his hand and walks to the rear of the truck, where the tailgate is missing. She slides back onto the bed and Brad plops down next to her. With its tires being flat, their feet easily rest on the ground.

Hidden below and behind the tall grass is a temporary license plate Erin crafted out of wood and paint. She made it after her father first got sick and placed it there until he gets better and revives the truck to its original glory—bringing it back to life—and gets a real plate. It simply reads, DADDY.

"Mm," hums Erin biting into her sandwich, "it's still warm. There's just something about eating or drinking something hot outside on a crisp, cold day. Don't you think?"

"Mm-hm," hums back Brad, sipping through his straw.

"Oh, how did the game go last night?"

"We crushed 'em." He swipes crumbs off his leg.

"Sounds like it was easy for you guys."

"Yeah, except for Big John. He got hurt."

"Big John? I didn't think it was physically possible for Big John to get hurt."

"Well, he did. Stretched the ligaments in his knee. But if he follows doctor's orders and stays off of it this week, he has a fifty-fifty chance of playing in next Friday's big game."

"I'm glad he's not hurt too badly."

"Me too." Brad takes another sip of his soda. "Okay." He places discarded fast food wrappers in the bag. "It's time for my favorite game."

"Oh no." Erin makes a half-hearted combination of moan and laugh, rolling her eyes. "Not *that* again."

"Aw, come on, you know you like it. Tell me something about you that I don't already know."

"I've told you everything," she retorts, in a lighthearted, sheepish manner.

"C'mon, I know there's more. You're way too complicated of a person."

"Hey, I'm not sure how I should take that."

"You know what I mean."

"Yeah, I know what you mean." She smiles. "Let's see. Oh, I've got it."

"What?"

"I'm probably the only person outside of Lucus's family who knows his actual name."

"Lucus isn't his real name?"

"Nope."

"What is it?" Brad asks.

"It's Leslie."

"Really? Leslie? Hmm."

"What?"

"Now that you mention it, I seem to sort of remember knowing that being his name. I'm not sure how or when, but at some point I do recall him being referred to as Leslie."

"Yeah, he got teased a lot about it as a kid, or so he told me."

"I'm sure that's why he changed it. Hey, wait a minute. *Why* do I care about this?"

"Well, it's something you didn't know about me."

"No, it's something I didn't know about *him.*"

"Look, I knew that about him and that's something you didn't know about me. Get it?"

"What I get is that you're trying to confuse me and change the subject at the same time."

"That's a very strong claim, Brad Ross. You got proof of that?"

"Hey—" He comes to a realization. "I don't think you've ever told me your middle name."

Uh oh, Erin thinks. This is now going down a path she did not intend.

"So," Brad continues, "what is it?"

"I've never told you my middle name?" She tries to think of a diversion, but nothing comes to mind.

"No," he answers confidently.

"I would rather not say."

"It can't be that bad."

"Oh can't it? As a matter of fact, it's as bad as Lucus's real name, in my opinion."

"What do you mean?"

"It's a guy's name."

"A guy's name?"

"Yes. My mom, Emily, and Elise all have the exact same middle name as well."

"What is it? You *have* to tell me now."

"No, I refuse, and you can't make me, even with your charm."

"Fine then, I'll just go ask your mom or sister." He moves as if to stand.

Erin grabs his arm. "Wait!" Defeated, she knows he will find out one way or another. "You promise you won't tell anyone?"

"I promise."

"I mean it Brad, you can't tell a soul!"

"Cross my heart."

Erin sighs and pauses. With her eyes closed, she finally mumbles it.

"What?"

"Todd. My middle name is Todd."

"You're joking, right?"

This time Erin really is a little taken back. She looks at him with an unmistakable expression. "You don't believe me?"

Brad now knows she wasn't kidding and goes into recovery mode. "Oh, what I mean is…is…that's not such a bad name and…I don't know why you made such a big deal about it."

"Oh, come on. Now I know you're lying. It's horrible and I hate it. Just listen to it—Erin Todd Gray. It's not feminine at all. Makes me seem like some hick backwoods tomboy."

"Well, you're definitely no tomboy. Why do you all have that as your middle name?"

"That's the one sort-of-redeeming quality about the situation; it's kinda like a family heirloom—a name from my mother's side that's been passed down from generation to generation."

"What's so special about it?"

"Well, I'm the descendant of some very famous people."

"Really? Who?"

"Non other than President and Mrs. Lincoln—you know, Mary Todd Lincoln."

"Really?"

"Yep."

"No kidding?"

"No kidding."

Brad sits still and quiet for a moment, staring off into the distance with a blank expression as if deep in thought. Erin looks at him, wondering if anything is wrong.

"What is it, Brad?"

He slowly gets up off of the truck bed, turns around and stands in front of her, looking into her eyes with an expression of utmost concern.

"Brad?" She's starting to worry. "What's wrong?"

"I…" he mumbles, then pauses a long time.

Her heart sinks. "Yes?"

"I…I didn't know that all this time that I, a mere…commoner, have been in the presence of…royalty."

"What?"

"Oh, your highness," he says, in the worst impression of a British accent Erin has ever heard, "I beg your forgiveness, m'lady." He reverently goes down on one knee.

"You're mocking me!"

"Mercy! Mercy, I beg thee, your ladyship!" He bows his head.

"You are such a dork!" She raises her foot, places the black canvas sneaker on his shoulder, and shoves, tipping him over onto the ground. His limp body lies there motionless for some time.

Erin, sure he's okay, patiently waits until she cannot take it any longer. "Okay, Brad, you can get up now."

No response. His eyes closed.

"Seriously, Brad. Get up."

Nothing.

Erin's hands cover her mouth. "Oh no, did I hurt you?!" She slides off and kneels to check on him.

A scream rips the air. It is Erin. Brad has grabbed her shoulder and pulled her down.

"You are such a faker, Brad Ross!" She tries slapping at his arms, but he's too quick blocking them. They tumble and laugh, tickling each other for a few moments. Erin ends up sitting next to Brad, who is lying on his back, as they pause to catch their breath. She leans over him with her left arm on the other side of his torso supporting her weight. After plucking a crisp autumn leaf from her hair, Erin pulls some rebellious strands back behind her ear. "And to think I thought I could hurt you." She rolls her eyes.

"Oh, you can definitely hurt me, Erin *Todd* Gray."

"How's that, Mr. All-American Football Star?"

"My heart; it's in your hands and at your mercy."

Erin is caught off guard by his poignant admission. For a moment she is lost in thought, back in the past, revisiting previous relationships when she was hurt both emotionally and physically. She snaps out of it, finding herself rubbing circles with her finger on Brad's chest, forming swirling patterns in his T-shirt. As a well-toned athlete, his muscles are solid as a rock. "I suppose it would be very easy for you to hurt me," she thinks out loud.

"Erin!" Brad sits up, gently holds her arms, and stares deeply into her eyes. "I would never, ever, do anything to hurt you! You have to believe me!"

"I do, Brad. I do."

Brad and Erin gaze into each other's eyes, just inches apart. The chemistry between them is growing stronger, and their emotions have pushed the couple's desires to a more intense level. Brad's expression reflects a conflict raging deep within his heart; a battle between what he wants to do versus what he knows he should not do. Erin's eyes, with eyelids dropped half way and her mouth slightly open, reveal a girl who is, at the moment, willing to give in to whatever Brad chooses.

But she knows what that will be. Their lips will not touch. Erin knows he has taken a vow, between him and his Maker, that he will not kiss until his wedding day. It is a gift he is saving for that once-in-a-lifetime moment with the one God has chosen for him. He has never been intimate with a girl, or even kissed one for that matter; a claim Erin cannot make. Not by a long shot.

Brad lays back down to get some separation between them before he gives in to temptation. He was successful again this time, but it's getting harder to control. He takes a deep breath and exhales slowly. Squinting and looking up behind him, the boy cocks his head and stares.

"What is it?" Erin asks.

"It seems we're being spied upon."

"Ugh, not my mother again!" She looks up just in time to see a curtain in her second-story bedroom window fall back into place.

"No, it was your little sister, Queenie."

"Oh."

"Since we're on the topic of names, why does she go by Queenie?"

"That's what Elise wants to be called. She won't answer to anything else."

"But why? Elise is such a beautiful name."

"It's because of the pigs." Erin stares toward the small, barn-like structure standing about thirty yards directly behind the house.

"The pigs?" Brad asks. "What do you mean?"

"Well, Queenie has always had trouble relating to people. The other kids at school think my sister's weird, and she has become somewhat of a social misfit. Emily and I were always on the outskirts of normality, whatever that is, but at least we found others who were like-minded; friends we hung out with. But Queenie, she's on a whole other planet. *I* even have trouble trying to relate to her."

"So, what does this have to with her name and pigs?"

"She's always loved animals—no problem interacting with them. She really comes out of her shell when around any type of nonhuman, but not long after Dad got his pigs, Queenie started acting strange."

"How so?" Brad asks.

"She began spending a lot of time with them. Way too much time, in my opinion. They even learned to follow her verbal commands. She would host tea parties for them in the barn. The pigs would all sit around a makeshift table, all decorated with fancy dishes and stuff, and they let her put big fancy hats on them. It was funny at first. But then one evening during supper, Elise announced that the pigs had elected her to be their queen. She was serious, not just pretending. When I asked how she knew that, she said the large sow told her."

"Thus the name Queenie."

"Yes." Erin sighs. "After that, Mom had her see a counselor

Harris County Public Library
Cy-Fair Library
12/10/14 05:07PM
12/10/14 05:07PM

****

To renew call: 713-747-4763
or visit: www.hcpl.net
You must have your library card
number
and pin number to renew.

PATRON: Muthurajah, Sinya

DUE:

_____

___

_____

___
The ghosts of Emily Gray : a
supernatural
CALL NO: Carpen
CALL NO: Carpen
34028085106731   01/02/15

_____

___

_____

___
Ghost wanted /
CALL NO: Hart X
CALL NO: Hart X
34028085764125   01/02/15

TOTAL: 2

for a few sessions, but the so-called expert said she was just going through a phase 'generated by a powerful imagination.' Huh. It's a phase that's still going on, with no sign of ending, I'm afraid."

"And it bothers you, doesn't it?"

"Yes, especially considering the pigs."

"What about them?"

"I know pigs are smart compared to other animals, but these here, they're scary smart. They don't act like other pigs."

"In what way?"

"Well, one night I found Queenie in the barn, sitting on the floor, talking to them, and they sat in a half-circle around her—like, listening intently. When I walked in Queenie stopped talking, turned around and stared at me without saying a word. I told her it was late and tried to coax her inside, and the large sow got up and walked toward me in a threatening manner. I still get chills thinking about it."

Brad frowns. "Wow, that *is* creepy."

"That's just the tip of the iceberg. These pigs don't roll around in the mud, either. They keep themselves really clean. I mean, relatively speaking. When they're not eating, they sit around looking at each other like they're communicating telepathically. I tell you, Brad, they're not normal."

"Are you sure they're actually pigs?" Brad is almost joking.

"I dunno. They don't look like normal pigs to me."

"How so?"

"They're nearly hairless. And their skin is much paler and softer than any pig I've ever been around. Their snouts and ears are smaller than usual. And their eyes…there's something about their eyes when they stare into mine. It's almost as if they're…human."

"Where did these guys come from?"

She crumbled a dry leaf in her hand and scattered the bits like confetti in the grass. "I'm not sure, but we were told they're some rare species from somewhere in Asia. I haven't been able to find a picture resembling them exactly anywhere on the Internet, though. When we first got them, Dad told us they were a research project for some company—he didn't tell us the name. All he had to do was inject them with some medicine or antibiotic, or whatever it is, once a week and feed them a special diet. Apparently we get paid pretty well for doing it and keeping it a trade secret. Once a month a couple of guys show up with cash, inspect the pigs in private, then leave without saying a word."

"Who takes care of the pigs since your dad…you know, can't?"

"Oh, Queenie gladly took over those responsibilities. The weird thing is, and I'm not joking, when it's time for their shots, Queenie tells them to line up and they do it, and always in the same order with the largest one at the front of the line. Each one waits patiently for its turn and she injects them one by one. They don't flinch at all. It's like they know the shots are good for them."

"That's something I've got to see someday," Brad says looking around. "Where are these odd oinkers now?"

"Either roaming the property or in the barn over there."

"Let's go check it out. I want to see these guys for myself."

"Okay, I guess. If you really want to."

"Yeah, it'll be interesting."

"All right." Erin stands up and helps Brad to his feet. She wipes the grass off his back as they make their way to the small wooden building.

Next to it stands a two-story rusted metal framework of legs supporting a large, barrel-shaped container.

Brad walks underneath it. "What's this, some kind of water tower?"

"It's called a cistern. Back in the day, when this was a working farm, it collected rainwater to irrigate crops. Now it's basically a mosquito hatchery full of stagnant water. The thing's pretty old and rickety. As a matter of fact, I wouldn't be standing under there if I were you. It's liable to collapse."

"Nah…looks pretty solid to me. Let's find out." Feeling a bit adventurous, he tests his theory by pushing up on a crossbeam.

"Brad!" Erin quickly takes a few steps back while looking up.

Holding his breath with eyes closed, he keeps pushing upward with all his might.

A squealing whine of stressed metal sends Brad dashing out from underneath the cistern. He stops and embraces Erin, and they both look up. It stands steady for now.

"I told you." She gives him a light slap on the back.

"Man, that would make for one monster of a baptism if it fell over. I still think it's pretty stable, though. Would probably take the strength of Samson to bring it down."

"Oh really," Erin says, "would you bet your life on it?"

Brad looks at her as if he's really thinking about it, then laughs. "No, not really."

"Good." She smiles. "Maybe from now on you will heed my warnings."

"Maybe," he says with a grin. "Just maybe." He takes hold of Erin's hand and leads her toward the barn's single oversized door, which is halfway open. "Let's go see these genius pigs of yours."

As they walk, Erin looks up to her dad's bedroom window to see if she can catch a glimpse of him. If he's up and around, that means he is feeling better, but there is no sighting.

They slowly make their way around the door, and Brad peeks in. "Nothing." Entering, he looks around. The barn is empty except for a layer of hay on the ground. Above the entrance is a loft with a rickety ladder leading up to it. Light pierces through the loft window opening, exposing the ancient rafters above as well as all the dust and hay particles swirling about in the air. "This is kind of small for a barn, isn't it?"

"Well, story has it that this was built small on purpose because it was a hideaway for the Underground Railroad."

"You mean to hide runaway slaves."

"Yeah. Its small size didn't attract attention because it didn't look big enough to house a bunch of people. A quick glance around would make anyone snooping think nobody was here. But the ground in here is actually a dirt-covered floor of thick wooden beams over a hidden dug-out room underneath."

"That's amazing. How big is it?"

"Oh, about the size of this room, maybe a little smaller."

"Can you still get down there?"

"Oh sure, here's the trap door." Erin walks over and pulls it open. "Down there is where the vials and syringes are stored, or rather, hidden."

Peering over, Brad sees steps quickly disappearing into pitch black. "Can I go down there?"

"Sure, if you want. There's a string hanging to your right once you get a few steps down. Feel around for it. When you find it, give it a tug and the light will come on.

"Cool." He slowly makes his way down and finds the light switch.

Erin stays above ground, looking over her shoulder at the door to make sure the swine are not sneaking up behind her.

"Whoa! It smells like death warmed over down here!"

"Yeah, I know. Why do you think I didn't follow you?"

"Well, thanks for the warning," he yells sarcastically.

"You're welcome." Her tone is equally sarcastic.

"It's just an empty room down here, except for a cabinet."

"That's where the pig juice is kept."

"Pig juice?"

"That's what I call it."

"Yeah, I'm looking for a label now, but there isn't one. So you have no idea what it is?"

"No." She peers over her shoulder again.

Brad replaces the vial of yellowish liquid and walks back up.

"I've tried to look up the license plate of the guys who come by once a month, but can't find anything on it."

"Let me know what it is." Brad steps back onto the floor. "I'll have my dad ask Sheriff Knox to look into it. He's got connections at the FBI."

"Okay, sure."

"Speaking of Sheriff Knox..." Brad hesitates. "I heard he pulled you over last night and that you were upset or something."

Erin heads for the barn door. "Oh, you heard about that?"

"Yeah, you okay? What happened?"

"Sure, yeah. It was nothing; just a misunderstanding, really."

"Nothing?"

"Yes. I didn't even get a ticket."

"Okay. Well, I'm glad you're all right."

"Thanks. Me too."

Erin recalls the beautiful moth she saw, and excitedly describes it in vivid detail—its light triangular body and bulging fuzzy legs—and how it landed on her chest. The way her face lights up while recounting the incident, almost in terms of it being a miraculous event, makes an indelible impression on Brad. It's a visual he won't soon forget.

Brad glances at his watch. "Oh…I've got to go."

"So soon?"

"Yeah, I've got a ton of homework to do before tonight's party. You're still going with me, right?" They make their way out of the barn and cross the yard.

"Sure, I suppose," she answers reluctantly.

"Well don't sound so excited about my birthday bash," Brad retorts.

"Oh, please don't take it the wrong way, Brad. It's just that Big John is throwing it for you, and I still don't feel comfortable around him. I know he doesn't like me."

By this time the two have reached the front of the house.

"Then I suppose"—he catches a glimpse of Rose staring at them through a window—"we'll just have to show him, and your mother, how wrong they both are about us."

Erin, knowing Brad has made a well-founded counter to her objection, concedes the point. "You're right. We just need to give it some more time."

"That's my girl. Speaking of your mom, I need to say goodbye. It's the proper thing to do."

"Oh no, no," Erin objects knowing full well that encounter might be worse than the first. "That's okay. Like we said, let's give her some time." As they walk, she notices the Corvette for the first time. "Is that your birthday present?"

"Can you believe it?" he answers. "I'm still not sure I do."

"It's gorgeous, Brad. I can't wait to ride in it tonight."

"I can't wait to pick you up tonight. See you around six, okay?"

"All right, see you then. And I'll have your present."

"I know I'll love it, whatever it is."

After a prolonged embrace, Brad gets in his car and pulls out of the driveway.

ERIN INTENTLY STARES AT HER REFLECTION in the mirror. Fresh from the shower twenty minutes ago and still wrapped in a towel, she sits at the vanity in her bedroom applying makeup. This is a quick and easy task, as her complexion is one most girls her age would die for. The smooth, blemish-free skin needs no help, but old habits die hard. The liberal application of blush, eye shadow, and lipstick was once Erin's way of gaining attention and showing the world who she was, but now all she uses is a light base and some eyeliner (but still a rather above-average thickness of the black border).

Leaning in closely, she pencils on the last dark stroke underneath her right eye, double-checks her face for anything missed, then places her products back in their bag and zips it up. A quick swipe of her hand across the dresser surface removes fallen powder.

She stands up and walks toward the closet, but something stops her: a thought, a memory. Turning back slightly, Erin peers over her shoulder into the mirror again. *How did I get here? How did I end up in a relationship with a guy like Brad? Do I really deserve to be with him?*

Such thoughts have plagued her since she first started having feelings for the hometown hero, but seeing how he treated her mom after she berated him really brought on doubts of her worthiness. Her reaction in a similar situation probably would have been the exact opposite of his. Present-day Erin usually feels comfortable around Brad, but Erin of the past knows it's not a match made in heaven.

She loosens the towel, lowering it behind her slightly. Exposed across her upper back are four scars, two on the left and two on the right. Each pair consists of one puncture wound next to another about three inches apart. The two sets, which have faded a little over the past year, are separated by a distance of exactly eight inches. Erin looks at them without any contemplation. There is nothing about the precisely aligned wounds that she hasn't already gone over in her mind a million times, and nothing is going to make them go away completely.

After staring a few moments, she lowers the towel farther from her right shoulder. Revealed is another pure reminder of her dark past—a black inverted pentagram bored into her soft, pale skin. Centered on her shoulder blade, the occult tattoo has not faded at all. It is as black and bold as the day she got it. Erin knows that at some point she is going to have to divulge all of this to Brad, but has yet to do so. She fears the consequences.

Not wanting to be reminded of it any longer, Erin immediately pulls the towel back up, turns, and heads for the closet. The time is getting close for Brad to arrive. Knowing him, he will be here on the dot, and another encounter with her mother must be thwarted.

Five minutes later, a fully clothed Erin applies some lip gloss, snatches her purse, and does a double-check in the mirror before rushing out of the bedroom. Bounding down the staircase, she passes her mother climbing up.

Alongside them on the wall, which is skinned in a busy floral-patterned wallpaper, hangs an original, one-of-a-kind photograph of Abraham and Mary Todd Lincoln along with their eleven-year-old son, Willie. The black-framed oval image, yellowed with age and spattered in mildew, was discovered in a box of junk tucked away in the corner of a barn on another Todd family farm long before Rose came into this world.

The Victorian-era parents, clad in dark clothing, stare out with haunting expressions of melancholy. Willie's cocked head, slightly drooped soulless eyes, and barely gaping mouth offer the voyeur clues that something is abnormal. At auction, the relic would easily fetch thousands, if not close to a million. Contributing to its exorbitant value, along with its being the only copy, is the fact that the young William, who is fully clothed in formal attire and propped up between his parents, is dead. All known copies of this fabled post-mortem photograph and the original metal plate were thought to have been purposely destroyed, but this one print, like baby Moses leisurely drifting down the river Nile, slipped past the destructive hands of historical revisionists.

Rose's distorted facial profile reflects in the picture's convex glass. "Where are you off to in such a hurry?"

"Going out. Don't wait up," Erin answers without breaking stride.

"But we're contacting Emily again tonight. Don't you want to be here?"

"Tell her I said hi," the twin mocks, opening the front door.

On the other side stands Brad, fist raised in the air, ready to knock.

"Hey Thmmmph—"

Erin quickly cups her hand over his mouth to silence him. Before closing the door, she takes a quick glance back to see if Rose heard anything. Not sure whether or not her mother is coming, she grabs his hand and immediately leads him away. Brad once again finds himself being dragged down the porch steps.

"Hey, how are you? You look nice," fires Erin rapidly, walking briskly and pulling Brad along.

"Fine. Thanks. Hey, isn't that Shep you told me about lying there on the porch?" He turns back, pointing.

"Yes. You two can get to know each other later. Let's get going, shall we?" She picks up the pace, heading straight for his car.

"See you later, Shep," Brad barks out, while being tugged farther away.

The old dog raises his head, gives a faint whine too soft to hear at this distance, and then lies back down. They reach his car and, after Erin is comfortably seated, Brad closes her door and gets in on the other side.

"You sure seem to be in a hurry tonight." He fires up the engine and puts it in reverse. "I thought you were hesitant about going."

"Well, you know. It sounds like a lot of fun, with the fireworks and all," she replies while he backs up. "Okay, you're clear," she says, looking in her side-view mirror. "You can go now."

He puts it in first, and as they head down the driveway, Erin looks back one more time. All is clear, and now she can finally relax.

That is, until they arrive at the party.

"Wow, you look absolutely beautiful tonight," Brad tells her.

"Thank you." Erin stares at him with a smile. She just keeps looking and grinning while Brad glances over now and then. "So?"

"So? So what?" he replies.

"Don't you want to know what it is?"

"What what is?"

She rolls her eyes. "Your present!"

"Oh, that. You going with me tonight is all the present I need."

"Don't be silly. You know I said I got you something."

"Yeah, I remember."

"Do you want it, or not?"

"Of course I do. I've been wondering about it all day. I just didn't want to seem expectant and greedy."

"Well it's not quite on the level of a fancy sports car." She reaches into her purse. "But it's the most valuable gift I can give you."

"You didn't spend too much, did you?" He knows they don't have a lot of money.

"No, not at all. I barely spent anything, actually. But it *is* something highly treasured—a piece of me." She pulls it out and holds it up. Worried what he will think, she waits for a reaction.

"Is that what I think it is?" he asks.

"It depends on what you think it is."

"A book of your writings."

"Yes. How do you feel about that?"

"Are you kidding? I love it!"

"Really? You're not just saying that?"

"No, I mean it. It's the best thing you could have given me."

Erin is a very talented writer. Despite her past and what conclusions others may have drawn from her actions and appearance, she is gifted and well-read. Drawing inspiration from Victorian gothicists such as Stoker, Stevenson, Shelley, Wilde, and Poe, her unique, eclectic work is saturated in themes of dark and profound contemplation, especially relating to spiritual influences on the human experience. Brad, however, reads mainly textbooks and sports magazines.

Much of Erin's work she considers to be explorations, journeys into her innermost being to discover who she is and what makes her tick, as well as the meaning of life. And some of these sensitive and frighteningly transparent searches are in the handwritten journal she has just relinquished to him—when he opens it and begins reading is the moment he dives into her very soul.

"You have to promise me, though, that you won't read any of these until after you take me back to my house tonight. I'm too nervous about what you'll think of them."

"Are you serious? That's not fair. I can't wait that long."

"I could always just keep it." She pretends to place it back into her purse.

"Okay, okay, how about a compromise?"

"Like what?"

"Pick one out and read it to me."

"Right now?"

"Just one, and you get to pick it out. Please. It is my birthday, after all."

"All right," she concedes, "but only one."

"That's all I'm asking."

Erin flips through the pages back and forth a few times until finally selecting one she considers the least revealing. She clears her throat, glances at Brad, and then begins to recite without having to read it:

Evening
As the darkness falls, darkness rises

Rises in the heart of man
Rises to destroy again

Spreading outward, all absorbing
Drawing inward, all destroying

Blind with lust, the blackness sees
All it desires, all it decrees

Undercover, dead of night
A trail of bones is its delight

Forever starved, never still
Satisfaction unfulfilled

Morning
As the sun rises, darkness falls

Brad stares forward, pondering the poem.

Erin takes a deep sigh of relief. "What do you think?"

"That was amazing, Erin. You have such a way with words. I don't know how you do it. Really, that was beautiful."

"I know," she responds in a playful tone to disguise her nervousness. "And I find *your* way of speaking, the common vernacular of an ordinary peasant in steerage class, quite charming as well."

Brad appreciates her playing off his royalty joke.

"It's not too depressing for you?" Erin asks.

"No, not at all." This is a good segue into talking about his faith. "In fact, it reminds me of the gospel of John in the New Testament. He writes about the darkness, how people love it and live in it. He also relates Jesus to the light and how people misunderstand and reject the light." He pauses for her reaction.

Erin is thinking of how to phrase her response. "Well, if you're subtly referring to me, then yes, I don't understand it." She won't reveal that she rejects it as well.

"What about Christianity do you not understand, if you don't mind us talking about it?"

She would rather not. "Oh, I don't mind. I can see how it makes sense for a few really horrific people to burn in hell for eternity; I get that. But I don't understand why normal, everyday, good people should suffer the same fate unless they believe in Jesus. And on the flip side, murderers, child abusers and so on can be forgiven if they just ask Jesus into their heart? That's not justice. I don't get it."

Brad swallows hard and grips the steering wheel a little tighter, his knuckles turning white. He is not prepared to tackle what she has thrown at him; that playbook has not been dropped into his lap. So he defaults to what he has been trained to say. "Not everything makes sense to me, either. You just gotta have faith. I do, and it has really affected my life in a great way. God has a wonderful plan for your life, too."

"That's great for you, Brad." She has heard something like this before. "And I know your faith has been important in forming who you are. Seeing that inside you is a big part of why I'm attracted to you. But there are many other faiths out there, other religions. I'm not sure what I am right now. I used to be one thing…but I moved on, even if I've temporarily landed in limbo. I want you to know, though, that I *am* a spiritual person. I *do* believe in God. But for me right now, the best thing would be to not be pressured into a certain specific direction. I have to discover that for myself. Does any of that make sense?"

Now it's her turn to take a deep swallow and nervously wait. The last thing Erin wants is for this to come between them. She understands the gravity of religious belief, and how an impasse like this can separate two lives forever. All this small-town girl wishes for is that they can shelve the topic, tuck it away in a locked room somewhere and proceed with the way things have been so far.

"Oh sure, I understand. I would never try to force you into anything. And if I ever seem that way to you, please let me know, because I wouldn't be doing it on purpose."

His words are a relief. Thank goodness he is not offended. "I'm sure that when God wants me to go a certain direction, he'll give me a sign."

"Me too." Brad is pleased that awkward conversation has finally died a merciful death. "One thing I like about your poem is the last line. What was it? As the sun rises, darkness falls?"

"Yes, that's right." She looks down at the book, which has remained open to the same page.

"I see that line as the light at the end of the tunnel. The whole rest of the poem is gloomy and depressing, but at the end there's hope."

"Very good." She looks a little surprised. "That's exactly what it means. I always believe in hope. You know, that's not bad for a jock."

"Hey now!" He looks at her, and they share a welcome laugh.

Erin, still smiling, looks down and scans the last line. Her eyes squint, then her brow furrows. Something is not right. She looks again more closely. There is, in fact, a scribal error; a misspelled word. Erin never misspells words, ever. Winning the junior high spelling bee three years in a row is proof enough the girl knows how to string together a line of correct letters in the proper sequence.

But this one is a doozy. Instead of *sun* it says *Son*. She reads it again slowly to make sure she is not seeing things:

As the Son rises, darkness falls

Before tonight, she must have gone over the entire book at least three times after penning it in calligraphy, and never once did she read this word as it appears now. And not only is it misspelled, the anomaly is also capitalized. Flubbed orthography for the straight-A English student adds insult to injury.

She goes over in her mind options to correct it, and, after a few seconds, decides there are none, really. She cannot make another page and add it in. She cannot erase the letter because it is written in ink. Erin decides to close the book and forget about it for now, but the insecurities have already been triggered. "I can't believe how nice you were to my mom after the way she treated you."

"Really?" Headlights far in the distance in his rearview mirror distract him.

"You're such a good person, Brad. Honestly, I don't know how I ended up with you."

"You act like you're some kind of monster and I'm an angel. I promise you, the two extremes are not accurate."

"I don't think I'm a monster. I know I'm not that bad a person. Sure, I've done some things, but you…I can't imagine you *ever* doing *anything* wrong."

"Trust me, I've done plenty wrong. You just haven't seen it."

"What, like not taking the trash out when you were told?"

"Well, yes, actually."

"See, that's what I mean. You're so good that that's the worst you can come up with."

Brad racks his brain, trying to remember the greatest iniquity he had ever perpetrated. "When I was little I stole candy from the store once. In the car my mom discovered I took it, turned around and drove us back. She made me return it and confess to the owner what I did. I cried all the way home after that."

"Ooh, Brad. I didn't know you were such a hardened criminal. I may have to rethink our relationship now."

Brad smiles.

Erin continues. "It's just that, compared to you, I feel people are judging me, that they see me as some evil presence who's going to lead you down the path of destruction. To be honest, it's a lot of pressure. I know they think I don't deserve to be with you."

"It doesn't matter what other people think, Erin."

"That's easy for you to say, you're not the one being judged. Why do people get off doing that, anyway? I mean, who are they to say what is right or wrong? What is the standard of goodness they're using, anyway? Their own opinions? Everybody has different views."

"I'm not sure why people are so judgmental. I hate it as much as you do."

"Oh, listen to me. This is your birthday." She reaches over to rub his arm. "I'm being such a downer."

"I don't mind. I like talking things out with you."

"Well, I just want tonight to be memorable for you, and not for the wrong reasons."

A horn blast from Brad's left startles them.

Another car has pulled up beside him. They're traveling down a two-lane highway, so the other vehicle is illegally headed the wrong way. Brad and Erin look over.

"Who is that?" Brad asks.

"I don't know. I've never seen that car before."

The car growling beside them is a brand-new, all-black Dodge Viper. Its windows tinted illegally dark so it's impossible to see who it is. The driver revs his engine.

"What's he want?" asks Brad.

"He wants to race," his streetwise girlfriend answers.

"Race?"

"You're not going to do it, *right?*" Erin asks.

"Of course not!"

The Viper guns it up ahead a little, then slows back even with the Corvette. Brad waves over, signaling that he is not interested. The black car guns it again, pulls over in front of Brad and taps the brakes.

"Whoa!" Brad shouts, braking quickly. "This guy is crazy!"

The car once again pulls over and slows down even with Brad, revving its engine even harder.

"No! Go away!" Brad yells, waving again.

Not taking no for an answer, the aggressor pulls to his left a little, then swerves into Brad's lane.

Brad jerks to the right to avoid being sideswiped. With nowhere else to go, he barrels down the shoulder, kicking up dust and debris.

Erin screams.

The black car moves back over, allowing Brad to reenter his lane.

Brad is furious. His competitive nature kicks in. He decides the only way to get away from this maniac is to outrun him.

"Okay, that's what you want?" he asks out loud. "Then that's what you'll get."

He floors it. The black car responds, accelerating instantly. The two cars run neck and neck, quickly approaching eighty miles an hour. Trading leads back and forth, they roar down the highway closing in on ninety.

"Brad, stop!" Erin cries out.

He shifts to another gear.

One hundred.

One hundred ten.

One hundred twenty.

Erin pulls out the cross pendant tucked in her shirt and grips it tightly with one hand. Preparing herself for impact, she grips the dash with the other. "Brad, please! It's not worth it!" she screams.

Realizing how fast they're going, Brad lets off the gas. They slow down, while the Viper keeps screaming down the highway.

Ninety.

Eighty.

The tail lights of the other car have already mysteriously disappeared, but it is not *those* lights Brad needs to worry about. "Oh no."

Flashing red-and-blues accompanied by a siren trail them close behind. Brad pulls over. Erin tucks her purse behind her legs on the floorboard. After sitting a few seconds, a bright beam of light streams into the Corvette's side-view mirror, slightly blinding Brad to what is happening outside. The sound of a car door shutting is heard, and then the shadowy silhouette of a large figure approaches. The person leans down, looking into the window.

Sheriff Knox.

Brad stares ahead, hands still gripping the steering wheel. His heart and mind are still racing. Knox taps on the glass. Disappointed in the situation in which he now finds himself, Brad slowly cranks the knob, lowering the window.

"Brad?" the sheriff asks.

"Yes, sir."

The lawman leans over and notices who is with his son's best friend. "Hmm," he lets out. "I'm gonna to have to ask you to shut off the engine and exit the vehicle." Then he leans over to get Erin's attention. "You stay right where you are."

"Yes, sir." Brad unbuckles his seat belt. He gets out, and Sheriff Knox leads him to the back of the Corvette.

"Son," he starts out, "I'm not going to tell you how fast I clocked you, but suffice it to say, it was in the triple digits."

"Yes, sir." The embarrassed teen looks down at his feet.

"This is more like some stunt my knucklehead son would pull off. What's gotten into you? Is it that girl? Did she put you up to this?"

"Oh, no sir." He looks up at the sheriff. "Not at all. In fact, she was trying to get me to stop."

"Then what gives?"

"Well you see, that black car, the one in front of me, it tried to get me to race but I wouldn't. Then it nearly ran me off the road, and I sorta lost it and took off trying to outrun it and—"

"A black car?" Knox asks.

"Yes, sir. You must've seen it. It was right ahead of me."

"I saw no such vehicle."

Brad is perplexed about that, but is not going to argue the point.

"Brad, this is not like you. Driving reckless, seeing things that aren't there. A word of advice, son." He places his hand on the young man's shoulder. "Be careful who you hang out with."

Brad glances back at Erin, who does not dare turn around.

"Yes, I'm talking about her. She's got problems, real problems. I've had many run-ins with her and her friends. I've been out to her house on more than one occasion. And there's that thing about her dad, I know you know about that."

"Yes, sir."

"Take my advice. Drop her. She's nothing but trouble and will drag you down with her."

This time Brad does not respond with *yes, sir*. He just looks down.

Sheriff Knox takes a deep breath and looks around. "You know I can haul you in for this?"

"Yes, sir."

"But this your first-ever offense, or anything even coming close to one. And because it's your birthday and you're like family, I'm going to let this one slide."

"Thank you, sir. It won't happen again, I promise."

"I know it won't, because I won't be so lenient next time. You got that?"

"Yes, sir. Thank you, sir."

"Now go on, get outta here. And drive careful."

As Brad returns to his car door, Sheriff Knox calls out, "Brad."

He faces the sheriff again who says, "I hope you'll take my advice…for your sake, as well as your family's."

Brad simply nods and gets into the car. Once inside, he exhales deeply.

"What happened?" asks Erin.

"He let me off with a warning."

"A warning? That's awesome! If it had been me, I'd be cuffed in the back of his car. It must be nice to have connections like that."

"Well, he assured that I'm entitled to only one get-out-of-jail-free card, and *that* was it. I can't believe I did that, I don't know what got into me. I'm sorry for putting you in danger like that. It was so stupid."

"Don't worry about it, Brad, nothing bad happened. Trust me, I've been through worse. A lot worse."

Brad starts the engine and pulls out onto the highway. In his rearview mirror he sees Sheriff Knox do an about-face and head in the opposite direction.

TEN MINUTES LATER THE COUPLE PULL INTO AN EN-TRANCE marked only by a large, open metal cattle gate with helium-filled balloons tied to it. The road they are now on is actually not a road in the truest sense of the word, but rather a double path in the foot-high grass formed by tires of vehicles that travel down it from time to time.

The still and crisp crystal-clear night, domed in a dazzling array of stars, is perfect for an outdoor party with a good fire and plenty of pyrotechnics. When they approach other vehicles parked off to the side, Brad turns next to the last one and kills his engine. They get out and head toward the revelry. As the two walk past cars, both on their left and right, they inspect each one looking for the black Viper. It is not here.

The party zone is marked off by a border of tiki torches. Almost everyone is already here, and the festivities have begun with music blaring and people conversing loudly, competing with extremely high decibels bursting from behemoth speakers.

As the couple approaches they hear, "Brad!" Big John comes toward them, performing some sort of wobbling skip with a brace on his leg and grasping a drink tumbler in his hand. "It's the birthday boy! About time."

"John!" Brad scolds. "What are you doing on your feet? The doctors said you have to stay off your leg."

"Doctors...what do *they* know?"

"You're joking, right? You should at least be on crutches."

"Crutches are for wimps, dude."

"Why am I surprised?" Brad thinks out loud. "But if you miss next week's game, you'll regret this."

"Yes, Mom," replies John in an overdramatically disgusted tone. "Look, everything's gonna be fine. There's a better chance of me being at the game than you, *that's* how good I am. And besides, is this any way to treat your host?"

Brad just stares at him, not changing his expression of disapproval.

John takes a drink and looks at the girl beside his best friend. "Hey, Erin," he says, just to be polite.

"Hey," she replies, just to be polite.

"Come on guys." John spins on his good leg. "The cooler's over here and dinner's roasting." John wobbles back, slower than when he approached, due to the increasing pain. Walking behind him, Brad and Erin cannot see him wincing.

Throughout the evening, everyone intermittently converses with Brad, wishing him happy birthday and talking about their chances in the playoffs, while Erin quietly holds his hand. Other than the occasional greeting from those approaching the football star, Erin does not engage in any conversation. The cheerleaders are especially cold to her. She is light-years away from her comfort zone and tired of feeling like a vestigial appendage, but endures it for Brad, as she wants him to have the best evening possible, especially after what happened on the way.

But Brad is not oblivious to his girlfriend's plight. He knows she is not at ease with his friends, and she's being a trouper about the whole ordeal. Wanting to rescue her, and desiring to spend some time with her alone, he nabs a couple of canvas camp chairs and leads her out farther into the field, beyond the torches, where the music is not as distracting and the area is not populated. After setting up the two seats with their backs to the party, he tells her, "You stay here. I'll be right back with a surprise."

Brad walks off and Erin is left sitting there all alone, momentarily abandoned, but enjoying the solitude. In front of her, about two hundred yards off, is the dark silhouette of a tree line, just barely visible thanks to the faint glow of the neighboring town behind it.

Peering into the trees, she can almost hear, or feel, a calling to enter; to return home, so to speak. A burst of fluttering wings explodes overhead and startles her. It is the flock of grackles, hundreds of them, heading toward the woods, their home. As she watches the massive swarm disappear into the night, the temperature quickly drops. Rubbing her shoulders, she can't take her eyes off the trees. The calling she once felt to enter has now turned into an ominous forewarning of danger.

"Hey!" comes a shout from behind.

Erin pops up in her chair and quickly rotates. Standing there is Brad, with two cups of steaming beverage and a couple of small blankets.

He chuckles. "Did I scare you?"

"Why yes, did you do that on purpose?"

"Yeah, sorta," he answers with a big grin.

"Well, your reputation as a good boy is quickly evaporating tonight, Brad Ross."

"Did you hear the coyotes?"

"Coyotes?"

"Yeah, the howling from the woods. We could hear them from all the way over there."

"You don't think they'll come over here, do you?"

"Oh no. They're deathly afraid of humans. They'll keep their distance."

"Promise?"

"I promise. Brought you some hot chocolate."

"Oh, that is so sweet." The hot mug warms her cold hands.

"Here." He holds out his arm with a blanket folded over it. "Take this and cover up."

She drapes the blanket over her legs. Brad sits down next to her and, after getting comfortably situated, reaches over. They sit together, hand in hand, sipping hot chocolate while gazing up at the nighttime sky.

"Thanks for being here with me tonight, Erin. I wouldn't be enjoying it near as much without you. I mean it."

"So you're having a good time?"

"Yes."

Erin is relieved to hear that her nervousness and discomfort is not putting a damper on his evening. She gazes up. "The stars are amazing tonight, don't you think?"

"Yeah. It's hard to believe there are billions of galaxies out there, each containing billions of stars. It's absolutely mind-blowing."

"They're so magical; mystical in some spiritual way. I can't stop looking at them."

"I can't stop looking at you."

Erin turns and gives him an *I can't believe you just said that* look, even though she loved hearing it.

"I know it sounds corny." He shrugs. "And I know I can't say things as eloquently as you can, but it's true. You are beautiful, Erin Gray. I hope you know that."

Erin smiles and slowly pans back up. "Do you think there's life out there?

"What, you mean like aliens?"

"Yeah, or something like that."

"Nah." Brad turns away and glances up himself. "I don't think so. From what I know, there are no other planets like ours suitable for sustaining life."

"Well I do. I mean, the universe is so huge, as you were just saying, there *has* to be some other life forms out there. The odds are for it. The real mystery, though, is whether they're friendly or hostile."

"Hey, look!" Brad points. "Falling stars."

"I see them! One, two, three, four, there's five of them. Wow! That is so cool!"

"Yeah, speaking of odds, what are the chances of five in a row like that?"

Brad and Erin watch the glowing projectiles, each the same exact size and distance apart, blaze across the sky above them one right after the other. Once the celestial procession streaks over, the couple stands up and turns to continue tracking them. All the partygoers have stopped what they were doing, captivated by the sky show as well. "It looks like they're headed toward my house!" Erin exclaims.

"Don't worry. The probability that they're heading directly toward your house is extremely low. And if they are, they'll disintegrate in the atmosphere before impact."

"Are you sure?"

"Yes Erin, I'm sure. Trust me."

The falling stars disappear over the horizon as quickly as they arrived, and everything goes back to normal.

"Hey Brad!" Big John yells from the party. "Come on, we're about to light your candles!"

Brad knows what his friend is referring to, and it is not birthday cake adornments.

"C'mon, Erin, let's go pop off some fireworks."

John's father acquired the fireworks from the local fire department. They were confiscated from people who were illegally shooting them off within city limits. And these are some *good* ones!

"Oh, you go. I'll sit and watch from here." Erin is not quite ready to rejoin the crowd.

"Don't you want to help me?"

"You'll have plenty of help, I'm sure. Seriously, I'm fine here."

"I'm not leaving without you."

"Brad, igniting runaway explosives does not thrill me, and you cannot talk me into leaving this chair." She folds her arms in defiance.

"Are you sure?" he asks.

"Absolutely. Go blow some things up and have fun. I'll observe from a safe distance." She takes another sip of her hot chocolate and stares at him across the rim of the cup.

"Okay, enjoy the show," he says, walking off. Then he turns back. "Oh, if the coyotes come sniffing around it's probably because they smell the hot chocolate. Just throw it at them, and they should leave you alone."

Erin's eyes widen and she looks back toward the woods. Brad walks off with a big grin. After contemplating a moment, Erin jumps up and runs to Brad and grabs his arm. "I've decided to join you after all. Sounds like fun."

"I'm so glad you changed your mind." He's pleasantly satisfied that his psychological manipulation actually worked.

Erin looks back one more time just to be sure. She has decided to take her chance amongst the wolves at the party rather than with the coyotes from the woods.

When they reach the edge of the crowd, Erin slips her hand out from Brad's arm just as the gang gathers around him to sing "Happy Birthday." She is content to be on the outskirts where the walls of judgment won't be felt closing in on her. After the chorus is finished, John leads him over to light the first rocket.

KABOOM!

The night sky lights up in a fiery array of bright colors followed by the distinct aroma of burnt gunpowder. Screams of primal delight fill the air as well. One after the other, each overhead detonation electrifies the audience in a dazzling display of pyrotechnic violence. Erin makes her way around the outer edge of gawkers and discovers an empty chair waiting for her near the fire and away from them. She parks herself next to someone whom she is sure will not judge her, and is, in fact, having a worse go of it with these people than she. It is a pig being roasted over the open flames.

"I know how you feel," she says, looking at it. To humor herself some more, she acts a little put off by not getting a response. "Fine, be that way."

She observes all that is going on, as if on assignment for National Geographic as a videographer hired to stealthily record wild creatures in their natural habitat. The whole scene brings back a memory, a recollection of what happened the night Emily died. It all started off not unlike this event: a clear starry night, a number of tiki torches, a gathering, an infestation of glowing, red-hot embers from a large bonfire slowly swirling around in the air, and a sacrificed animal. And there were plenty of fireworks, except the sparks generated then were from a sibling rivalry rapidly exploding.

"HOW COULD YOU!" Erin screamed.

"I'm sorry, Erin. It just happened."

"Just happened? Things like this don't 'just happen,' Emily!"

"What do you want me to say?"

"Lucus is my boyfriend! Mine! And you…you are my sister!"

"Look, let's not be overly dramatic about this."

"Overly dramatic? My own sister is fooling around with my boyfriend behind my back, and I'm supposed to not be overly dramatic?"

"Look," Emily said, "It's not like you two are married or anything. Who's to say we can't share him?"

"But I love him! You know that." Erin sobbed. "I'm not going to share him, with you or anybody else like that. That's just wrong!"

"Well, maybe according to you. But Lucus is all for it."

"You liar! Liar!"

"Oh, don't believe me? Just ask him. Here." Emily offered her phone. "Call and ask him yourself."

Erin took the device and hurled it into the nearest tree with a crack. The phone lay fractured, rendered useless. Overcome with emotion, she broke down crying.

"My phone!" Emily hollered.

"I don't care about your stupid phone! I've lost so much more!" She knew in her heart that Emily was telling the truth about Lucus and his desire to be with other girls. Through her sobs she asked, "How long...how long has this been going on?"

"A while."

"Are you going to stop seeing him?"

Emily did not answer.

"Well, are you going to answer me?"

"Lucus and I are together now. Nothing is going to change that."

"Not even for your own flesh and blood sister?"

"Think about it, Erin. I'm more suited for Lucus than you. I'm the one who's been eager, like him, to take our rituals to the next level. Like tonight for example. You're the one who couldn't handle killing a stupid cat and ran off like a sissy to puke your guts out. I, on the other hand, am the one who stayed behind and dismembered it. You should have seen the look in Lucus's eyes. It was obvious he got the same thrill out of it that I did. Sharing that experience with him is something I'll never forget. You see, baby sis, he and I are soul mates. You...well you just don't have what it takes to keep up with a man as charismatic as...Luc."

Pronounced *Luke*, that was Erin's own personal pet name for him.

Erin stood there shaking. "This is not fun and games anymore, Emily! Our little gatherings are more than trendy, rebellious amusement now. We're getting into things that are just not right, and I'm terrified at the results we're getting."

"This is what I'm talking about, Erin. Lucus and I are ecstatic about the results we're getting and want to grab hold of the power out there to teach those who mock us, who abuse us, a lesson, like those stupid cheerleaders, rich kids, jocks…everyone who's considered 'popular' by conformists' standards."

"Not if it means slaughtering innocent animals and all the other stuff we're doing. I'm sure I can convince Lucus of this. I demand that you stop seeing him. Is that clear? I demand it!"

"Luc and I are not going to change. You can either adapt and share him, or lose him altogether. Those are your only options."

Erin stood still for a moment, then slowly lifted her head and peered at Emily through bloodshot eyes with a look of determination brought about by committing to a nonnegotiable decision. "You're wrong. I have another choice." She turned and walked away.

"What's that?" Emily called as Erin opened her car.

"I can lose the both of you." She got in and cranked the engine.

"You're not going to leave me here, are you? Everyone's already gone. I don't want to have to hitch a ride home!"

"I hate you, both of you!" Erin shouted as her parting shot. "As far as I'm concerned, you two can die excruciating deaths and go to hell!" She put it in gear and disappeared into the night, leaving Emily stranded out in the middle of nowhere.

It was the last thing Erin ever said to Emily.

ANOTHER BLAST FROM ABOVE brings Erin back to the present. Their fireworks are getting bigger and louder heading toward the finale. The girl's heart is pounding and her mood has swung dramatically. On the verge of tears, Erin tries to compose herself for Brad's sake.

Her senses heightened, she begins to notice things as if in high definition and slow motion. The warmth of the crackling fire draws her attention. She watches the tiny orange glowing embers rise up into the nighttime sky as they zigzag back and forth, riding the column of heat toward the heavens. A big one way up high catches her attention. But it's not an ember; it's a flaming piece of paper, about the size of a dollar, from the last detonation. It drifts leisurely down to earth, slowly rotating in a counter-clockwise motion. Passing overhead, it methodically floats toward the pig and lands squarely on its chest. From there, Erin pans up to the swine's face.

Squee! Squee! The pig screeches. Its eyes snap open, and the carcass flails wildly to free itself from the metal rod piercing through its gutted body.

Erin screams, jumping up, knocking the chair into the fire.

Everyone turns to look at the girl standing alone with her eyes tightly shut and hands over her ears. All is quiet except for Erin's bloodcurdling shrieks of terror. "Brad! Brad!" she keeps calling out. "Brad!"

He bursts through the crowd and latches onto her. "What is it, Erin? What's wrong?"

"The pig," she shouts, pointing without looking, "it's moving! It's alive!"

Brad glances over to see a very still and very dead hog nearly roasted to perfection.

John has made his way to them and overheard Erin. He gives Brad a look that is unmistakable.

"Come on Erin, it'll be all right. Let's go home." Brad hugs her.

The two start walking off, but not before they hear the crowd murmuring about how strange she is. Erin is shaking, and Brad has to hold her weak body up as they make their way toward the car.

Big John follows closely behind. "I'll get the door." He hobbles ahead to the passenger side. He opens it, and Brad slowly lowers Erin down into the seat.

She sits curled over, whimpering, still not willing to look up. Brad assures her everything is going to be okay and gently closes the door. He makes his way around the back of the car to the other side.

"Thanks, John, for helping here. I'm sorry if your party got ruined."

"It's *your* party, Brad. But it's not the party I'm worried about, it's you. Don't you see this girl has some major issues?"

"You don't know her like I do, John. Okay? Everyone has a bad day now and then."

John snaps, "I guess what they say is true after all. Love *is* blind."

Brad counters with a look that makes it very clear that now is not the time or place to discuss this. He gets in, starts his car, and takes off.

Driving down the highway, he asks, "What can I do for you?"

"Nothing. Just take me home." Her voice is a whimper.

Brad sighs out loud, frustrated at not being able to do anything to help her.

She misjudges his expression. "I'm so sorry I messed up tonight for you."

"You didn't mess it up," he says in a comforting tone. "I'm just worried about you."

"You believe me, don't you?" she asks. "You saw it moving too, right?"

Brad does not answer. Erin knows how to interpret his silence.

"You must think I'm crazy. But I saw it, Brad, with my own two eyes. It squealed and tried to escape."

"I…" he pauses, trying to collect his thoughts. He wants to comfort her but will not sacrifice the truth to do so. "I didn't see it move, but I believe that you believe you saw it move."

"So you *do* think I'm crazy."

"I didn't say that."

"Then what exactly *are* you saying, Brad?"

"Your eyes could have been playing tricks on you. With the lights from the fireworks, tiki torches, and the cook fire…I bet the shadows moving back and forth on the pig made it look as if it was moving. And you were already nervous with my teasing you earlier about the coyotes coming around. So it's really my fault."

"No, Brad, I saw what I saw. And that doesn't explain the pig squealing."

"There was a lot of yelling out there. And you know, the cheer-leaders have pretty high-pitched voices." Brad's attempt at using humor to diffuse the situation does not work.

As the whole incident keeps replaying in Erin's mind, she starts crying again, repeating, "It was real. It was real," while rock-ing back and forth. The memory of Emily's last night claws its way back into her consciousness and fights for attention as well. It is getting hot and becoming more difficult to breathe. The car feels much smaller than she remembers. Finally, she cannot take it anymore. "Stop the car."

"What?" Brad asks.

"Please, stop the car. Now."

Thinking she's going to be sick, he pulls over onto the shoulder. Erin swings the door open and grabs her purse. Exiting the car, she orders, "Do *not* follow me."

Brad watches her disappear into the trees. All he can think to do is give her some privacy and send up a quick, desperate prayer. He patiently waits for her return.

In a small clearing, Erin paces back and forth, hyperventilating. What is happening to her has all the earmarks of a panic attack. She fights for sanity but feels she is losing the battle.

"What is happening to me? Am I going crazy? Or am I cursed?" She repeats to herself out loud, "I just need some time. I just need some time."

But about ten minutes later her nerves are not any better. Brad debates in his mind what to do, and finally concludes that he should go check on her. He gets out and makes his way down the same path. As he enters the clearing, Erin is standing eerily still on the other side with her back facing him and head slightly bowed.

"Erin?" he calls out.

She immediately turns around with a look of fright on her face, and it's all too clear why. She has been caught lighting a joint. "I told you not to follow me!"

"Erin! Is that what I think it is?"

"Brad, please. Don't be upset."

"You told me you quit all that!"

"I *did* stop, I promise."

"Then what are you doing with marijuana?" Brad has never been around alcohol, much less illegal drugs.

"It's an old one—found it in one of my other purses a few days ago. I don't know why I've kept it since, but now I need it to calm my nerves. Just this once. Please!"

Brad shakes his head. "You know it's illegal. What if we get caught?"

"Hey, what's going on down there?" bursts a deep tone from the direction of the highway.

A beam of light breaks through the trees, panning back and forth. The voice is all too familiar. Erin drops the contraband and places her foot on it. Sheriff Knox makes his second appearance of the night.

"Brad? Is that you?"

"Yes, sir."

"I came across your car on the side of the road thinking something had happened. What in the blazes are you doing out here?"

"Well, sir, Erin here wasn't feeling well, and she needed some fresh air."

Knox raises his flashlight and shines it directly in her face. Erin squints tightly and raises her hand to block the glaring light.

"Some fresh air, huh? This deep in the woods?" He turns back to Brad.

"Yes, sir."

The sheriff inhales deeply through his nostrils and exhales just as hard out his mouth. "Okay, I think you two have gotten enough fresh air. It's time to call it a night and head on home."

"Okay," Brad replies, all too ready to do just that. "Come on, Erin, let's go."

The two walk past him and head for the car, both thankful they weren't caught. It was a close call indeed. The ride back to Erin's house is quiet. Heavy tension between them is new territory for their relationship. Neither one says a word until, almost to her house, Erin finally breaks the silence.

"I don't know what to say, except, I know I let you down. I'm not sure what came over me tonight, but it doesn't matter, because there are no excuses for my behavior. Maybe they're right, all of them. Maybe we shouldn't be together. We come from different worlds. I…It would be fair for you to want to break up with me. I wouldn't be mad at you. I'd understand."

This is important. Brad pulls over on the side of the road and shifts the engine into park. He turns and looks at her. A defeated Erin turns to face him…to face the consequences. "Erin, when I decided to be with you I knew you had a past. Now, I know there's still some things you haven't felt comfortable sharing—you've been up front about that, and I am willing to wait. But I have to know that what you've told me so far has been the truth." A pause in his speech clues Erin in that he is waiting for a reply.

"It has. What I told you about the marijuana is also true."

Brad nods slightly. "Okay, I believe you. And one bad night isn't enough for me to want to break up. I mean, look at the stunt I pulled earlier. You didn't put our lives in danger like I did. I care for you deeply, Erin, and I'm willing to try and make this work if you are, no matter what anybody else thinks."

His words are shocking, shocking in the sense that his response is pretty much exactly the opposite of what everyone else in the world would say if they were in the same situation. Brad's attitude is so very selfless, Erin was sure she had lost him. She has strong feelings for him as well, maybe even loves him, which itself is shocking because the concept of love, as she understands it, has been slain and buried with Emily this whole time.

"I want us to work too, Brad. If you're willing to keep trying, so am I."

"Of course I do."

He warmly smiles and she smiles back, wiping away a tear. Brad leans in and Erin reciprocates. They silently embrace for several minutes.

"Okay," says Brad finally, but begrudgingly, breaking away, "let's get you home."

"Sure," Erin replies with a big exhale.

Brad puts the car back in gear and pulls out onto the highway.

"I want you to come in," Erin announces.

"Where? In your house?"

"Yes. I want to find the piece of paper where I wrote that license plate number. You know, the one I told you about; the guys who own the pigs and supply their medication."

"Sure, sure. What about your mom? You've been hesitant about us meeting again."

"Oh, that. I'm not worried anymore. I can tell she's not going to be able to run you off. I mean, if I didn't tonight, then I don't know what will."

Brad chuckles, and the two are relieved that things seem to be getting back to seminormal and that the night is going to end on a good note.

AT ERIN'S HOUSE THE NIGHT IS JUST GETTING START-ED, with Rose and her spiritual advisor finishing preparations for the séance in Emily's room. As Madame Zelda sets up the video cameras, Rose continues recounting the bizarre event that transpired earlier.

"…and it was about twenty minutes before you arrived when I was in here meditating like it says in that book you sold me."

"You got a great bargain on that book, Mrs. Rose," interjects Zelda, the consummate saleswoman.

"Yes. Anyway, I was sitting on the floor in the lotus position with five candles around me and opening myself up to the spirit world, like the book teaches, hoping it would help tonight with Emily. I was in a deep trance, I think, when all of a sudden there was a brilliant light. Actually, there were five bright flashes, one right after the other, which lit this entire room."

"Interesting. Go on."

"Even with my eyes closed, the light was blinding. It was so unbearable that I had to actually cover my face with my hands."

"Did you hear anything at all while this was happening, dear?"

"No, except our dog downstairs wouldn't stop barking for ten minutes. What do you make of all this, Madame Zelda?"

The professional medium pauses for a moment, not to search her memory banks, but to think of how she can spin this incredible story to her advantage.

"Well you see, light is good…always good. I believe it was Emily's way of announcing that she will be communicating with us from the other side once again, but that's not all."

"Really? What?" Rose asks excitedly.

"She will be bringing good news." Zelda knows her clientele always want to hear good news.

"Good news? About what?"

"I don't know. We'll have to wait and see."

"Oh, I'm so excited! I can't wait! Let's finish putting everything in its place." Rose looks around puzzled. "Where is all your other equipment?"

"We won't be needing any of those after what happened last night." Zelda picks up the old radio and places it on the table where they will be seated again. "Emily proved she is a strong spirit, very strong indeed. She also demonstrated her preferred method of communicating, through this here radio, so we had better stick to that. All the other equipment might cause interference, so I didn't bring it."

"Ah, I see. Do you think we'll get to actually see her tonight?"

"Oh, not hardly. You see, ghosts themselves are very skittish creatures. They are afraid of the physical world, like many people here are scared of theirs. Emily is going to have to get to know me much better before she realizes she can trust me and decides to materialize. It's a great honor to have spirits show themselves, you know."

"How long will that take?" Rose hopes it won't be too long.

"Well, with regular, consistent contacts, through séances like this one, it could be as quickly as oh, six months." That would bring in a nice steady sum of money.

"Six months!"

"My child," Zelda starts off, somewhat condescendingly, "Emily is going to have to get to know and trust me. She has to become confident that I intend her no harm, and *that* is going to take some time."

"Okay, but you did say we would be hearing from her this evening, right?"

"Absolutely, Mrs. Rose, one way or another we will receive audible contact tonight. Don't you worry."

The lady showman always has a backup plan.

They take their seats at the table like last time, only with the radio strategically planted in front of them instead of behind. Zelda goes into her usual opening routine with heavy breathing, summoning of spirits and deep hums. The pair then becomes intensely focused on the radio, hoping it will once again be a channel to the other side.

Emily's room, like before, is dark with the faint glow of a few choice candles. However, they are not the only smoldering objects in the vicinity. Unknown to them, above on the roof, are five burn marks, still emitting faint columns of smoke, equidistant in a circular pattern on the shingles. They are in the same alignment as Rose's candles were earlier when she was meditating, and are the result of the fallen quintet of celestial entities that Erin and Brad observed from the field.

"Mom?"

It is Emily's voice, crystal clear, without interference or static of any kind. Unlike last night, her words are not transmitting through the radio. But exactly like last night, the spirit summons them from behind. Rose and Madame Zelda slowly turn and look at each other, then continue all the way around. Levitating just above the bed, gazing down at them, is the corporeal form of Emily Todd Gray.

She appears just as Rose remembers, except for the faint aura of pale blue light radiating around her shadowy silhouette. With hands extended out slightly and palms facing upward, she appears angelic as her light gown and long hair gently flow about as if in a weightless environment. Emily's relaxed feet dangle with toes dipping downward, and her content smile conveys a peace that surpasses all understanding. The shocked mother is so mesmerized she does not hear the deep muffled thud beside her. Madame Zelda has become dislodged from her chair and taken up residence on the floor in an unconscious state and horizontal position.

"Emily, is it you? Is it really you?"

"Yes, Mom, it's me, Emily."

MADAME ZELDA'S CAR catches Erin's attention as Brad pulls into the driveway.

"Oh no, I forgot about that."

"Forgot about what?" asks Brad.

"It's my mother. She's hired a psychic to contact Emily."

"Emily?"

"Yes, Mom hopes to reconnect with her spirit. They're holding a séance in her room, probably as we speak."

"Really? Right now? Wow, that's...I have to tell you, the Bible warns against doing things like that."

Erin laughs. Brad is a little taken back.

Erin notices Brad's negative reaction. "Oh no, I'm not laughing because I don't believe the Bible. As a matter of fact, that may be at least one area where I agree with it."

"Then what is it?"

By this time they are out of the car and making their way to the front door.

"It's Madame Zelda; she's no psychic or medium. She's just a snake-oil-selling charlatan. With her it's all hocus pocus and trickery. I tried to warn Mom that she was throwing money down the drain, but she wouldn't listen. She's too obsessed with getting my sister back, blinded by her objective and unconcerned with the cost."

"So none of it's real?"

"Not with this woman, not by a long shot. Trust me, Hollywood is more real than the great, magnificent, one-and-only Madame Zelda!" Erin quotes this last part with overly dramatic zeal and fanfare with a touch of Transylvanian accent while twirling to mock the woman. They both share a laugh, entering through the front door while dozens of geckos watch from the porch ceiling.

Sitting at the bottom of the staircase to their right is Shep, focusing on something that demands his attention.

"What is it, Shep?" Erin asks.

He does not flinch. Like laser beams, his eyes stare straight ahead and up.

She walks over and gently rubs the back of his head.

"Shep! You're shaking! What's wrong, boy?"

He glances over momentarily then directs his focus back upstairs. Erin looks up but sees nothing.

"He seems frightened," Brad says.

"Oh, it's probably Madame Zelda. I can't say that I blame him for acting strange around her. Come on, Brad, let's go on up so I can get you that license plate number."

They climb the stairs while Shep anxiously watches from the landing. When they're about halfway up, the dog gives out a yelp, seemingly just audible enough to get them to look at him but not so loud as to draw any unnecessary attention from whoever, or whatever, may be on the second floor. Erin turns back to Shep, who anxiously patters his front paws up and down on the floor in an attempt to get them to change their minds about going any further. She smiles. "Oh Shep, don't worry. Madame Zelda's bark is worse than her bite."

As they make their way up and approach Emily's bedroom, the door is cracked open just a little, allowing flickers from lit candles inside to dance across the wall on the opposite side of the hallway. Murmuring is heard within, but the words cannot be made out, nor can the participants of the conversation be seen. Erin and Brad look at each other. She takes hold of his hand and leads him quietly into the dimly lit room. Once inside, the two at first spot nothing unusual. Then it becomes apparent that the voices are originating from the opposite side of the room. They turn to see Rose kneeling on the floor looking up. Standing in front of her is Emily. She is wearing a white gown and barefoot.

The spirit quickly turns its head and scowls at the two intruders, then immediately disappears with a gush of wind that extinguishes the candles and slams the bedroom door shut with immense force. Erin screams. In the dark, Brad struggles blindly to locate the light switch. Downstairs, Shep barks frantically, pacing back and forth, but still refuses to come up. The few agonizing seconds in pitch black seem like an eternity, until Brad finally locates the toggle and pops it up. But the light flickers, sporadically strobing as the old, faulty wiring struggles to make full contact. Amidst the flashing, Emily's ghost appears intermittently in front of Rose. One moment she is there, the next, vanished.

Then, after a brief period of sustained darkness, the room finally becomes saturated in a sharp light. Emily's manifestation has departed. However, inexplicably, Erin is now in front of Rose, where Emily's spirit stood, across the room from Brad. Rose is still kneeling and looking up. It takes her a few seconds to realize that something is different.

"Emily? Is that you?"

"No, Mom. It's me, Erin." The puzzled girl looks toward Brad, wondering how she got here.

"Erin?" the confused mother asks, emerging from a mental fog. "Oh yes, Erin." Rose reaches up and touches Erin to confirm that the girl is actually present in physical form. Rose has not yet noticed Brad. Madame Zelda starts coming to.

"Mom, what is going on here?"

"Did I miss anything?" The groggy psychic struggles to prop herself up on the floor.

"Did you see her, Erin? It was Emily!" Rose hugs Erin's legs and keeps talking. "She's back. Emily's back. Oh, thank God! She told me so much, *so* much. And she's coming back. Coming back for good, she promised. In just a little while, when everything is set up, whatever that means, my darling Em will return to be with us. Oh, isn't it wonderful!" She hugs Erin's legs tightly again. "I'm so happy."

Erin looks at Brad, who is at a loss for words, too. They both know they saw something—exactly what, though, remains a mystery. However, it's apparent the events that took place here were unnatural. Erin walks over to the closet and peeks in, careful to not open the door wide enough for Brad to see in. She confirms that *it* is still in there. Erin closes the door and turns around. "Mom… where's Queenie?"

OUT IN THEIR BARN, the youngest daughter sits on the ground surrounded by her five subjects. The large sow is plopped directly in front of the young girl, communicating in a series of deep low grunts. Queenie stares quietly in a mesmerized state, taking it all in, until the pig finishes its message. After a moment of silence and with a deadpan look, Queenie responds, "Yes."

A MOUTH-WATERING AROMA OF BAKED HAM still lingers in the air along with that of thoroughly seasoned black-eyed peas, mashed potatoes prepared with a hint of sour cream, and butter-saturated bread. But the dishes of this Sunday noon meal have been plucked off of the dining room table and are being loaded into a dishwasher, and the leftovers have taken up residence in the spacious double-door, stainless-steel refrigerator.

Unlike most other Sabbath days' rest, the afternoon nap ritual this week for Mr. Ross is postponed, if not abandoned altogether, to take care of some urgent business—family business. Brad's father closes the French doors to his home office and locks them in order to have complete privacy with his son.

Outside in the hallway lie two pair of shoes, Brad's and his father's. Only bare feet are allowed in the office due to Mr. Ross's affinity for what Mrs. Ross declares as the ultimate blasphemy of interior design decisions. It is an understatement of biblical proportions to say she does not share her husband's affinity for white shag carpet. To him it is a twelve-foot square patch of heaven, holy ground that is only allowed by the lady of the house if hidden behind his closed doors, the glass panes of which are completely veiled with opaque curtains that block detection by any guest who might pass in the corridor. The carpet is unsoiled, pristine, without blemish, and Mr. Ross aims to keep it that way.

Brad sits in a chair wondering what this is all about, one socked foot fidgeting atop the other. Jack makes his way past, anchors himself behind the large executive desk, and pulls open a drawer. Landing on the surface in front of Brad is a small clear plastic bag, the contents of which are, at first, unrecognizable to him.

"Care to explain that?" his father asks.

Brad grabs the mysterious object and holds it up to get a better look. Then a burst of adrenalin shoots through his body. Now it is crystal clear what this is all about.

"I know how this looks, but there's a reasonable explanation," the nervous son replies with a shaky voice.

"I'm listening," Mr. Ross leans forward on his forearms, hands clasped.

Not wanting any more association with it, Brad returns the marijuana cigarette to its resting place on the large mahogany desk, then clears his throat.

"Well, you see…um…there was this incident and um—"

"It's hers, isn't it. That girl's."

Brad already feels defeated without getting the first snap off. He was hoping to figure out a way of putting it more…diplomatically. All he can do at this point is concede and try to pick up the pieces.

"Yes, sir."

"John gave it to me this morning in the church parking lot." Dad retrieves the contraband and drops it in the trash can. "Said he found the two of you alone in the woods just off the highway late last night and came across this thing exactly where she was standing. And don't try to tell me it was just a coincidence that a joint was on the ground where you two were standing, because the tip is freshly burnt, and John could smell it in the air." Jack stops abruptly and stares at his son waiting for a reply.

Brad rubs his thighs in a nervous attempt to dry his sweaty palms. He talks to the floor. "You're right, it was hers. She used to do drugs, but not anymore. She did find that one in an old purse, and last night something disturbed her, and she's been under a lot of pressure lately, and she's had a hard life, and everybody slips up every now and then, and—"

This is all true—Brad is trying to throw as much stuff up as possible, hoping the sheer number of excuses will weigh heavily in his favor, or that at least one of them will stick to the wall as being legit.

Having been a lawyer for many years, Jack knows every debate tactic in the book and recognizes what his son is attempting. In one fell swoop, Jack brings down his son's house of cards. "Brad, none of that matters. It is illegal and immoral, and you know that. If any officer other than John had come across you two and discovered what was going on, I would have been bailing you out of jail last night."

"You do believe me," Brad says, "that I wasn't doing anything?"

Jack stares into his son's eyes. "Yes, I believe you. But that doesn't matter; you would have been guilty by association."

"Yes, sir. For what it's worth, she was just starting to light it, and I stopped her right before Sheriff Knox showed up. So nothing really happened."

"What else are you having to make this girl stop doing?"

"This was the only time Erin has done anything remotely wrong."

His dad clarifies, "That you've seen, right?"

"Well, yes, but I trust her."

Jack sighs and gazes at Brad for a few moments. "Son, I'm not sure this girl is right for you. Far from not being a Christian, she doesn't even attend church at all."

"She met me at youth service last Wednesday night, but feels she wasn't welcomed by the others because she's different."

"That may be true to an extent, and it's a shame that it happens, but I would be willing to bet there is something deeper, something spiritual, going on there. Take this to heart, Brad, but an unregenerate sinner is no more comfortable in church than a criminal is in a police station. In other words, she probably felt conviction over her sins and doesn't want any part of that. The whole 'not feeling welcome' thing may be just a convenient excuse to stay away."

"Then that's all the more reason she needs a good influence around her, right? As a matter of fact, I had the chance to share the gospel last night."

"Really? How did she respond?"

"Well…she didn't totally reject the idea, and I probably could've done a better job, but at least we touched on the subject. I can tell she's looked into these things, and she's a smart girl, Dad. I feel we made some real progress."

Brad is omitting the rejections Erin brought up, partly out of his desire to not weaken his case for staying with her, and partly due to embarrassment that he didn't really know how to respond to them.

"What did she actually say, son?"

"Erin says she's willing to go wherever God leads her, and I believe I'm supposed to be a part of that plan."

"But wasn't your sharing the gospel, in fact, God leading her?"

Brad pauses to think. It makes sense. "I guess she's just not ready yet, or it's not her time, or whatever."

Reality is starting to sink in for Jack. He was once his son's age, too, and was overcome with the same lures and emotions. Nothing he says is going to convince Brad that pursuing his relationship with Erin is ill-advised.

Jack is also wise enough to not do what he wants to in this situation. "Son, I'm not going to demand that you stop seeing her. You're old enough to make those decisions for yourself. All I can ask is that you pray hard about it and make sure that *you* are the one who is the leader; don't let her influence you away from God."

"No, sir, I won't."

"Oh, and one other thing."

"Yes, sir."

"Promise me that if you catch her with drugs again you will call it off. Will you do that for me?"

"Oh, yes, sir. She promised me that she doesn't do them anymore, and if that's not the case, then she's lying to me, and I won't tolerate that."

"That's very wise, son. Well, I guess we're done here."

"Actually, Dad, there is one more thing." Brad reaches into his pocket.

"What's that?"

Brad pulls out a piece of paper and holds it out across the desk. "Can you have someone run this license plate number for me and see who it's registered to?"

Jack reaches over, and the exchange is made.

"What's this about?" Dad reads the number through bifocals perched on the tip of his nose.

"It's for Erin, actually."

"Erin?"

"Yes, she's curious about the people her family has an arrangement with to take care of some pigs."

"Why is she inquiring into these individuals? Doesn't she know who they are?"

"She says the pigs act strange and believes discovering the identity of the owners may shed some light into their unusual behavior. And no, Erin doesn't know who they are. Apparently her father made some secret deal to keep it all hush, which is part of the agreement to get paid for taking care of them."

"Well, I would presume that he's not going to divulge any of that information any time soon."

Brad looks at his dad silently and nods.

"Okay, I'll pass it along to John. He's got deeper contacts at the bureau than I."

"Do me a favor?" Brad asks.

"Sure son, what is it?"

"Please don't tell Mr. Knox it's for Erin. Let him know you're doing it for me, which *is* the truth. I would just like to protect her privacy." He also doesn't want to cause any more undue tension between the law and his girlfriend.

"Sure, I can do that."

"Thanks, Dad. I know I can always count on you."

The two get up and hug for a moment, then Jack reaches to unlock the door.

ERIN STRUGGLES TO UNLOCK THE DOOR and has labored at the undertaking for some time. Queenie's room is purposefully sealed shut while she and her mother are in town buying groceries. Sundays are great this time of day, because so many people are still at church or eating lunch afterwards, which makes for a less crowded experience, and that suits Rose just fine.

"Come on, I know this works." Erin sighs, jiggling the long brass key inside the antique lock. Rattling from the attempted break-in ricochets off walls and floors throughout the unoccupied house.

Erin discovered not long ago that Queenie had begun locking her door, a feat that, until recently, had been literally impossible due to the fact that no key for that room existed.

Late one night, during one of the girl's fellowship gatherings with her adopted family of pigs, the large sow enlightened her as to its yet-undiscovered resting place. Queenie had to crawl on her belly underneath the house, through a massive entanglement of cobwebs, over a slight hump in the ground, and claw the key up out of the dirt with her bare hands.

It had been hidden there for over nine decades, the result of a small child's thoughtless prank on his parents. But like all children do, he became distracted and soon forgot about the object and later could not recall what he had done with it. One evening his dust and sweat-covered father, upon returning home from laboring in the fields all day, beat him severely in a drunken rage after learning what had happened.

The little boy died as a result of his injuries.

Sometime later his parents reported the child missing, and a massive search was launched, with the whole community involved in the hunt. The months-long effort, spawned by a fraudulent claim, had expected results. The tot's remains still lie there today, under the house, buried just three feet away from where Queenie unearthed the key.

Click.

"Yes!" Erin exclaims as the latch finally gives way, rotating counterclockwise, allowing a breach into Queenie's private abode. Erin pulled off this covert task with a skeleton key, able to unbolt every lock in the house—that is, except for one. She stumbled upon it in less dramatic fashion than Queenie did her key, yet miraculously, on the very same day at the same exact moment in time, two levels up, discovering it tucked away in the corner of her closet's top shelf.

Erin is the only one aware of its existence.

She gradually, softly, nudges the creaky door open, pokes her head in for a quick glance around, and then enters cautiously. All is deathly quiet and still inside the vacant room. She tiptoes around, searching for anything unusual, which may be difficult since the room is bizarrely littered with all sorts of unique collectibles—specifically, pig paraphernalia. Stuffed pig animals, pig posters, pig buttons, pig books, pig toys. If it's pig-related, Queenie probably has it in her room, as part of what Erin calls the Swine Shrine. A full-sized latex Halloween hog mask, with holes cut out for eyes, hangs on the bedpost near her pillow. A worn-out hardcover of George Orwell's *Animal Farm* stands at attention on a nearby bookshelf near a cheap plastic beauty queen tiara.

Bzzzzzzz.

A rattling inside one of the drawers startles Erin. It goes off again. Bzzzzzzz.

She walks over and cautiously pulls a drawer open. The unsettling noise emanates from a cell phone switched to vibrate that is intensely knocking against the inner wooden frame of the bureau.

Bzzzzzzz.

Erin immediately recognizes it as Emily's old phone, the one she furiously smashed against the tree and busted that night. Officials returned it to the family after Erin gave her testimony about the altercation between herself and Emily before the accident. She reaches in and picks up the device, then flips it open. Lit up across the cracked screen is a text from someone called Babe18. The message: *I love you.*

Who on earth is Babe18? she wonders. *And how is this phone possibly working?*

Another message pipes through, causing the device to unexpectedly quiver in her hand. She hits the OK button immediately. This text much longer; it appears to be instructions specifying how to perform some sort of ritual, but the details are hard to make out since many of the words and letters are cryptic symbols Erin has never seen before. Sensing that something is not right, and worried for her little sister, Erin becomes fearful.

What is Queenie getting into?

Staring at the phone, she starts to ask herself questions. *Who is possibly teaching her these things? Where did they come into contact? When do they possibly have time to meet?* Answers keep coming up blank. Queenie is a loner with no real friends. She does not go out and socialize. Rather, she is a homebody from whom a peep is rarely heard. It just does not make sense.

Then Erin gets the idea to snoop through all of the past messages in the phone's history. She starts scrolling and reading them randomly. Some are similar to the one she just read, mysterious and hard-to-follow instructions for cult-like procedures, and others proclaiming how her little sister is loved, and that she is somebody special; something every tween girl wants to hear from anyone and everyone.

Erin keeps scrolling down farther and farther, deeper into the past. The further back she travels, the fewer occult instructions turn up and more flowery praises there are. She keeps scrolling, hoping to get to the very first text, but she never reaches it. The list keeps going on for what seems forever. Giving up, she starts scrolling back up and a certain title catches her eye: *TONGUES (untranslatable) THE SWINE.*

This is different. Erin selects it and presses the OK button. Nothing happens. She presses it again; still no response. Pushing down with greater force and quicker repetition, Erin is determined to make the thing work, but the phone persists in not giving up its secret.

Vrrrrrr.

Erin shrieks as the phone suddenly quakes within her grip again. Startled, she drops it on the wood floor and it bounces a couple of times, landing face down. The device lays there for a couple of seconds. Then: bzzzzzzz.

The phone takes on a life of its own as it vibrates again, causing a slight shift in position, rotating on the rigid surface.

Bzzzzzzz. The apprehensive girl reaches down, picks up the phone and turns it right side up to see a new message. Again, it is from Babe18.

Who's holding Queenie's phone? the newest text demands.

How could the sender possibly know that someone other than Queenie has it in their possession at the moment? Erin stands petrified, not knowing what to do.

Vrrrrrr. *You're not Queenie! Who are you?*

Every new message is accompanied with the irritating vibration against the soft, smooth skin of her hand. It is a sensation that makes the device feel like a living, breathing creature, a gigantic wasp, perhaps, that will attack if released from her secure grip. Erin dares not reply.

Vrrrrrr. *Well, aren't you going to respond?*

With her heart now throbbing violently, Erin looks all over the room feeling a dangerous presence close to her. The messages pour in at a rapid pace.

Vrrrrrr. *Answer me!*

Vrrrrrr. *Who are you?*

Then comes the most disturbing declaration yet.

Vrrrrrr. *Do you think it's right for a person to go through someone else's personal belongings like this? Do you?*

Erin turns pale, with terror in her eyes. The texts pop up without Erin having to tap the OK button.

Vrrrrrr. *Leave Queenie's room right now!*

Vrrrrrr. *Get out now or I will kill you!*

Vrrrrrr. *Kill you!*

Then the vibrating intensifies in strength, unrelenting with no more pauses. One phrase begins echoing on the screen:

GET OUT!

GET OUT!
GET OUT!

The blood drains from Erin's face and she starts hyperventilating. Her senses become overloaded and the room begins spinning. Then the unthinkable happens. Voices begin transmitting through the speaker: loud deep voices hurling an unknown language in an aggressive, threatening tone. It's as if the bowels of hell are threatening her. She flips the phone shut immediately, tosses it back into the drawer, slams it shut, bolts for the door.

During her panic-stricken escape she happens to notice something. There, next to the wall behind the door, is a black velvet bag. Somehow Erin finds the courage to stop. She kneels down, opens it up, and peeks in. Some candles, papers, and other artifacts typically employed in rituals are concealed within. Erin is all too familiar with such items; her heart sinks.

Slap!

A book has slipped (or been pushed) off the shelf, landing flatly on the floor.

Animal Farm.

Erin spins to see what happened. Overlooking the literary classic, she spots the hanging mask with eyes, human eyes, staring right at her. She instantly jumps up and runs out of the room, slamming the door shut behind her. In the hallway, she nervously fumbles with the skeleton key trying to lock the door to hide the fact that she has been in there, as well as to maybe keep anything, or anyone, from getting out. The key finally clicks in place.

Erin, believing she is now safe, turns around and leans her back on the door. A deep exhale with eyes closed aids in calming her nerves. Slowly, over the next few moments, her heartbeat and breathing decelerate back to a normal pace.

"Erin!"

She slowly opens her eyes and rotates her gaze toward the direction of the voice. No one is there. It takes a moment, but soon she realizes it is her father summoning from his bedroom. She makes her way, legs still shaky, over to his door.

"Yes, Daddy?" she responds softly.

"What's going on out there? Is everything all right?"

"Nothing Daddy, everything's fine."

"Are you sure?"

"Yes. You don't need to worry about a thing, except getting better. How are *you* doing?"

"Oh, that's what I wanted to tell you, darling. My legs are growing stronger every day. I'm walking around in here quite a bit, now. It's probably the new medicine; with it I'm able to keep food down."

"That's great! Everything's going to be back to normal before long, isn't it?"

"Yes, Erin, it will all get back to the way it was before I got sick, I promise. And when I'm fully recovered, I think you're old enough to go dancing with me at Jake's in Cedarville. Now I know you don't really care for country music and all, but it would sure be a hoot to dance with my daughter—let all my friends see how pretty she is."

"I'm definitely willing to put up with country and western music and go boot scooting if it motivates you to get better."

"And you're going to help me resurrect that dead old truck of mine, right?"

"You bet, Daddy. I can't wait." Erin pauses for a moment, then asks once again, "Can I…can I come in now?"

"No, it's not quite time. I'm just not ready for that yet, and I may still be contagious. I know that's not what you want to hear, but I just can't let you see me as I am right now. I hope you understand."

Erin does not answer. She pulls the skeleton key out of her pocket and looks at it with an expression of longing, then glances at the lock. Ultimately, she decides not to try it again. If it hasn't worked all of those other times, why would it possibly work now? They say the definition of insanity is trying the same exact thing over and over expecting different results. Erin is not insane, or at least, she is going to fight its progression with everything she's got.

She slips the key back in her pocket.

"Erin…I said I hope you understand."

"Sure, Daddy, it's okay."

"You don't sound okay. I can tell there's something bothering you. What is it?"

"It's Queenie. I'm worried about her, Daddy. I'm afraid she's in trouble."

"Queenie is just fine, sweetheart."

"How can you possibly know that?"

"I'm standing at the window right now. They must be back from the store, because Queenie just ran into the barn."

Downstairs, the front door whisks open and a scream from Rose races up the staircase. "Erin, we're back! Get down here and help me bring in groceries!"

SUNDAY EVENING GRADUALLY SETTLES over the Gray residence, methodically snuffing out a day that, thankfully, did not give witness to any more surprise events. As a spattering of clouds is gently nudged across the nighttime sky, their faint shadows cast by lunar radiance slither along surfaces below at the same leisurely pace. Subtle gusts of a gentle ongoing breeze brush up against patches of tall, dormant grass and remaining thinned-out tree canopies, giving them life as they dance in rhythm to the soft wind's fluctuating lazy tempo.

Only two rooms in the quaint farmhouse bear any signs of life in the dark night: one on the second story, the other below, each emitting, through their respective windows, flickering light from opposite ends of the color spectrum.

Up top, sequestered in Emily's room with door closed, sits Rose on the floor with five candles encompassing her position. The warm-colored light bouncing about goes unnoticed by the meditating woman as her eyes are effortlessly closed and mind transported light-years away from current events.

On the first floor, at the front of the house next to the porch, a neon-bluish hue flashes quickly and erratically through the thin veil of curtains hanging in front of the living room window. Plopped down on the couch, in a non-ergonomic position, Queenie is taking in all the television has to offer. She, too, is voluntarily whisked away to another world, away from this present reality.

Erin stealthily perches on the staircase underneath the Lincoln portrait, observing, through the banister railing, her little sister. So much is running through Erin's mind at the moment, as it has all day, concerning Queenie. Much of her contemplation is centered on guilt. Guilt for maybe not trying hard enough to connect with her little sister on a more personal level. So preoccupied with her own worries, Erin has considered her unplanned baby sibling to be really nothing more than another long-lost relative, like one you might get temporarily reacquainted with at a family reunion and make small talk with just because that is what is expected.

It is also becoming clear that her mother has also had the same mindset toward the girl for some reason. Now it is coming back to haunt her. The little sister who has been just too young, or too different, or both, for Erin to take the time and make the effort to build a relationship with, is now in danger of plunging down the wrong path with disastrous consequences, and at a much, much younger age than when she and Emily got initiated into the lifestyle.

Erin has already lost one sister; she does not want to bury another. But is it too late? Will any advice coming from pretty much a stranger be well received, if received at all? These are questions Erin grapples with while sitting on the stairs.

Queenie laughs at a scene in the movie.

Something has to be done, if nothing more than igniting the tiny spark of a relationship's genesis. If some mentoring does not take place, the young girl will become a pawn, thrown into the boiling sea of spiritual battle, tossed about to and fro by powerful opposing forces clashing to take advantage of what she may have to offer to their side.

Erin stands up and makes her way down the stairs. One hand sliding along the wooden rail, she keeps her focus on Queenie.

All the while, Emily's apparition stands still at the top of the stairs, unnoticed, and tracks Erin's movement into the living room.

Out of the corner of one eye, Queenie notices her big sister approaching and lunges for the remote.

"I was here first! We're not changing it!" She clings the device with both hands close to her chest.

"Oh no, I wasn't going to try and change it."

Queenie stares at Erin, waiting and wondering what is going to happen next. "Then what do you want?"

"May I sit and watch with you?"

This is unusual. Queenie studies her big sister a bit longer.

"I don't care."

"Thanks. What are you watching?"

"Babe."

Erin already knew the answer to that question. Queenie had watched this movie hundreds of times and could pretty much quote it verbatim.

"Oh, is that the one about the talking pig?"

"Of course."

Erin sits down next to Queenie, who slides over and sits up straighter to maximize personal space.

"At what part is the movie?" Erin asks.

Queenie remains glued to the TV. "It's the part where Ma the sheep is dying from being attacked and Babe is standing there with blood on his nose. It's my favorite part."

Taken back, Erin asks, "Why's that?"

"I don't know. I guess because farmer Hoggett thinks Babe did it. I think that's funny."

"Oh," Erin responds.

"What's *your* favorite part of the movie?" asks Queenie.

"Oh, I don't know. It's been a long time since I last watched it, but I'm sure glad farmer Hoggett didn't shoot Babe. That would have been horrible."

"Well, if that had happened, maybe the other animals would have attacked Hoggett and ripped him to shreds," Queenie adds.

"Would that be a good thing?"

"Oh, I don't know. Who's to say, really?"

"Hm." Erin watches her sister focus on the TV. "Queenie?" She brushes some strands of hair behind the girl's left ear. "I want to talk to you about something."

"Un huh." She merely raises her eyebrows, staying focused on the screen.

"Our relationship hasn't been what it should be, and it's totally my fault. I haven't been the big sister I know I should be, and I want to change that starting right now."

Queenie slowly turns to Erin with a puzzled look. "What do you mean?"

"What I mean, is…I want to start spending more time with you.

Doing things that sisters should do together."

Queenie responds slowly in an exaggerated way, stretching out her words. "Liiiiike whaaaaat?"

"Oh, I don't know, just girl things, really."

Again, in the same measured tone she asks, "Why?"

"I think you need some guidance, some direction that only a big sis—"

Queenie suddenly whisks her head around and up, looking in the direction of her room, which is on the other side of the house. She stares without flinching, with the same mind-numb gaze usually reserved for the boob tube. With eyes darting back and forth ever so slightly, she looks as if she is watching, through walls, other events taking place.

"Queenie?" Erin gently calls out.

No response.

"Queenie?" she calls out again reaching over and gently squeezing her arm. "What is it, sweetheart?"

The young girl jerks her arm away, hops up, and sneers down at Erin. Her facial expression is one of anger, hatred…evil.

"Don't you ever go in my room again!" Queenie yells. "Do you understand me? Stay out or I will kill you!"

"Queenie, what's gotten into you?"

"Kill you!"

The young girl dashes away, bounds up the stairs, and barricades herself in her room. Erin is left sitting, wondering what just happened. One thing is now for sure, the door to Queenie's trust is going to take much longer to unlock.

THE NEXT MORNING KICK-STARTS ANOTHER week of school for Brad and Erin, one that will dramatically alter their lives for eternity. Each teen performs similar weekday morning routines that are accomplished in different ways: They both get dressed and have breakfast, but Brad spends time with his family during the most important meal of the day while Erin nibbles at a bagel or piece of toast alone unless Queenie just happens to be in the kitchen at the same time.

They also both drive their little sisters to school; however, the Ross siblings unreservedly engage in a volley of stimulating conversation en route, while the Gray sisters barely grunt a word to one another. Also, Brad usually does not pick up Jessica after classes let out due to scheduling conflicts, typically sports; Erin always gets Queenie unless her mother happens to be in the area, which is quite rare but not unheard of.

Until that which is about to take place, today, for the most part, has been a typical day at school.

Between bells and before the final class period, Brad and Erin flow with the current of students streaming through the crowded hallways and make their way toward his locker. Word of Saturday night's meltdown at the party has already permeated its way throughout school with the story of how Erin *actually* behaved being greatly exaggerated in some circles. But as the day has worn on, stares and snickers have subsided.

Actually, what the two have had to endure today has been nothing like the Friday they revealed their romantic connection. While making small talk, they come to a crowd and are unable to pass. It is a large gathering near Brad's locker at the corner of an intersection. Giggles and snickers can be heard. It is the beginning of a carefully planned offensive.

Brad turns to Erin and asks, "You have any idea what this is about?" Erin shrugs. He gently slices his way through the swarm with Erin in tow. Emerging on the other side, it becomes quite clear what all the clamoring is about. Taped to Brad's locker is a retouched photo of him that flaunts an irreverent Goth version of the straight-laced young man.

The stinging satirical piece portrays the popular boy with long black hair swooping across half of his face and forming a gap, exposing the only visible eye which is darkly outlined in an overly excessive application of liner. Unnaturally pale skin showcases the look, along with a few strategically placed facial piercings. His usual beaming smile has been replaced with a smirk of jet black lips that scarcely embrace the dangling vice of a lit cigarette.

As for attire, the alter-ego sports a black football jersey with gray trim and the number 666 in a grunge font plastered on the chest. Another detail, now getting more personal, is the inverted pentagram tattoo, with a heart placed in the center of it, that is on his arm, with Erin's name arching above it.

But the most offending element of this noncommissioned portrait is the wide, black leather dog collar, with large sharp protruding metal studs, that is securely buckled around the circumference of his neck. Attached to this is a leash with Erin on the opposite end gripping it with one hand. She is displayed in a provocative pose, standing dominantly with feet a little more than shoulder-width apart and clenched fists confidently perched on her hips. Erin's petite frame is tightly wrapped in a shiny black full-leather body suit buttressed by a pair of matching six-inch stiletto heels. Clasped in her other hand, a whip dangles down her side and slithers across the floor.

The telling image of Erin is not doctored at all. It was merely clipped from a previous photo, and is a stark memory resurrected from the girl's muddy past, which persistently comes back to haunt her like an undead pursuer.

As horrific as it is that an intimate detail of her former aberrant lifestyle is now laid bare before the discerning eyes of her idealistic, chaste boyfriend, as well as everyone else, Erin is more fixated on the small pentagram subtly placed on his arm.

The skin on her back crawls. She imagines that everyone can clearly see through her shirt, witnessing her own "tramp stamp" expand aggressively across the whole of her back, growing larger like a wildfire. Centered in the pentagram on her back is the astrological symbol for Pisces; Emily had an identical one. And in this damning vision, she watches Brad look in horror at it, shake his head and walk away forever.

Nothing like this has ever happened to Brad before, and it takes a moment for it all to sink in. He finds his self-reflection turning outward, his astonishment bubbling into anger. Mocking him is one thing. He can take the abuse, but dragging Erin into this is a whole other matter.

Everyone has a good idea as to who is probably behind this passive-aggressive slur of a pseudo-psychoanalytical nature. Erin, however, knows exactly who is to blame. Only one person has ever had access to that image of her, and that person is a monster.

"Hey, Ross!" A deep voice reverberates down the hallway.

The sea of people surrounding Brad and Erin parts, revealing Lucus approaching, his small band of disciples flocking close behind as if he is leading them to the Promised Land. Also exposed is the fact that a copy of the image is affixed to each and every locker down both sides of the long corridor. As he gets closer, eyes fixated on Brad, without looking Lucus snatches one of the small posters and comes to a halt in front of the couple. Erin wilts behind Brad, gripping his hand tighter.

Clinging onto Lucus's arm is Erin's replacement, Scarlet. She is a gorgeous girl with a full mane of long, curly blonde locks whose looks far outweigh Lucus's. Scarlet would not even be with the less-than-handsome lanky fellow except for his bold rebellious confidence, rock-star-like status among local people of the alternative lifestyle, and shared interest in occult practices.

His money is also footing the bill to develop her band.

Scarlet peers at Erin with a look that expresses both high satisfaction, proud of what she has snagged, and also that of arrogance, knowing she has what Erin lost. But Erin misses not what Scarlet has procured; she actually pities the poor girl. She knows Scarlet has Lucus like an innocent woodland creature is in possession of the cold metal trap painfully digging into its shattered leg bone—in which the only way to escape is for the desperate captive to self-mutilate and leave a piece of itself behind.

However, knowing how the game is played, she stares back aggressively with slightly squinted eyes, not daring show any sign of weakness. As this silent battle of glares takes place, a war of words, and wits, is about to be waged between the guys.

Brad is ruthlessly outmatched.

Before Lucus can launch his opening salvo, Brad rushes in, going on the offensive. "If you had anything to do with this, so help me…" He jabs a finger at Lucus.

Lucus throws up his hands, feigning surprise. "Whoa there, partner. Hold your horses. I'm just as appalled here as you are. I can't believe someone would be so callous as to do something like this. A public school, where we, the next generation and future of mankind, come to be educated in a safe, comfortable environment, is no place for harassment such as this."

Everyone knows that he does not mean a word of what he is saying, but every remark is calculated to avoid self-incrimination, and to drive Brad over the edge.

Lucus continues. "I came to offer my support as soon as I learned of this dreadful caricature, and it is my desire that the person, or persons, responsible for this mockery are caught and brought to justice. I give you my word that I will do whatever it takes to help apprehend these…agitators. As a matter of fact, let me begin right now." He holds up the photo snatched off the locker earlier and scans the gathered students. "Who did this?" he asks out loud. "Who is the cruel architect of this senseless abomination? I pray, turn yourself in! Turn yourself in now and the authorities may go easy on you." Then he adds in a shallower tone, "Although it will surely be on your permanent record."

The crowd snickers. Brad's anger grows as Lucus continues his thinly veiled façade.

"You know who you are! If you do not surrender now, your

conscience will get the better of you and you won't be able to sleep tonight! Oh, for the love of—"

"Stop it!" Brad shouts. "You're mocking us! I know you did this, and pretending otherwise won't change that."

It's about time, Lucus thinks. Brad was more patient than he had planned, and he was about to run out of antagonisms. His expression turns cold. "You got any proof that I had anything to do with this?" He takes a step closer.

Brad does not reply.

Lucus sarcastically inquires, "Is this any way to treat someone who has come to you and generously offered assistance? It doesn't seem to be the 'Christian' thing to do, now, does it? Maybe this photo of you is accurate after all—at least of what you are really like on the inside, just like all the other religious hypocrites out there."

"I think you had better leave, now," Brad says.

"And," Lucus continues as if he were not just addressed, "isn't bearing false witness a no-no? I mean, it's one of the 'big ten' from Moses, if I'm not mistaken. Oh, Scarlet, my sweet." He turns to her. "Would you get your Bible out of your purse and check on that for me? I wouldn't want to say something that isn't accurate."

"Oh shoot," she replies, with her hand on her cheek, "I totally forgot it and left the darn thing on my bedside table. Oopsies."

Brad's fists are tight. "I'm warning you, Lucus. I mean it."

"Ooh, a warning! Well, if you're going to be that way, then I may have to consider suing you for slander—that is, unless you're willing to recant your baseless accusation against me right now in front of all these eyewitnesses."

Brad remains tight lipped.

"Suit yourself. Pun intended, by the way," Lucus quips with a big grin. Of course, he is bluffing about a lawsuit. "Hey, that sure is a nice cross hanging from your neck. Is it twenty-four carat gold? Ouch, that must have cost a pretty penny. I wonder how many starving children you could have fed with that kind of money. But it is sorta small. Not nearly the size of the one Erin has tucked in her shirt right now."

This catches Brad off guard. He glances over to see Erin's hand rise up to her chest. Not wanting to discuss her recent liaison with Lucus, Erin has not told Brad about her acquisition of Emily's necklace.

Lucus takes his index finger and places it on Erin's chest in the picture. "Oh, it's there, all right, you can take my word for it." He stares at the picture longingly. "Dangling in a place that is near and dear to my heart. She *does* look sinfully delicious here, now doesn't she?" His finger slowly slides down her torso. He turns back to Brad. "So answer me this, Bradford, since her cross is larger than yours, does that make her holier than thou? It must, right?"

"There's no need to drag Erin into this."

Lucus concocts an expression of bewilderment. "I'm not sure what you're talking about. What is this 'this' you speak of?"

"Your animosity toward me. It's obvious, don't try to deny it."

"Brad, Brad, I feel no animosity toward you. In fact, we can both relish the shared experience of having known Erin on an… intimate level."

Brad feels the prized self-control within his grip slipping away as Lucus plows ahead.

"We've both had the chance to discover her lovely hidden attributes, a privilege that no one else has: the haunting beauty of her personal poetry…the comfort of her warm embrace on a cold evening…the tantalizing sensation of her soft lips pressed against our own."

At this, both Brad and Erin glance away from Lucus, an involuntary action that does not go unnoticed by the antagonist. Lucus's eyes dart back and forth between the two as it becomes clear to him.

"Hold on a minute," he says in a tone of developing revelation. "Don't tell me you two haven't even kissed yet."

No response from either of them.

"Ooh, that's just delicious," he belts out. "You haven't even made it to first base with her? Wow, I have to give you credit, Bradley; it seems you have tamed the tiger."

"You're crossing the line, Lucus! For the last time, I will not allow you to treat Erin this way!"

"Allow me? Allow me! You're not in a position to allow or disallow anything. Besides, I have nothing but the utmost care and concern for her." Then he turns straight to Erin and, with a phony look of compassion, asks in a sickeningly sweet tone of sympathy, "So, how is your dad doing these days? Is he getting any better, or has his recovery hit a…speed bump?"

Brad loses it and lunges for Lucus.

Erin screams, "Brad! No!"

Big John, who had earlier slipped his way into the inner circle where this drama is unfolding, intercepts his friend before irreparable damage is inflicted. He is the only person on campus, including staff, strong enough to restrain his friend at this moment. Brad continues to struggle toward Lucus.

"Let me go, John!"

"No! It's not worth it! She—He's not worth it!"

"Well, if it isn't big bad John to the rescue," taunts Lucus.

"Shut up, Marilyn. It's *your* neck I'm saving here!"

"Ooh, you are so pregnant with masculinity, aren't you big fella?"

John wisely ignores him. Lucus continues.

"Erin taught me that little saying. She has a way with words, don't ya think? Let's see, what else did she used to say…Oh, yeah. Something about jock brains being full of emptiness or crammed with ignorance or something like that; sheer poetry."

Brad likewise ignores this obviously loaded statement. Realizing he is not going to overpower his way past someone who benches nearly three hundred pounds, he gives in and reluctantly steps back. John remains latched onto him just to be sure. Lucus confidently and arrogantly continues his verbal assault with an air of superiority.

"Oh, my! I'm aghast and don't know what to say. Is this the way a *Christian* is supposed to behave? I'm pretty sure your holy scriptures mandate that if you're insulted, which I haven't tried to do, but obviously I have inadvertently, for which I offer my sincerest humble apology, then you must forgive and forget, turn the other cheek as it's said. Quite honestly I'm shocked at how you've reacted here, how you've represented our Lord and Savior. It's disappointing, really."

A red-faced Brad, still secured by John, breathes heavily through his flaring nostrils and glares at Lucus, whose words ring true, to a point. Brad has never lost control like this. He is caught between reacting Biblically to a verbal insult, like Lucus pointed out, and defending Erin's honor.

It is frighteningly diabolical how evil can twist scripture to suit its own needs, leaving in its wake a swath of wounded Christians and tainted witnesses.

"What's going on here?" a faculty member shouts, pushing through the barrier of packed students. "Make way! Make way!"

"Can you believe this, Mr. Cooper?" Lucus responds to the emerging science teacher while holding up the picture. "Look what some punk did. I'm appalled, as we all here are, at the maliciousness of such an action. And we were trying to figure out who did it. Isn't that right, Bradford?"

Mr. Cooper looks at Brad, who is halfway hidden behind John's massive frame. Brad does not respond.

"What I believe needs to be done," continues Lucus, "in my own humble opinion, is that the hall monitor needs to be tracked down and interviewed. I mean, how can something like this happen on his or her watch? I daresay I will not be able to sleep until the guilty party is nabbed. Oh, the nightmares I'll have." Lucus is confident that the incompetent adults will not catch the deliberately obvious contradiction in his last two sentences. To his twisted delight, he is right.

"I assure you, we will do what we can to figure this out," replies Mr. Cooper.

"If I can be of any assistance, sir, please let me know."

"I don't think that will be necessary, young man. Now you all need to move along it's about time for the—"

Rrrrrrrring.

The horde of students instantly scatters, bolting for their classrooms. Today an unprecedented number of tardy slips will be issued, but to everyone who witnesses the event, their citation will be well worth it.

As Mr. Cooper slips into his classroom behind his students, the main players stay for a few moments longer. With no impartial witnesses around, Lucus changes his tune. "We will battle 'this' out, Brad. Of that, you can be sure. But it will be on *my* turf, *not* yours, and there you won't have a chance in hell."

John steps in. "Marilyn, how do you sleep at night knowing you're such a freak?"

"I don't sleep, don't need it. I'm an insomniac, slightly more evolved than the rest of the species hominid. By the way, how's the knee? Still a bit...tender?"

"I could have half the bones in my body broken, and I would still be able to tear you apart limb from limb."

"Be careful what you wish for, jock. I can have that whole 'broken bones' thing arranged. And you"—he turns to Brad—"you should be on your guard as well. Better keep your antenna up." With a smile, he points his closed umbrella skyward.

"Get to your classes immediately, or I'm taking you to the principal's office!" demands a voice from the nearest classroom.

"Yes, sir, Mr. Cooper," Lucus responds in a sweet tone. "We were just brainstorming how we could catch the perps. We'll be on our way; sorry if we disturbed your class."

Lucus gestures a kiss to Erin and walks away.

Brad turns to John. "Thanks for holding me back. You're a good friend."

"Listen, Brad. I did it for purely selfish reasons, not for you. You're the one putting yourself in this situation by staying with her." He glances at Erin. "But our team needs you Friday night. This game is too important. Our playoff hopes ride on it, and we can't do it without you. So please, don't thank me. If you're really grateful, make sure you keep out of trouble for the rest of the week."

With that, John grabs his book for the next class and bangs his locker door shut, leaving the picture of Brad still attached to it. As John walks off, Brad quietly removes it himself, as well as the one on his locker. He won't have to snatch any more, as all the other narrow metal doors are bare, each one eagerly plucked clean by passing students frantically scurrying to class.

The two stand alone in the empty hallway, a bit dazed. For the first time since he can remember, Brad has trouble making a decision, choosing exactly what to do at this point. He just can't think straight. Erin waits patiently. One thing is for sure, she is not going to her Government class. Brad has similar feelings.

"Come on." He leads her down the hallway.

"Where are we going?"

"Out of this place."

Erin realizes they are headed for the school entrance.

"You're skipping class?"

"That's right."

"But you told me you've never missed a class before."

"So what? The world is not going to come to an end if Brad Ross doesn't have a perfect attendance record in high school."

"Then where are we going?"

"I haven't decided yet. I'll figure that out once we get to my car."

Brad bursts through the entrance door with Erin following, and they zig-zag through the parking lot toward Brad's car. Approaching his Corvette, Brad notices something wrong right off the bat.

"Oh, no!"

"What is it?" asks Erin.

"My antenna; it's gone."

Erin looks down to see that it has been cleanly snipped at its base. Brad thrusts his hands up, covering his face.

"Are you kidding me?" he belts out. "What else is going to happen today!"

Erin can only watch his frustration and think that this is all really her fault, and since the cat is now partially out of the bag concerning that period in her life, she reluctantly decides to go ahead and tell him about the picture of her and where it came from.

"Brad, I want to explain the photo of me in that leather suit. I'm not going to make excuses, I'm just going to tell it like it is. There was this—"

"No," Brad interrupts. "I don't want to hear about it."

"But you deserve to know the truth, no matter how ugly it is."

"Look, Erin, I know you have a dark past. I know you're not perfect, and I don't want you to think you have to tell me every little past sin, especially if you think that's necessary to earn my trust or for me to keep liking you. I don't care about your personal history when it comes to that stuff. All I care about is our relationship now. What you did in your life before coming into mine is not going to change how I feel about you."

"Oh, Brad." She lunges forward and hugs him around the waist.

"I don't deserve you." With her ear to his chest and eyes closed, she squeezes him firmly. He just lifted a massive load of guilt and shame from her shoulders, a burden she has endured ever since she started having feelings for him. "I feel so light. Hold me, Brad. Hold me tight so I don't drift away."

"Oh, I'm going to keep you from floating off?"

"You are my anchor," she responds. "Rather than dance among the clouds, I would rather be grounded with you here on terra firma, frozen in time." Her eyes remain shut. Her smile, beaming.

Brad grins and begins to embrace her but instantly stops short, realizing he was about to make contact with her upper back again, and that would have been disastrous. Without Erin being able to see, he rolls his eyes at himself.

"It's okay," she says.

"What's that?"

"You can hug me there, now."

"Wait a minute, I thought you—"

"I know, but I'm over it."

"Are you sure?"

"Yes, I want you to. Go ahead."

With the gentleness of a young father holding his newborn for the very first time, he slowly, carefully, wraps his arms around her with bated breath and his eyes bouncing around, not knowing what to expect.

"Tighter," she insists. Brad grips Erin more firmly, bringing her closer, like a soldier embracing his wife for the first time after a long tour of duty in some God-forsaken land halfway across the world. His chin rests on her head, his eyes glassy.

Such a small, simple, seemingly insignificant gesture, yet such a huge impact it has on the both of them. Their relationship in this short moment has progressed light-years. They are becoming one.

After a few moments Erin softly asks, "What do we do now?"

"We keep doing what we're doing. Come to school, go out in public, be seen together. We can't let what others think dictate how we live our lives."

"No," Erin replies.

"No?"

She turns her head and places her chin on his chest, grinning up at him. "No, I'm talking about right now, this very moment. We have almost a full hour to kill before school lets out."

"Oh, I see what you mean." He looks around the parking lot while the memory of what just happened in the hallway resurfaces. "We can't leave campus, that's a given. I've got a lot of energy that needs to be burned off and was thinking about heading to the field house and lifting weights, but they won't let you in there now, and I want you with me—or at least in my eyesight—until you leave the grounds when school lets out. So I think I'm gonna jog around the track. What about you? Do you ever run?"

"Are you kidding?" she says, with a slight tone of disgust. "Even when I'm sick I don't run a fever."

Brad laughs. "You're funny. And amazingly beautiful."

"Are you sure you're not staring at your own reflection in my eyes?"

"Are you kidding?" he says with a smile. "I get *lost* in your eyes. Come on, let's go."

The two walk across campus, hand in hand, to the field house, where Erin waits for him outside while he goes in and changes into sweats and running shoes. The door opens a few minutes later, and Erin takes a step toward it thinking Brad is coming out, but she is mistaken. It is one of the coaches, but not the head coach. He is a fairly obese man wearing a baseball cap and white-collared pullover shirt, both displaying the school's logo. Gray shorts loosely wrap around his pasty white legs. Mercifully, tall double-striped tube socks conceal the bottom half of his stocky pale lower limbs up to his knees.

"Can I help you?" He holds a clipboard at his side.

"Oh no, I was just waiting for someone."

"You know you can't go in there."

"I know."

"Okay, as long as you know."

"I do."

The large man stares at her a few seconds as if sizing her up. "Okay, carry on."

"I will." She stands there, perfectly still.

Just as the portly priest of this religion known as football rounds the corner of the field house with his cleats clacking on the sidewalk, Brad emerges from the door.

"Hey, it's you," Erin says.

"Hey, it's me," he responds. "Were you expecting someone else?"

"Oh, no." She grabs his arm as they walk to the track. "Did you know I'm not supposed to go in there?"

"Yes. Why? Did you want to go in there?"

"Are you kidding? Please. I'm sure I would drown in the testosterone."

Brad laughs. "You do have a way with words."

The two make their way onto the track encircling the football field.

"So, you're just going to sit up in the stands and watch me jog?" Brad asks.

"Don't flatter yourself, jock-boy. As exciting as watching you run around in circles sounds, I'm going to get a head-start on my homework."

Brad smiles and shakes his head. "Okay." He walks onto the track and stretches while Erin plants herself several rows up on the cold metal bleachers. After a few minutes, Brad makes his way around the first lap and notices that Erin is, after all, watching him. He waves with a big grin and she reciprocates with a brief gesture back, embarrassed that she got caught doing what she said she wouldn't. Then she digs down into her book bag and pulls out a spiral notebook to do some writing that is not related to school assignments.

Unable to come up with anything creative enough worthy to pen, Erin spends her time just doodling. She can hear Brad coming around again and she makes sure not to look up, although the urge to do so is strong. As the thuds of Brad's footsteps fade in the distance, Erin hears another sound reverberating behind and above her.

Tang…tang tang tang.

She whisks around to witness a grackle near the top row, pecking on the stands, striking at an unfortunate insect of some kind that happened to be at the wrong place at the wrong time. The rigid spikes of the bird's claws scratch across the metal bench while it relentlessly pursues its meal. Squinting, she finally makes the prey out to be a wounded butterfly, sporadically flopping about in hopes of escaping in some miraculous turn of events. *What a cruel world,* she thinks, *where the strong prey on the weak, vulnerable, and wounded. Why does it have to be this way? What is the purpose of it all?*

Tang.

The distinct loud ping jostles Erin from her thoughts. The grackle has finally prevailed. The victor stands proudly with his prize securely fastened within the crushing tongs of its beak. After a few quick jerks of his head, surveying the area for others who may want to steal his morsel, the bird bursts upward in a flurry of beating wings, flies over the top of the stands, and is gone. As quickly as it began, the whole violent ordeal is over, which gives Erin pause.

She will not be a helpless victim. She will not just wait around for another surprise attack. Erin makes up her mind to turn the tables, go on the offensive, striking the predator.

LUCUS DRIVES AS IF HE IS a graduate, with honors, from the Grand Theft Auto School of Defensive Driving, or better yet, as one of its tenured professors. With little or no regard for his car or other drivers on the road, he zips in and out of traffic, only concerned with getting where he wants to be, when he wants to be there—which is especially hazardous at nine-thirty at night. Turn signals are merely vestigial appendages from a bygone era.

By his side, Scarlet endures the intense aggressive maneuvering by sealing her eyes and plugging into an MP3 player. Only every now and then does she ever gasp, reacting to a sharp turn or quick stop that is more forceful than usual.

There have been several gasps tonight.

A rift between the pair began earlier when Scarlet voiced her irritation over the way Lucus spoke about Erin at school previously that day, as if he still wanted to be with his ex. Lucus assured her that was not the case and that it was all part of his plan to get under Brad's skin, but Scarlet would not believe him. She insisted that it sounded like more than that to her and it got under *her* skin. She warned that he had better keep his distance.

The more Lucus tried to convince her otherwise, the more Scarlet became defensive, aggressively and relentlessly issuing threats of retaliation. That clash of unwavering opinions brought Lucus to the boiling point. He clammed up and started venting his anger with the gas pedal, and she, in response, crawled into her dark hole with the classic Rolling Stones and their man of wealth and taste.

An incoming text to his cell phone triggers a ring tone that is assigned to only one person on the planet, a ring tone that has not gone off in a long time. Lucus immediately taps a button that brings up the new message:

I'm at the park alone, leaving in 20 minutes.—Erin

This is highly unexpected. Lucus glances at Scarlet who, with eyes tightly shut and head lightly bobbing up and down, braces herself with feet firmly pressed against brakes that are not there and white knuckles clenching the door handle on one side and seat cushion on the other.

He smiles menacingly and immediately hangs a hard right, crossing over the path of a car in the outside lane, an act that elicits an extended horn blast from the offended motorist. Scarlet gasps, eyes popping open. Her hands slam onto the dash in front of her, involuntarily bracing for impact. As Lucus aggressively enters a convenience store parking lot, the front of his low-riding sports car scrapes on the inclined driveway entrance, and the impact jolts Scarlet violently in her seat. Her head knocks against the side window when Lucus hangs a tight left, pulling up next to a gas pump.

"Lucus! Was that really necessary?" She yanks out ear buds and massages her sore temple.

He drops a twenty on her lap. "Go in and get me some smokes while I fill up."

"You know they won't sell cigarettes to a minor."

"The clerk in there owes me a favor. Tell him they're for me."

Scarlet rolls her eyes and lets out a sigh.

"Come on girl, I don't have all night!"

She reluctantly grabs her purse along with the money and begrudgingly climbs out of his car. As she walks, Lucus lets down his window and drops a handful of candy wrappers onto the ground: his trash. About halfway to the door, Scarlet hears tires squealing. Spinning around, she witnesses the black car zooming out of the lot and disappearing into the night, with glowing red taillights keeping watch from behind and the littered candy wrappers sucked in its draft dancing about, failing to keep up.

Scarlet throws her head back with eyes closed and mumbles. "Not again."

Lucus's mood has instantly swung from one extreme to the other, but delight does not compel this narcissist to drive friendly.

In fact, he barrels down the road at breakneck speed in anticipation of his meeting with Erin, wanting to be sure to get there before she changes her mind and leaves. Tapping his phone and swiping his finger across the screen to unlock it, Lucus hits speed dial and waits for the other end to pick up. After the third ring, there's a click, and he begins issuing orders before the person even gets a chance to say hello.

"Get your idiot cousin and the video camera and get to the park immediately!"

An incoming call is from Scarlet. He hits *ignore* and continues talking.

"You'll see Erin there. Drive in inconspicuously, if you have enough brains to do that, and make your way around to where you can get a good shot of her. Just pretend like you're lovers making out in the car out until I get there. What's that?...I don't care if it would be awkward...Yes, I know both of you are guys...I don't care, just do it! When I arrive, she'll forget all about you, and that's when you can start filming. And make sure you have everything set up correctly. You two brainless idiots almost messed up the whole thing last time."

Lucus pauses to listen while the other party delivers regretful news. He reacts in frustration. "What?...What do you mean it's not charged?...When I bought it for you I gave you explicit instructions to keep it charged and with you at all times!...I don't want to hear how you're sorry. Listen, just use the car plug-in adapter. What's that?...Your pet ferret chewed it up?...No...No, your phone camera will not work good enough, you fool! You need a better zoom and night mode as well! Excuse me?...Drive to your friend's house and get his? We don't have time for that you..."

He growls and throws his phone on the floorboard. This is one covert operation Lucus won't be able to carry out. After a few minutes, he surmises that he has enough evidentiary ammo to use anyway and that all is not lost. He still gets to meet with Erin in private, and the possibilities of what might come out of the get-together erase his irritation.

The idea of their impromptu hook-up takes over his thoughts and excites his senses. Never satisfied, though, he complements these feelings by indulging his sweet tooth. Leaning over, he fumbles with releasing the glove box door, which finally pops down. Just as he grabs for a candy bar, the lights on his radar detector flash, accompanied by the unmistakable high-pitched squeal alerting him that he is possibly caught in a cop's telling beam. The speeder immediately sits up straight and hits the brakes. Fidgeting in his seat, an irritated Lucus reluctantly goes the speed limit with his hand at the ready on the knob that controls his headlights. If the officer pulls out in pursuit, he will black out his car and outrun the lawman while concealed in the dead of night—a move that has been successful on more than one occasion in the past.

"Come on. Come on," Lucus mutters, scanning the roadside for a patrol car and tapping on the steering wheel to cope with his g-force addiction, as he calls it. Driving sixty miles an hour feels like barely moving at all, which grates at his nerves to no end. Finally, he spots the patrol car hidden off to the side. As Lucus passes, he can make out the distracted officer talking on his cell phone and eating a burger—a good sign. A few seconds of observing in his rearview mirror after safely clearing the trap confirms that he has once again successfully skirted the law.

Biting into a chocolate candy bar packed with peanuts and chewy nougat, he smugly takes delight in being cunning enough to avoid detection in this ongoing cat and mouse game between speeders and police. It also helps that he has the best radar detector Dad's money can buy. He floors it once again.

ERIN SITS SLUMPED ATOP A PICNIC TABLE with her right foot nervously tapping the bench below. Each passing car on the highway spikes her heart rate, which then subsides after none of them turn into the park. They keep traveling down the road to their own destinations. She feels very alone, isolated, vulnerable. The worried girl scans around for anyone or anything that might be able to come to her defense if needed, or at least be a witness should she end up missing the next day, but there is nothing. No people, no squirrels, no birds, nothing.

There is also, strangely enough, a lack of noises one would associate with being outdoors, except for an unseen dog, which sounds huge by the resonance of its tone, somewhere in the distance furiously barking at something it deems a threat. Probably an invader encroaching upon its territory. A train some miles away can be heard off in another direction. But these remote echoes make her feel even more secluded and exposed.

What she does not notice, though, is a battle being waged close by. The streetlights high above are blanketed with swarms of insects that are overpoweringly drawn to their hypnotic glow and frantically fly in erratic patterns, evading ravenous bats in an aerial dogfight for survival.

Down below, Erin's craving for the drag of a nerve-calming cigarette graciously takes her mind away from thoughts of what may happen in a few moments when Lucus appears. But she is determined to go through with it; there is no alternative as far as she can conclude. It *must* be done. Erin hopes that the short notice she gave him will restrict his ability to concoct anything devious, and maybe throw him off balance a little. But the twenty minutes are almost up. If he does not show by that time, then something is probably up, and she is bolting out of there.

A pair of headlight beams sweeps the park from one side to the other, flashing across Erin's face, as a car pulls into the drive. The vehicle heads straight for her, illegally cutting across on the grass, and comes to a stop a few feet away from the picnic table. The lights go dark. She does not recognize the car, but there is absolutely no doubt who this is.

Erin stands, steps down, and walks toward him as a front of confidence. At first there are no signs of life in the vehicle, no movement at all. Then, in the dark interior, a glowing orange point of light quickly grows in intensity then fades back to its normal radiance. She knows he is in there watching her, studying her. Then, cigarette in hand, Lucus finally exits and approaches. The skin on his hands and face almost appears to glow, matching the moon's hue.

"*Salve,*" he says, in a gleeful tone.

Standing with arms crossed, she does not respond.

Lucus waits a few more seconds.

"*Silentium est aureum?*"

"I'm not conversing with you in Latin."

"Aw, come on," he pleads, "for old times' sake, my sweet?"

"The past is the past, Lucus. I'm not going back there."

He looks down at her chest. "What's with Emily's cross hanging on the outside of your shirt now? Am I a blood-sucking vampire to be warded off?"

If this was an attempt at humor, it is lost on Erin.

Lucus quickly surmises this is not a friendly visit, nor one of surrender, but he does what he can to try and woo her back the only way his lost soul knows how. "Sorry I couldn't get here sooner. Scarlet wouldn't let me get away; she's very jealous of you, you know. I can't say I blame her, she doesn't fill out that black leather body suit the way you do."

"Is that all your carnal mind can focus on?"

"Of course not, there's alcohol, drugs, and sugar," he replies with a grin.

She is still not amused. "Regardless, I couldn't care less about Scarlet or your relationship with her."

"Scarlet means nothing to me," Lucus declares.

"Well that's one thing coming out of your mouth that I can actually believe."

"She's just a cheap substitute for you." Lucus is sure she will take that as a great compliment, especially coming from him.

Erin responds, "Is that what Emily was? Or maybe I'm just a cheap substitute for my dead sister?"

The quick dig causes Lucus to pause. He pulls out a pack of cigarettes and offers one to Erin while he takes the final drag of his. She shakes her head. He exhales smoke in her direction and flicks the butt off to one side.

"So, you've given up smoking too?" he asks.

"I want you to stop," she responds.

"I can't, I'm addicted."

"Don't play stupid with me. You know what I mean."

"Oh, you mean stop harassing you and your little boyfriend. No, sorry, I can't do that. I'm afraid I'm addicted to that as well."

"What do you hope to accomplish? Because I can tell you right now there's no way I will ever get back with you."

"Who says that's what I want? I'm not going to lie, that would be icing on the cake, but there's a bigger picture here."

"And what is that?" she asks.

Lucus bends down and picks up a fallen autumn leaf. It is big, about nine inches across. "That, my precious, is only for those in the inner circle to know." He holds the leaf up, blocking Erin's view of his face. "It's privileged information." He extends it halfway between them. "There's a wall between us now, Erin. A wall of your own making."

She does not reply. She does not move.

"Of course," he continues, "you can tear down that wall and come back. I've left the door open, but it's your choice."

"Like I said, I'm never coming back to you, but that doesn't mean we have to be enemies. Why can't we just both go our separate ways and live our own lives?"

"I'm afraid it's not that simple."

"Why not?"

Lucus slowly crumbles the brittle leaf in his hand until a fist is all that remains for Erin to stare at. "You are either with me or against me; there is no middle ground."

"Then so be it, Lucus. You leave me no choice."

"And what is that?" he asks condescendingly.

"If you don't stop harassing us, I will go to the police with everything I know."

"Is that so? First your boyfriend levels threats against me, now you?"

"I mean it, I will do it."

"So what are you going to tell them, that I sacrifice animals now and then? What are you going to offer as evidence?"

"I'm referring to the drugs, Lucus."

"Oh please, you can't be serious."

"I am. I'll tell them about your so-called parties and how you freely hand out narcotics to people in order to enslave them and bring them under your control."

"Really, Erin? Is that what I do?"

"That's exactly what you did to me and Emily, and I've seen you do it to others too. Don't try to deny it."

"*You* wanted the drugs, Erin. I did not *force* them on you. You took them of your own free will. And, as a matter of fact, you even helped me give them out on more than one occasion. Now isn't that so?"

She does not reply because what he said cannot be refuted.

"Go ahead, go to the police and tell them how I use drugs to ensnare unsuspecting victims into my sticky web of a cult and how we perform satanic rituals and kill animals. Be sure to give them all the grisly details; don't leave anything out. And don't forget to draw pictures and diagrams; make it as tantalizing as you can."

Lucus pauses as a stunned Erin looks in disbelief. He continues. "Do you really think they're going to believe you? It's too outlandish, especially in a podunk God-fearing perfect little white picket fence community like ours. Things like this only happen in the evil big city, as far as they're concerned. And who are you going to go to? Sheriff Knox? You know how he feels about you. He thinks you're completely out of your mind as it is."

Lucus waits to see if Erin has any more fight left in her. Her body language suggests otherwise. He comes in close and goes for the kill. "Little girl, don't mess with me. You're way out of your league. You know I cover my tracks too well. You know none of that can be traced back to me. And if you should ever try to pull this little stunt you're fantasizing about, I'll go to Brad and spill the beans on you. It's only because of my feelings for you I haven't done that yet."

Erin looks up with tear-filled eyes. "I'll have you know that Brad told me he doesn't care about my past, so your threat of telling him is useless. And don't give me that bull about your not spilling the beans yet because of your *feelings* for me. You have been holding that over my head as a way of trying to control me. Well as you can see, it won't work…not anymore."

Lucus laughs. "Don't be so naïve, Erin. If he told you that, it was out of pure ignorance! Do you really believe your perfect little sheltered Christian boyfriend is going to be okay with you being a Wiccan?"

She now knew that what Lucus taught his followers wasn't really Wicca, but it wasn't worth arguing about again. "I *was* a Wiccan—not anymore."

"Once a Wiccan, always a Wiccan. I guarantee you that he and his holier-than-thou family will forever paint a scarlet *W* on your chest once they find out. They'll see you as an evil girl damned to the pits of hell for eternity. And more than that, what about our satanic rituals, which you gladly took part in? Huh? That is, until we got into the animal sacrifices. They were still satanic nonetheless. That's a whole other level of depravity in their book, Erin. And what about the tattoo on your back? Has he seen it? Or even know about it? Does he even have the slightest idea of what we used to do for amusement?" He waves his arms about as if he is a marionette dangling from strings.

She does not answer.

"Be honest with yourself. If you really believed that Brad would not be shocked and leave, you would have already told him everything by now."

Erin's shoulders slump under the weight of guilt and shame once again. Lucus is right. She sobs, hands covering her face in a feeble attempt to shield herself from the verbal onslaught. Seeking refuge in the darkness, she says in her heart, *God, please help me.*

Erin begins to feel comforted after praying this. Her emotions subside, and the warm sensation of being gently held by a loving father envelops her body. She has heard before that God is a father and all are his children. Maybe God really does care about her; it certainly feels like it now. The sensation is like being under the influence of a drug, but a clean, natural one that is pure and without lasting negative effects. Her whole body feels comfortably numb, weightless, yet at the same time her senses are fully active and tingling.

At this very moment Erin is in a place she feels she would like to be in forever. It reminds her of how she feels when alone with her beloved Brad, as if she is in heaven.

But after a few moments of welcome peace help clear her thoughts, she comes to a realization that wrenches her stomach. The sickeningly sweet stench of chocolate and cigarette breath hits her in the face. The girl's delicate fingers slowly curl inward, exposing her eyes, which take in a horrifying vision.

She is in the full embrace of Lucus. He has been hugging her body against his this whole time. The terror of this revelation stuns her for a moment, then she pushes away. This time, Lucus does not fight to keep her in his grasp. Erin doubles over, hyperventilating and trying to not throw up.

"Can't you see what all this is doing to you?" Lucus asks. "Trying to be something you're not is killing you. *I* accept you for who you are. Don't you see that?"

She looks up without responding.

"Here, take one of these." He extends his hand. "It'll make you feel better." In the center of his outstretched palm sits a tiny pill. Erin recognizes it immediately. It is one of the really good ones. "Come on, you know you need it. I hate to see you like this."

Erin glances up at him then back down to the pill. She slowly reaches over and takes it between her thumb and index finger.

"That's my girl. I knew you'd come around." He tenderly slides some stray hairs behind her ear, delicately rubs her cheek as his hand retracts, then gives her a comforting look and softly says, "Go on, take it."

Erin gradually raises the pill to her mouth, locks eyes with Lucus and ever so slightly nods. Then, without notice, she rears back and hurls it as hard as she can. Lucus follows the tiny object, lit up from above by nearby streetlights, as far as he can but eventually loses it in a dark patch of grass. He then turns back to Erin.

"That was stupid," he says in an irritated tone. "You're hopeless."

"You look here." She steps forward and gets in his face. "I am not falling for your deceptions anymore. You hold no power over me. I am no longer your 'sweet.' And another thing—lay off Brad and me. If anything happens to him, so help me God, I will make you pay. This sweet little thing will turn to a bitter poison in your mouth and take you down." She spins and marches toward her car.

If Erin thinks this is over, she is sadly mistaken. When she gets about halfway, he says something that stops her dead in her tracks.

"How's Queenie doing these days?"

A petrified Erin stands motionless with her back to Lucus.

"Cute kid. I've noticed her around. That little girl is growing up fast. Has some of your same features, and she's going to be as delicious as you are in a couple of years. Don't you think?"

Erin dares not let Lucus see the shock and fear in her eyes. She knows all too well that was a classic veiled threat from this monster. She simply turns her head slightly to direct her voice toward his position and warns, "If you touch her, or even get near her, I will *kill* you."

"Oh, so *now* you care about your little sister? That's not how it used to be. What changed?"

She cannot answer.

"The deeper I descend into the abyss, the stronger my abilities grow," he says. "You and everyone else are powerless against me."

Erin waits a moment silently then declares, in an uncompromising tone, "You have been warned." She continues walking to her car.

As she opens the door, Lucus says, as ominously as he can, "*Memento mori.*"

Erin pretends not to hear. She gets in, closes the door, and drives off, forgetting to turn on her headlights.

To amuse himself, Lucus throws his hands up and yells while she pulls out of the park, "Why do our reunions keep ending up like this? And if a poor innocent little squirrel ODs on that pill you tossed, it's *your* fault!"

A THICK CURTAIN OF FOG LOWERS as Erin drives down the road, navigating her small car with both trembling hands firmly latched onto the steering wheel at ten and two, her headlights now on. She is determined to keep a safe speed this time, bearing in mind her limited visibility and frazzled nerves. And considering her recent run of bad luck, Sheriff Knox is probably up ahead waiting to bust her and haul her off to jail for the slightest infraction.

Memento mori. Memento mori…*Remember, you will die.* She ponders his words.

No doubt the common Latin phrase imploring one to contemplate one's own mortality was an indirect warning, but for whom? Herself? God forbid, Queenie? Erin's mind starts to wander, and then it launches into an all-out sprint. Queenie was the last one spoken of before Lucus uttered the phrase, so it had to be directed at her. But surely he would not involve someone so young; that is one boundary he has never crossed. On the other hand, he probably no longer has any boundaries—they were becoming thinner and grayer throughout the course of their relationship.

Referring to himself as the Minister of Sin, Lucus would often gather his flock and, among other things, preach to them about how the real world is, about how the strong, with bloodstained teeth and claws perfectly designed for ripping into flesh, prey on the weak with violent efficiency—and no so-called "god" was either loving enough or powerful enough to do anything about it.

Sometimes his rants would go on late into the night, teaching an odd mixture of evolution, quantum physics, pagan spirituality, Gnosticism, Native American religion and Crowleyan Magick—

with a heavy dose of Christian-bashing Satanism thrown in for good measure.

He believes, and has convinced his followers to accept, that humans are soulless creatures, nothing more than fleshy bags of chemicals responding to stimuli, but at the same time beings who can learn how to control the forces of nature on the path to becoming something like gods, although not in a supernatural sense. To him, the spiritual world is nothing more than another state of the physical universe occupied by those who have evolved highly enough to discover and enter it through the attainment of hidden knowledge that can be applied upon death. Those who do not learn these dark arts simply become worm food as their lifeless bodies decay postmortem.

For Lucus, this is a unifying theory, one that perfectly explains a violent and unjust natural world, one in which religion could arise with its many gods and unexplained "miracles."

According to his theology, the beings in this other realm are pure forms of light or energy, with some more powerful than others, able to manifest themselves to us. He is convinced a war rages in this other dimension between Yahweh and Lucifer. They struggle over enlightening those of us trapped in our dimension, disagreeing over whether or not to show us how to reach their side.

Yahweh, the one the Bible misrepresents, he believes, has blinded people to the truth by keeping their natural desires suppressed and convincing them to wallow down the path of rules and regulations, striving toward some sort of mythical moral perfection to escape divine judgment and an eternity of searing torture in the underworld of hell. Satan, on the other hand, whom the Bible also lies about, is actually the good being who aspires to share his world with us. The Dark One knows that ultimate freedom of the individual, not suppression of desires and instincts, is the tool humans need in order to evolve highly enough to discover it and cross over.

And that is exactly what Lucus intends to do. It is his goal to reach that place someday, but unlike any who have gone before him—without dying. Once there, he plans to learn and grow powerful, living forever (or at least until the universe implodes on itself again—unless he becomes powerful enough to control even that). It is also his aim to spark a rebellion against both of its warring leaders so he can take over and rule their world, as well as this world, himself.

Erin knows that in Lucus's worldview there is no universal morality, no omnipotent lawgiver waiting to reward or punish those who do right or wrong. It is the only thing that makes sense to him in a materialistic universe, one without any supernatural presence. There is no inner conscience, just instinct. There is no justice, only revenge. There are no rules, merely desires. There is no mercy, only wrath.

Terrified that something may have already happened to her sister, Erin plucks the phone out of her purse and calls home, but no one answers, which is typical. But that fact still does not alleviate her fears. The more she agonizes over Queenie's safety, the more her body tenses up and the heavier her right foot becomes, easing the gas pedal closer and closer to the floorboard.

The fog is unnaturally thick now, concealing trees on both sides of the road. With no points of reference, and getting lost deeper and deeper in thought, Erin has no clue that she is now driving at a dangerously high speed. The distracted girl is looking forward, but sees no further than her corneas. Only witnessing what is in her mind, she is, in effect, blinded.

Death approaches.

Then, for some reason, Erin's train of thought is disrupted, and her eyes focus just in time to witness a rather large dark figure, about the size of a tall man, quickly swoop down in front of her car. It is so startling that Erin screams and her hands involuntarily withdraw from the steering wheel. She immediately places them back but stays focused on the thing out in front. Her mouth hangs open in disbelief.

The shadowy presence hovers above the ground, maintaining a fixed distance in front of Erin's car barreling down the highway. Details of the anomaly are hard to make out, but what can be seen is the shadowy outline of a humanoid-like being, somewhat resembling a black angel, waving its arms, or wings, whatever they are, as if to get Erin to stop; but for what purpose? Does it want to attack? Surely it could easily break into the car if it wanted.

Erin vigorously rubs her eyes for a moment but the ominous figure remains. She now knows this is not her runaway imagination playing tricks. The manifestation is real. Somewhat in shock, and not knowing what to do, she glances down at the speedometer, discovering that her small car is hurtling down the road at over ninety miles per hour.

The road…what road? Where is it?

Erin cannot determine where her car actually is. She sees nothing except for the gray haze of smothering fog and the persistent creature out front, just on the boundary of her headlights' beams. It is as if she has been transported into the nighttime sky, up in the clouds where winged demons frolic.

Erin shuts her eyes tightly, takes a deep breath, and slams on the brakes. After an extended skid, the car comes to a screeching halt. At the exact location where she stops, the flock of grackles perched in trees on both sides of the road bursts away and flies off into the night. But Erin neither sees nor hears them.

The frightened girl remains frozen to her steering wheel, eyes closed. She sits in self-imposed blackness, like small children do when scared of something they see and hoping that the threat will disappear if they can't see it. But Erin is merely waiting for that thing out there to make its move. Clutching Emily's cross, she sits still for some time listening for the shattering of glass or ripping of metal, but all she hears is the quiet hum of her engine running, which causes small vibrations that can be felt through the fingers of the one hand that remains on her steering wheel.

Other than that, all is deathly quiet.

After a few more anxious moments, she slowly opens one eye, which takes a couple of seconds to focus. To her surprise the demon, which she is convinced that it is, stays out there at a distance. It remains steadfast several feet in front of her car but no longer waving. Even without moving, the nebulous creature is still hard to make out, having ill-defined edges.

But one thing is clear; the entity has stopped trying to wave her down—mission accomplished. It remains above the ground with its appendages fully stretched out to its left and right. It does not flinch. Erin glances all around outside through her windows, then returns her attention back to the front. It is strangely motionless. She stares, trying to make out details, or witness it move even a little, but nothing happens. Then her curiosity gets the better of her. She unlatches her seatbelt, gently pulls her door handle and cautiously gets out of the car, staying focused on the apparition.

The smell of burnt rubber still lingers in the air.

She stands motionless for a moment, quickly looks behind her, spins her head back around, then walks to the front edge of her car, one deliberate step in front of the other, leaving the door open in case she needs to quickly jump back in for safety.

The engine continues to idle in park.

Even after taking a few steps toward it, the creature does not stir. The dark, ghostly being is still unrecognizable. Erin decides to test the waters by going in closer to see what happens. Doing so, she inadvertently wanders in front of her headlight's beam. All of a sudden, the creature vanishes. Erin squeals and twirls around; afraid it will reappear behind her. She frantically scans the area but cannot locate it. She knows if this thing is what she thinks it is, it can materialize anywhere at any given point in time.

While spinning in circles, Erin steps closer to the middle of the car, between the headlights, and it reappears exactly where it was before. She squeals and stands frozen in fear. But like before, it does not move. Erin decides she has had enough and that inside the car with doors locked seems like a good place to be right now. She takes a step to her left slowly, so as not to startle it, and then notices something odd. Now half of the creature has vanished, its left side.

Then it dawns on her. She ponders for a moment, looks down and, stuck to the headlight is a moth: a rather large one she recognizes. It is the same one, or at least the same species, as the one that landed on her when she was pulled over by Sheriff Knox the other day.

"Are you kidding me?" she says aloud. "Did I get all worked up over a moth?" Erin looks back at the dark figure then walks toward it to make sure it is just a shadow being projected into the fog. As she approaches, surely enough, it begins to fade.

But then, just beyond where the being should have been if it were indeed real, she notices something. A terrifying revelation.

Lying dead on the road stretched across her lane is a full-grown wild boar—the one that attacked her in the woods behind Emily's roadside memorial. Had she hit it going the speed she was driving, surely the impact would have sent her car flying, tumbling end over end. The crash would have been fatal.

Erin is breathless thinking about what could have been. She slowly walks over and reverently places her hand on the poor animal. It is still warm. There is no blood or obvious injuries, only an oversized limp tongue dangling out of its mouth. Surely, if another car had hit it, the vehicle would still be at this location in a mangled heap.

There is no way this tiny girl can pull the massive beast off the road. She does not even try. With arms crossed, Erin walks back to the front of her car and squats down next to the front of it. Swirling miniscule vapor droplets are illuminated by the light's beam. She holds her hand in front the moth, and its shadow spans her palm.

"You saved me," she says out loud.

But the savior's life was not spared.

Erin gently pinches each wing and plucks the creature off the headlight. Its feet, stuck to the glass, resist separation for a moment then, one by one, they break loose with quick retractions. She holds the amazing insect for quite some time, cradling it like water cupped in her hands. It is as exquisite and beautiful as she remembers from before, only this time it will not be ascending into the heavens.

Keeping her gaze on it, Erin treads softly to her open car door and backs onto the seat, then swings her feet around, making sure the moth does not fall out of her palms. As if laying a dead loved one to rest, she gently places her hands onto the passenger seat and separates them, allowing the moth to gently descend between them and lie there in peace.

Erin is in a daze, a mild case of shock perhaps. She reaches over to the car door, feeling for the handle, keeping watch over the moth as if hoping it will miraculously revive.

Erin eventually latches onto the handle but it feels different, warm and somewhat pliable. She then comes to the realization that it is not the handgrip she has grasped, but the arm of someone or some thing! It is large, muscular, and carpeted in thick, bristly hair.

There are no sounds coming from that direction except for deep, partially obstructed breathing that is balmy and moist on the back of her neck. It sounds inhuman, whatever it is, and the rotten stench of its breath is nearly overpowering.

Trembling and defenseless, Erin forces herself to slowly turn around and look upon what it is next to her, which apparently came out of nowhere. As her eyes fall upon the startling sight, she recoils. To her surprise, and relief, sort of, it turns out to be Sheriff Knox standing there, bending over looking into her car. It is almost as if he materialized out of thin air, just like she thought the phantom demon would do earlier. This guy seems to be everywhere—at least everywhere she is. Erin now realizes that there are bright flashes of blue and red lights coming from the patrol car parked behind hers.

Even at night, he wears those mirrored sunglasses.

"Are you trying to get yourself killed?" he asks in a gruff tone then immediately turns and sneezes into a handkerchief. John is fighting one nasty cold.

"What?" she replies with a big swallow.

"The other day you nearly ran head-on into my car, now you're sitting still in the middle of the road on a night foggier than I can ever remember. Seriously, you must have a death wish or something…" He sneezes loudly.

"Well, there's a dead hog just up ahead blocking my path."

"I know." He wipes his nose. "We got a call about it at the station earlier. Only because I was looking for it is why I was driving slower than normal. Otherwise, I might have plowed into the back of your car and killed both of us. And did you know, in the short time since I've been here, another car drove by as well?"

"No, I didn't."

"If I hadn't been here with my lights flashing, they wouldn't have known to slowly pass on the other side. That's another person or persons who might have had a tragic encounter tonight because of your carelessness."

"Right." She turns her attention away from his stare, and germs.

"You didn't run into it, did you?" he asks.

"The hog? No."

Knox leans over and spots the moth laying on her other seat. "Is this what has you parked here in the middle of the highway—a bug?"

She does not answer.

He shakes his head and stands up. "You stay right here."

Erin watches him make his way around and inspect the front of her car, probably making sure she didn't lie to him. Then he disappears into the fog up ahead with his flashlight leading the way. As she sits there, Erin thinks about how these days she just can't seem to escape being under the microscope of the law, which always seems to be around watching when she does not realize it. It is a smothering feeling, almost one of claustrophobia. She is also tired of seeing her reflection in those wretched mirrored sunglasses.

The sheriff's silhouette materializes in the vapor, becoming more distinct the closer he comes. The man leans down into her window, wiping his nose again.

"That's a boar all right, a big one at that—biggest one I've ever seen in these parts. I can't tell what happened to it. Died of natural causes, I suppose. How is it that you didn't hit the thing? How did you see it?"

"Careful driving, sir."

"Hmm." He doesn't know what to think. "Well, you can go now. Just slowly pull out and ease your way around. I've got someone on the way to remove it."

"Okay." She puts the car in gear.

Before she drives off, he says one last thing. "Ironic where this happened."

"Excuse me?" she asks.

"Right here, with you."

"I don't know what you're talking about." She squints her eyes.

"You don't know where you are?"

"Uh-uh."

Knox takes his flashlight and shines it toward the back of her car. "That right there is mile marker number 279." He can tell by the expression on Erin's face that she still doesn't get it. He then points the light in front of her car. "Exactly where that boar is, off on the side of the road, is your sister's memorial. This is the precise location where she…um…passed away."

Erin's eyes immediately widen and she glances around with her mouth slightly open, but visibility is practically zero.

"I'm sure glad you didn't meet your sister's fate."

She turns back to him and finds herself looking directly into his eyes. He has removed his sunglasses and stares with what she can only interpret as an expression of…compassion. Her mind does not know how to process this as they gaze at one another for a moment.

"Now you drive careful, Erin. It's real dangerous out there tonight. Okay?"

"Um…yes. I will. Thank you."

"You're welcome. Now go on home."

Knox steps away, and Erin slowly depresses the gas pedal and drives off. In her side-view mirror she sees him watching her as he dons his reflective spectacles once again.

FAINTLY GLOWING LIGHT from a couple of windows is all Erin can recognize in the haze of vapor as she carefully walks toward her house with the moth securely cupped in both hands. Queenie is on her mind as she detours around the side and toward the back, where a large floodlight fastened high up in an oak tree illuminates the area with an eerie radiance, casting shadows on the ground of the tree's gnarly branches.

Erin cautiously makes her way to the barn door and puts her ear up to it but hears nothing. She steps a few feet over and peeks through a knothole in one of the boards of the wall. Just enough ambient light filters through the window opening above that she can make out slight movements within. As her eyes adjust, the pigs are gradually revealed to be standing in a circle in the middle of the barn, all silently facing one another with their heads slowly bobbing up and down in unison. Their eyes shut.

A shiver quakes down Erin's spine, but she is relieved that her sister is not in there with them. Hopefully she is in the house safe and sound. Erin goes to the back porch, pulls open the screen door, careful not to drop the moth, and then pushes the main door open. At that moment she hears a slight whimper.

"Shep? Is that you?"

The nervous dog once again lets his feelings be known as he

timidly emerges from the shadows.

"What's wrong, boy? Come here."

He hobbles up to her side and sits down.

"Are the pigs freaking you out too?" she asks with a half-hearted smile.

He looks up and whines again.

"I don't blame you. Come on inside, you'll be safe in here."

He looks through the open door for a moment then up at Erin without moving.

"Go on."

Shep peers into the house again then finally makes his way to the doorway guardedly. Erin has to slightly nudge him with her foot to get him to go in all the way. She closes and locks both doors as Shep goes into the kitchen and sits anxiously waiting for his master. Erin walks past and is about to exit the kitchen on the other side when she notices Shep not moving. She stops and addresses him. "You're not getting anything to eat tonight. You can wait until morning."

Shep stares past her down the hallway toward the front of the house.

"Stay here all night if you want. I need to go check on Queenie." Erin turns and walks down the dark hallway and comes to the stairs near the front door. She makes a U-turn to start ascending the staircase. She looks up before taking the first step and beholds Emily.

Her deceased sister is halfway up, standing alongside the Lincoln portrait, looking down at her. She is barefoot and motionless in a long white cotton nightgown with hands by her side. There is a warm smile on her slightly tilted pale face, but it does not ease Erin's fear. She stands trembling and working hard to keep from dropping the moth still cupped in her hands.

"Erin, it's me, Emily."

She does not respond. The girl is speechless trying to make sense of what is going on. With Emily blocking her view, Erin is also unable to see the top of the stairs. Up on the second floor, her mesmerized mother stands looking down at Emily as well, however she is also inexplicably staring into the vision's face at the same time. The ghost's body is two in one, somewhat like conjoined twins fused at the back, only the merging goes much deeper. There is only one body, two arms, two legs and one head with two faces, one on either side. The unnatural illusion is flawless as neither Erin nor her mother is aware of this dual vision, or each other. All they see is the front of the Emily that is facing each one of them.

"My dearest Erin, do not fear. My presence here is a gift, a gift to you and to me from God. I don't have much time now, but soon, and very soon, something wonderful is going to happen…a miracle."

Up above, tears stream down Rose's face as she converses with the Emily she sees. "Oh, I miss you too, baby," she replies, apparently already in a conversation with the spirit.

Rose's vision holds out its arms. "Oh, how I long to be with you, Mom."

"Me too! Come, come be with me. You are welcome here."

"I can't."

"Why not?" asks Rose.

"Because of Erin."

"What do you mean, Emily?"

"My sister is still jealous of me. You know she is the reason I died, don't you? If she had not left me stranded that night, we would all still be together. It all happened because of her envy and hatred, which she still harbors against me."

"But it was an accident. She didn't mean for you to get killed," Rose answers timidly.

"Oh, she didn't? We know the thoughts you have about the incident, and they are correct. She left me on purpose, and you know in your heart of hearts this is the truth. Don't fight it." Emily's expression turns to one of a pitiful worry. "You don't love her more than me, do you?"

"No! Of course not."

"Then stop defending her! If you want to honor my memory, don't insist on turning a blind eye to what happened that night. And then there's that boy she's with now."

"Brad Ross?"

"He is an obstacle, Mother. You know what kind of family he comes from. You remember all too well what his father and his friends did to you on prom night."

Rose is taken back. "I never told any of you about that night. How do you know this?"

"We know much about you, Rose. We also know that together Emily and Brad are creating such negative energy in this place that I am unable to cross over to your side. It's their fault we cannot be together like we should. If you don't believe me, just ask Madame Zelda. She will corroborate what we are saying."

"Why do you keep saying 'we'?" Rose asks.

"You will find out *only* if you do something about those two. There are many wonderful things I want to share with you, but I can't under the current circumstances. Please, Mom, I want to be with you again. Do something about them."

"What?"

"You can start by getting rid of Brad. We are doing all we can from this side, but we can't do it alone. After you take care of him, we will discuss what to do with Erin."

"Wait, what do you want to do with Erin?"

The apparition ignores Rose's inquiry and serves up a diversion.

"Tonight you will be given a special gift, as a good-faith offering to show all we can do for you *if* you do what we say."

This is altogether different than what Erin is hearing down below.

"You are so beautiful, my darling sister. You need to know that your goodness is the reason I am able to visit like this. I know things have been difficult for you recently, but keep an open mind and heart, and all will be well. Listen, there is something I have been wanting to tell you for a long time. Something I know you want to and need to hear. About that night—"

Suddenly an eruption of vicious barking and growling breaches the heavy silence. Rose and Erin both look over and see Shep, with raised hair on his back and fangs protruding from a snarling, drooling mouth, fixated on the spot where the vision of Emily stands. The temperate dog has never shown any aggression remotely close to this for as long as they have had him. He is going wild, snapping and barking violently, yet backing up a little as if he is unsure whether or not an attack on him is eminent.

Then all goes quiet. As quickly as it started, the barking stops and Shep meanders back to the kitchen licking his chops. After he disappears from view, Erin and Rose look back to the middle of the staircase and discover Emily is gone, vanished into thin air. They now see each other for the first time.

"Emily?" asks Rose.

"No mom, it's me, Erin."

"Oh."

The two stare at each other for a moment, then Rose quietly turns and walks out of view, heading for Emily's room.

A stunned Erin stands motionless, then leans to her left, looking down the hallway and through the kitchen, where she sees Shep curled up next to the back door. He appears to finally be at peace, at least enough to get a nap in. She leans back and surveys the stairs once again before heading up to the second floor. Every step elicits a creak, each with its own distinct moan. As she passes the spot where Emily was standing, next to the Lincoln death photo, she feels nothing out of the ordinary, no coldness or gust of air like she thought she might.

Pausing at Emily's old room, Erin spies her mother already crawled into bed, but not alone. She curls up next to a stiff body that is nearly her size and strokes the long hair that is the exact same color as Erin's. Rose does not lie there quietly; she converses with it. "My darling Emily…Oh, I love you so much and miss you with every ounce of my being. Thank you for showing up tonight. Of course I will do whatever it takes to get you back for good. You hear me? Whatever it takes."

This bizarre spectacle does not faze Erin in the slightest. She is used to it by now. Desensitized. Numb to it all.

The surviving twin then makes her way to Queenie's room and carefully cracks open the door and looks in. To her relief, Queenie is sound asleep in bed. A quick scan around the room reveals nothing out of the ordinary. Erin closes the door and sneaks to her father's room. She can still hear her mother mumbling down the hallway. An ear to the door here exposes nothing but silence on the other side. Dad must be out as well.

She rests her forehead on the door and starts thinking about how if Brad knew all that went on in this house, and with her, he would surely walk away. In fact, Erin sometimes thinks about leaving; going off to some distant place to begin another life as a new person altogether, or maybe even a new creature, if that were possible. She looks down at the moth in her hands. Who is she kidding? Erin has not the guts to do it. She is a coward. However, if she loses Brad, that may be the motivating factor in her going over the edge and throwing it all away for good…forever.

THE FOLLOWING DAY AT SCHOOL is uneventful, a welcome relief of normalcy for Erin. And time with Brad always seems to draw her back from the edge of insanity. That Lucus has kept his distance is comforting as well, albeit a little unnerving at the same time. Was he busy with other "projects," or lying low to build up a false sense of security in her? Erin tells herself it is the former, though she is not convinced of it.

A text message comes in as she walks to her car: *I'm picking up Queenie. She has a doctor's appointment.—Mom.*

Not at all surprising. Queenie's health has been fragile ever since she was born, so she has needed regular checkups three or four times a year. Erin is grateful; now she can drive straight home and get some rest from the exhausting weekend instead of having to double back after retrieving her little sister. She replies *ok* and pulls out of the parking lot past the football field where Brad and his teammates have already begun practice. The game of their life is this Friday night. Win it, and they make the playoffs for sure.

LUCUS SMIRKS AS HE taps his phone's touchscreen to close out of Erin's reply to what she thought was her mother's text. His sleek sports car slowly pulls up in front of the junior high school building where a few stragglers still wait to be picked up, including Queenie. His dark tinted window slides down with a distinct whirring sound.

"Hey Queenie," he calls out. "Come here."

A wall of tweens slowly divides in two as the students turn

around to stare at Queenie, who stiffly loiters alone in a corner with a canvas bag hanging from her right shoulder and books clutched against her abdomen. She looks up and points to herself and quietly asks with a mouth packed full of braces, "Me?"

"Yes you, gorgeous. Come here."

She recognizes Lucus, as do all the others viewing this spectacle. He is well known even in the lower grades. Despite his unorthodox appearance, or maybe because of it, Lucus is highly revered among these kids, like a dark super hero in a graphic novel, and they can't believe what is happening right now—that he would lower himself to enter their world and call out to one of their own.

Queenie slowly makes her way past her classmates as they track her with mouths gaping wide open. Standing at his window looking down at Lucus, she coughs into a handkerchief, waiting for him to speak.

"Listen, Queenie, Erin asked me to come pick you up and take you home. Her car is having problems, and she can't get hold of your mom."

The girl turns to see what her classmates are doing. Of course, they are staring. She faces Lucus with handkerchief still pressed against her nose and lips. "I thought you and Erin weren't speaking to each other," she mumbles through the cloth.

"Sure we are. As a matter of fact, Erin and I met the other night and had a pleasant conversation. She didn't tell you about it?"

"No."

Erin never confides in Queenie, and Lucus knows this.

"Look, we may not be together as a couple anymore, but we're not enemies. And as a friend, she asked me to take you home this one time."

Queenie stares for a moment and tries to process all this to make an on-the-spot decision. "I don't know…"

Lucus calls out to the audience, "Hey, should she go for a ride in my car? Would you do it?"

The faces of all the girls light up and they nod approvingly with wide-open smiles, also sporting grills of orthodontic handiwork. The boys, on the other hand, jump up and down in a tribal display, fists pumping high in the air as primal hoots and grunts obnoxiously squeak out from their underdeveloped diaphragms.

Queenie is a bit uncomfortable with all this attention, but at the same time is enjoying the feeling of being envied by her piers. The overwhelmed girl finds her feet walking around the front of the car almost involuntarily. She pulls the door handle, then slips into the black leather bucket seat. Though you can't tell from the way she sits bundled up with her bag and books, her senses are highly activated. Lucus reaches over. She shifts away slightly.

"Don't worry," he says, laughing. "I won't bite." He depresses the glove box button and the door flops down. Grabbing a candy bar, one of many, he holds it up in front of her. "Afternoon snack?"

After a short pause, "Sure. I guess." Queenie takes it from his hand but does not open it.

Lucus smiles, grabs a handful more, and tosses them out his window. The kids outside all go wild, diving and fighting for the scattered sweets, which are way better than any birthed by a birthday party piñata. Once the last bar is snatched, the horde of candy sharks stands back up to discover that Lucus's car is gone.

Purring down the highway, the engine's muscle can be felt through Queenie's seat with vibrations resonating deep within her chest. It is both exhilarating and intimidating. For some time there is nothing but awkward silence: no conversation, no music, just Lucus driving while looking straight ahead. Queenie stares down at her feet, stealthily glancing over at him from time to time. One last time she looks, and he turns to gaze directly into her doe eyes. She snaps back and stares straight down again.

"You know, Queenie, I can tell you're going to be way prettier than Erin." This proclamation is accompanied with a gesture of reaching over and tucking hair behind her ear, an intimate moment of physical contact he knows will be a new, exhilarating experience for the innocent young girl. He also wants to be able to see her expression.

Queenie finds herself in a mild state of shock, forgetting to exhale. She has never been in a situation remotely resembling this, except in her daydreams. She does not know if she is supposed to respond or not. And if so, what should she say? Lucus stares at her and she can sense it. Feeling pressure to say something, anything, she finally blurts out a sentence, the only thing she can think of.

"I like your car."

"Yeah?" he responds. "Check this out."

He floors it.

The engine revs higher and higher as the car picks up speed. The candy bar in Queenie's hand suffers the full force of her clenched grasp as she attempts to hold on for dear life.

"I know this car can outrun Brad Ross's old clunker!" Lucus shouts over to his frightened passenger, competing with the loud engine. "I tested it out the other night! Blew him away!"

Queenie, eyes shut, does not respond. The mangled candy bar no longer in any way resembles its original shape. Lucus lets off the gas, and the car steadily slows back down to its original speed. "You can open your eyes now."

The girl's eyelids sporadically flutter open. Her deep breathing is reminiscent of just having finished laps around the basketball court in gym class.

"What'd you think of that?" he asks.

"Cool," she responds not knowing what she actually thought of the terrifying experience. As her adrenaline and breathing taper down to normal levels, she starts into another one of her coughing fits, probably brought on by all the excitement. She raises the handkerchief up to her mouth again.

"There, there. You gonna be all right?" Lucus reaches over and pats her shoulder.

Queenie nods as she continues violently hacking into the rag with a red face. Reaching into her bag, she pulls out an inhaler and takes a deep puff between coughs. A few moments later, the bronchial storm subsides.

"There you go," Lucus says, as if he had anything to do with her getting better.

"Sorry," the embarrassed girl responds.

"No, no. Don't apologize. It's not your fault that your health is not what it's supposed to be."

This statement puzzles her.

"I know what will help calm you down further."

"What?" she timidly asks.

"You like music?"

"Sure."

"I've got something I want you to listen to." He pulls out an MP3 player from the center console and hands her the headphones. "Here, put these on. I want your opinion on this new music I got. It's different, but should help calm your nerves."

"Um, okay." She loosens the grip on her books and bag. They start to fall over.

"Put those on the floorboard," Lucus orders. "Then lean your seat back a little."

She complies and places the headphones over her ears. Looking over, she sees Lucus telling her something but can't hear what he's saying. "What?" she asks lifting the left one off of her ear.

"I said just close your eyes and let the music do its thing."

At first she is hesitant about not being able to keep an eye on their whereabouts, but realizes that though there are still a few miles until they arrive at her house, there are only two more turns, a left and then a right. Queenie is confident she will be able to feel the car's motion to determine if they are still on the correct route. "Okay."

Leaning back, she is interrupted by Lucus again just before placing the headphone back on.

"Relax, breathe normal, and concentrate on the music. Got it?"

"Yeah. Sure."

The willing participant settles back down into the seat and shuts her eyes. Lucus hits the play button and increases the volume a little. After a few moments her eyes pop open and she looks over with a furrowed brow. Lucus motions with his hand for her to close her eyes again. After adjusting her skirt, she does so.

What is now coursing into her ears and mind are a psychedelic blend of music, loosely defined, and strange tones that seem to almost pulsate from one side of her brain to the other in rhythmic motion. The dark dissonant earworm, a harmonic digital Trojan virus of sorts, burrows its way past the outer surface of her mind and deep into her subconscious, where it will lay dormant until deciding to surface.

Lucus can see her countenance morphing into an altered state of relaxation. After raising the volume a little more, he takes his foot off the gas and slows down a bit, then gently speeds back up. Again he slows down then speeds back up. He continues this ritual, creating a rhythmic motion back and forth that helps Queenie sink deeper into the abyss.

At some point Lucus looks over to see an elderly lady in the next lane staring in disapproval at him and his erratic driving behavior. He sticks his long pointy tongue out at her. The insulted senior citizen harrumphs, turns forward, and speeds ahead.

Returning his attention to Queenie, he can tell she's finally out. Her head is limp off to one side, and her hands have fallen down next to her thighs, palms up, relaxed fingers loosely curled inward. Lucus slowly reaches over and places his hand in between her legs. She is oblivious to what is happening. He carefully unzips her backpack and deposits a folded sheet of paper. As he sits back up, the back of his hand accidentally scrapes her bare knee, but she does not flinch.

"Queenie. Queenie," the young girl hears off in the distance some time later, fighting to raise her heavy eyelids. "We're here at your house."

Lucus removes the headphones as Queenie slowly reaches up like a sloth in a confused attempt to do the same. After realizing the headphones are gone, she rubs her eyes.

"Did I fall asleep?" she mumbles.

"Yes. How do you feel?"

"Good, I guess." She squints around, trying to get her bearings.

"Don't forget your backpack."

Queenie's head bobbles around then she remembers the bag is on the floorboard. With a deep breath she picks it up and fumbles for the door handle.

"Let me help." Lucus reaches over and pops open the door.

The dazed girl starts to get out, but he grabs her arm.

"I want you to know, Queenie, that I can cure you of your sickness."

"Really?"

"Yes. I also want you to know that I would never leave you or forsake you. Do you believe me?"

"Mm-hm." She nods slightly.

"I will never abandon you, like some close to you would. You are a precious jewel worth keeping. Will you remember that?"

"Um, sure."

"All right, shut my door and go inside now."

"Okay." She follows his order.

Lucus takes off down the road, leaving Queenie standing at the end of their hundred-yard-long dirt driveway. She slowly meanders her way toward the house, rubbing her head and trying to remember anything of the last thirty or so minutes. She slips into the house unnoticed, and neither Rose nor Erin ever become aware of how she got home.

IT IS NOW APPROACHING TWO A.M., and Erin is finally getting ready for bed. The effect of a prolonged nap earlier in the afternoon kept her up later than usual. Queenie herself only went to sleep about an hour ago. She had been unusually energetic following the ride home with Lucus—that is, once the cobwebs in her head cleared out.

Erin stands at the bathroom sink and partakes in the nightly ritual of cleansing her face of makeup and checking for emerging blemishes. One swipe of an alcohol-soaked cotton ball does indeed reveal a crimson pimple on her cheek.

She sighs and leans in to get a better look. Like any girl her age, the slightest imperfection is seen as a grotesque deformity the likes of which has never been seen by man, outside of science fiction movies. A face with acne might as well be the hairless red buttocks of one of those baboons they saw pictures of in Biology. Erin, as well as every other teen with this problem, does what she has been told again and again not to do. She picks at it with her fingernail. The action does not help, but makes her feel like she did something to speed its disappearance.

Erin dips her hands into the water and splashes her face. Leaning away from the sink, she catches a glimpse of something behind her in the mirror. A squinting of eyes and more determined focus reveals that it is not a *what*, but a *who*. Standing somewhere in the midst of light and shadow, he is clothed in a thick but tattered brown, dust-covered robe of coarse material, like one might see in Bible times. His resolute eyes, inset into a sunbaked leathery Middle Eastern face plowed with deep trenches carved by time, are draped on either side by gray hair streaked with experience and wisdom. One of his large, strong hands confidently grasps the tall wooden staff at his side.

Strangely, Erin is not terrified, as the intruder does not appear to offer any ill will. Her feeling can be more accurately described as reverent fear. She asks, "Who are you?"

The mysterious prophet does not speak. He simply responds with an extended arm and callused finger pointing straight at her. No, not straight at her—off to the side slightly.

Erin turns back around to see in the mirror ten red streaks, each a finger width wide. They are in two groups of five, four vertical lines with a diagonal mark running across—resembling what a prisoner might etch into his prison cell wall to mark off passing days.

The girl then lifts her hands to discover they are now covered in blood, dried blood. She rubs them together vigorously in vain, attempting to remove the crimson stains from her fingers. Then a ghastly reflection in the mirror captures Erin's attention; a vision of her highly decayed face. Maggot infested gray rotted flesh is partially melted off her skull and only one eyeball has moderately survived the decomposition process.

Erin shuts her eyes and screams, "No!" She then feels her hands being gently guided down into the water. After a few moments of darkness and silence, Erin looks again to see her restored beautiful face staring back in the mirror, which no longer has any red marks on it. The old man is gone, and her hands are cleansed of blood.

Movement in the water. Concentric rings radiate outward from a splashing center. It struggles to stay afloat, eight pointy black legs thrashing furiously. The red hourglass a warning of its deadly potential. Erin plunges the sink's stopper handle and water flows in a vertical river. Observing from above, she watches as the venomous creature is pulled into a vortex and sucked down the drain. A quick pull of the stopper's handle seals the spider's fate.

These bizarre incidents are followed by a quick retreat to her bedroom, where Erin slips under the covers, quietly mumbles, "Please God, make this all go away. I'm sorry. Dear God, if you're real, make this all go away. Dear God, if you're real, make this all go away. Dear God, if you're real, make this all go away," a chant that eventually tapers off into unconsciousness.

ERIN FINDS HERSELF BACKED INTO A DARK CORNER of the barn, enveloped in a blanket of blackness that camouflages her presence. A small table with seven chairs around it, one being much larger and more ornate than the others—a throne—sits in the middle of the floor.

The tabletop is clothed in a fancy cream-colored satin table-cloth, topped by a fine tea set adorned with painted red roses. Off to the side is the old radio from Emily's room, playing the lullaby "Rock-a-bye Baby." The static-littered recording appears to be a performance from the 1930s, maybe even the '20s. It loops over and over without ceasing.

Erin spots Queenie at the edge of the light. She is clothed in a very formal dress, like something out of a Charles Dickens novel—very Colonial. Her hair is styled as well, with huge ring-lets buttressed upward and fenced in by a gold tiara liberally adorned with precious stones and jewels. She appears to be con-versing with someone who is just off in the darkness, but cannot be heard.

Queenie curtsies and reaches out her delicate hand, which is swallowed by the blackness. She then turns and walks toward the table. It is soon apparent that she is holding the hand of a tall bulky man canvassed in a vintage black tuxedo with tails. Imme-diately four others follow, stepping into the light, their faces still masked in the shadows. Queenie points at chairs, directing where each one should sit. As they follow orders and some orbit around the table to the other side, faces are revealed. They are not human.

Erin gasps, and all activity at the tea party stops. The men, all with hybrid pig-man faces, stare in her direction. Queenie peers as well, but they do not see Erin and continue about the business of their formal party. Erin exhales a sigh of relief as she watches Queenie go to the edge of the darkness and begin speaking again. Queenie's expression turns to one of irritation as it becomes ap-parent that a disagreement is at hand. The song is louder now.

When the wind blows
The cradle will rock

Queenie stiffens up and points with dictatorial resolve to a chair across from the throne on the opposite side of the table. After a few moments, the standoff ends when a rather large foot, cupped in a shiny black patent leather high-heeled shoe, breaches the light, and out steps a very rotund woman. She is huge, towering over the girl and dressed to the nines as well. There is no way she could ever fit in the chair Queenie has reserved for her. The woman's face is every bit the same species as the hog-men still camped around the table. She makes her way to the setting, but pauses for a moment halfway there.

When the bough breaks
The cradle will fall

The sow changes direction and paces to the throne, where her large backside takes up residence. Grunts of excitement fill the air, but Queenie does not share the hog-men's joy in what has just taken place—a coup. Indignantly shocked, she stomps over and yells at Madame Pig while pointing to the other chair. Her ranting falls on deaf ears. Once Queenie determines that words have no affect, she rears back and slaps the sow across its snout. The celebratory grunting stops abruptly.

And down will come baby
Cradle and all

A loud squeal bursts forth from the sow, and her minions jump to their feet, swipe all contents off the table, and storm around Queenie. They grab her and slam her body onto the table, holding her down. Queenie struggles, but the young, frail girl is no match for the large beasts' inhuman strength. The sow slowly stands up, walks over, and plucks the crown off the frightened girl, slinging it back without aiming. It skids across the floor and falls into the open basement entrance, bouncing down the steps and coming to rest in several pieces next to the cabinet.

Erin watches in horror as Queenie is stretched out on the table, pinned down by her captors. A huge knife arises above the girl's chest, held there by the large sow. Erin is paralyzed with fear, unable to go to her sister's rescue or even scream. The knife rises then starts to strike when a moth, the angel moth, flutters by, distracting the attacker, who stops midmotion. Then the moth rises out of a crack in the room, coming to rest outside on the cistern.

The sow returns her attention to Queenie, raises the knife again, and somehow Erin is able to let out a blood-curdling scream. "Nooooo!"

All attention is then focused in her direction. They definitely now know someone is there lurking in the shadows. The female makes her way over, leaving Queenie in one piece for now. Erin struggles to bolt, but realizes she is chained to the wall. After a few more steps, the sow stands before her. Erin notices something. The pig's face—it does not look real. Then she realizes it is a mask—the eyes beneath, human.

This is an actual person, not some sort of freakish human-animal monster. But who could it be? The only person who comes to mind is Madame Zelda—a much larger version of her, which is an unsettling thought in itself. Then, for some unknown reason, Erin feels the cuffs slip off her hands. She is now free and going to find out who is behind this madness. She reaches up, clutches the mask, and rips it off.

What she sees captures her completely off guard. Beneath the mask lies the face of a hog. It was one of the creatures the whole time. Erin cannot comprehend the meaning of all this. The sow snarls, raises the knife, and strikes her in the chest.

ERIN SITS UP IMMEDIATELY, clutching her damp T-shirt. She looks down, fearing it is blood-soaked, but discovers only perspiration deposited by her body during the nightmare.

Once she gathers her thoughts, the concerned sister gets out of bed to go check on her sibling. She peeks her head inside Queenie's door to thankfully discover the girl safely sleeping like a baby. Someone else sound asleep is their father, snoring up a storm down the hall. Still concerned for Queenie and reflecting on her dream again, Erin gets an idea. It is worth a shot.

She returns to her room and goes straight for the vanity. On it, the angel moth rests in a glass jar. She picks up the container and a straight pin, grabs her chair, and returns to Queenie's room. Perched on the chair in front of the door, pin clasped in her lips, Erin lifts the glass container, causing the moth to gently slide out onto her outstretched palm. She sets the empty jar between her feet on the chair and raises the moth, placing it just above Queenie's doorframe. She then takes the needle and pierces its body, pinning the creature to the wall.

Maybe, just maybe, this will help protect Queenie. It is an act of desperation.

Stepping down off the chair without looking, Erin bumps into something unexpected. Startled, she looks down to discover it is a nervous-looking Shep with the leather gloves in his mouth again.

"Shep! Oh, you startled me."

She quickly notices something is not right.

"What is it, boy?"

He turns his head, pointing toward the stairs. Erin glances over and notices that a light is on down below. Shep plants himself on the floor and whines. He is not going anywhere. Erin gives him a pat on the head and makes her way down to the first floor. She cautiously walks into the den, where Rose is seen from behind in the rocking chair. An all too familiar sound that has been resonating in her head now eerily filters through her ears.

"When the bough breaks / The cradle will fall / And down will come baby / Cradle and all."

Is it just a coincidence that her mother would be singing the very lullaby from that horrific dream? More importantly, *why* is she singing it? Erin slowly makes her way closer and notices an unbelievable sight in the mirror. Cradled in her mother's arms is a curled-up, sleeping four-year-old little girl. And not just any girl; it is Emily. Erin is sure, because there is that telltale birthmark on her face that she had until it disappeared on its own a couple of years later.

Erin rubs her eyes and looks again, but it does not wipe away the startling vision. She makes her way around to the front and it is slowly revealed that her mother is not holding Emily after all.

A quick glance back to the mirror confirms this. Her mother sits with arms outstretched as if she is indeed holding the little girl, but there is no one there. Rose keeps looking down and singing with an expression of pure joy as if all this was happening for real—except that she sees the little girl alive, asleep.

"Mom?"

Rose looks to her right noticing Erin for the first time. "Oh hi, baby," she replies in a hushed tone. "Quiet now, you'll wake her."

"Mom, what are you doing? What's going on?"

"Isn't it wonderful, Erin? It's Emily. It truly is. You can tell by the birthmark." She motions as if softly rubbing the little girl's face. "I was asleep upstairs. You know, with Pretend Emily. And I was awakened by a girl's voice. When I opened my eyes little Emily here was standing there next to my bed. She told me she couldn't sleep and wanted me to rock her like I used to."

Erin stands there, not knowing what to make of all this.

"Oh Erin, this is so much better than I thought it would be. You two are now complete again. We are complete again. I've never been so happy, at least not since I can remember."

Erin looks back in the mirror, and Rose now appears different sitting in her chair. Aged and much thinner. Skin leathery, wrinkled. Emily is now not Emily on her lap, but a baby. It is small, *very* small, with no birthmark. And drenched in blood. By the infant's gaunt appearance, and body sinking listlessly into her mother's cupped hands, it is obviously dead. Rose's eyes are closed and her head eerily pivots back and forth as if to say *no*.

Standing behind the chair, just within light's faint exposure, is Emily, the teenage one, holding hands with four-year-old Emily. Both standing. Smiling. Living.

THIS WEEK HAS BEEN A TOTAL BLUR FOR ERIN, who finds herself at the end of the next day sitting at home and slowly trying to plow through a mountain of homework. Exhausted both physically and emotionally, she attempts to recall details of that day, especially time spent with Brad, but only fuzzy clouds of memories briefly appear in her mind and evaporate as quickly as they materialize.

Along with all that has happened to her, this mild form of amnesia is probably also due to the fact that she has kept her conversations with Brad guarded, carefully censoring everything that she and her family have gone through, making deep, memorable conversations all but impossible. Brad has not noticed her being somewhat distant because he has been preoccupied himself, constantly thinking about this week's big game.

Erin sits on her bed, surrounded by books and papers, with Shep curled up at the foot keeping a watchful eye on the door. He has spent much more time with Erin lately, following her every move and keeping his distance from other occupants of the house, both living and otherwise.

The phone downstairs rings. Rose or Queenie will get it, as Erin does not receive calls to the house phone anymore, only to her cell, and those calls are only from Brad these days. Shep gets up and makes his way to Erin, rudely trampling on everything in his path. One step on the calculator wipes out the math problem she was working on.

"Shep, you crazy dog, you're wrinkling my papers!" She picks him up with a grunt and moves him over to her side. "Wait a minute, this is not the right answer," she says holding up the calculator. She turns to Shep. "Did you do this?"

He looks up with a whimper.

"Now I've gotta start all over again. Do you know how long it took me to get to that point?"

He keeps staring at her, not understanding a word she is saying but knowing he is in a bit of trouble. She lets out a sigh. "Oh Shep, you know I can't stay mad at you." She rubs behind his ears. He lays his head back down. "One thing's for sure," she continues, "you're as bad at algebra as I am."

Erin's door bursts open, startling both her and her sheepish canine companion. It is Rose. "Erin, quick, meet me outside at the car. It's an emergency!" Rose disappears as quickly as she arrived, her shoes stomping frantically down the hallway.

"Wait, what is it? Is it Queenie?" Erin shouts at the open doorway.

"No!" comes a distant but clear reply. "It's Emily!"

ERIN AND HER MOTHER STAND AT THE EDGE of Emily's grave, or rather what is left of it. Rose inhaled three cigarettes en route from their house and is currently lighting up number four waiting to hear what Sheriff Knox has to say about the vandals who dug up her daughter's grave.

"When my deputy arrived, the casket had been opened, but we closed it back for your sake, ma'am."

The culprits also toppled the statue. The fallen angel lies on its back with both wings snapped cleanly off.

"What did they do to my Emily? Did they steal her body?"

"Fortunately, it appears your daughter's remains were untouched. However, there were some items placed into the coffin that I feel you need to be aware of."

At that moment, a car rushes up and barrels to a skidding stop on the gravel drive. Out of the hatchback pops an animated Madame Zelda. "I'm here! I'm here!" she shouts, waving a handkerchief to get their attention while doing her best to jog up the slight embankment to where everyone else is. She continues yelling, "I came as soon as I heard! I'm not too late, am I? Don't start without me! Yoo hoo, I'm here!"

They all watch Zelda approach huffing and puffing, seeing more than they ever wanted of bodily bounce action—heels digging deep into the soft sod. She comes to a rest between Rose and Knox, doubled over trying to catch her breath and unable to speak for a moment.

The sheriff says, "I told you before, Mrs. Zelda, if the department needed your psychic abilities to help locate missing persons or solve cases that we would contact you. But we don't need your help. In fact, there's no missing body."

Madame Zelda, still sucking for oxygen, raises one finger, indicating she'll respond once she is able.

Rose takes another deep drag and chimes in as streams of smoke pour out of her mouth and nostrils, dissipating upward. "I called her. She's my spiritual advisor."

Zelda nods and points at Rose.

Both Sheriff Knox and Erin simultaneously ask with a hint of surprise and disapproval, "Spiritual advisor?"

"Yes, anyone got a problem with that?"

Erin and Knox's eyes meet for a split second, then bounce away.

"Ahem, as I was saying, Rose, there were some items left in the casket."

Zelda springs up with an, "Ooh!" And then a longer, "Oooooh, I'm a bit dizzy. Nice."

Knox grabs the elbow of the swaying woman to make sure she does not inadvertently bury herself in the pit next to them.

"I'm okay. I'm okay." She tugs her elbow away. "Whatcha got?"

"First, there was a dead rabbit. Its blood has been drained. I figured there was no need in showing you that. Then there was this." The sheriff shows them what appears to be a small, thin layer of metal and a nail. He continues. "This sheet of lead was rolled up into what I can only describe as some sort of scroll with this here nail pierced through it. There's some kind of writing on it. Greek, I suppose."

"No, it's Latin," says Zelda.

"Greek, Latin, it's all the same to me. I don't care what language it is. Do you have any idea what this is and what it's about?"

"Sure do, it's a *defixione*."

"Defi...defi...well, what is that?" he asks.

"*Tabulae defixione*, to be exact," Zelda says. "It's a curse tablet."

"A curse tablet?"

"Yes, in ancient times they were used to convey messages to influence spirits, or even gods, usually asking them for victory over an adversary or enemy by binding them up in some sort of horrific trouble."

"What about the nail?" asks Rose.

"It is pierced through the rolled up sheet to reinforce the binding nature of the curse."

"Let me see that." Erin takes the object and studies it.

Knox continues probing. "So it's a curse. Who's the intended target? Can you read it?"

Erin's eyes grow wider.

Zelda responds to the sheriff's inquiry. "Oh yes, I read it. It appears that someone named Brad Ross will be the recipient of some unforeseen tragedy."

Both Sheriff Knox and Rose turn their attention to Erin, who is still fixated on the artifact.

"Brad Ross?" Knox looks back at Zelda. "Are you sure?"

"Oh, I'm sure all right." She takes the artifact from Erin, who is finished with it. "But that's not all."

"What?" asks Rose. "Someone else is mentioned as well?"

"Who?" asks Knox.

"I'm afraid...our little Erin, here."

Erin hugs herself, staring deadpan down into the grave.

"What about Queenie? Is she mentioned?" Rose spins around to check on her youngest daughter, still safely sitting in the warm car.

"No, no mention of her, just Erin and this Brad fellow. But don't you worry, Rose, I can counteract this curse for you...for a nominal fee, of course."

"But why go through all the trouble of digging up a grave? Emily's grave?" asks the sheriff.

"I can think of two reasons. First, it is a place relevant to Erin since it is the final resting place of her identical twin sister. Second, probably to take advantage of the strong miasma here."

"Miasma?" he asks.

There is one thing you have to hand to Madame Zelda, she may not be a true psychic with actual supernatural abilities, but she knows her stuff. "Miasma is a form of bad air. It was believed that close contact with miasma generated by the decaying dead and the cursing tablet would produce a more potent form of noxious and mysterious mist, thus polluting the intended victim even more by empathetic magic."

Rose flicks her spent cigarette on the ground and steps on it, twisting her foot back and forth. As tobacco smoke with chemical additives rises from the damp dead grass, Knox blurts out, "You don't really believe this stuff, do you?"

"I most certainly do," replies Zelda. "Don't you, sheriff?"

"Of course not! It's all hogwash."

"Then why do you inquire of it?"

"Because the more I know what is believed by this loon, the better chance I have of discovering who it is."

Erin is sure of who it is beyond a shadow of a doubt. Sheriff Knox's next statement confirms it even more.

"We also found a candy bar wrapper in the casket. Now it was probably blown in by the wind, but we're gonna dust it for prints just in case."

Erin knows they will not find any. Lucus will have been way too careful for that when leaving his calling card.

Knox continues, "And there's one last thing we found. Quite unusual. It's a car antenna, from an older model by the looks of it. I don't suppose you would have any insight on this, would you, Madame?"

"Oh yes, yes indeed. This is an object that belongs to one of the two intended victims. It was placed here to help insure the curse is successful."

"Is this yours?" asks the sheriff.

"Hold on." Zelda snatches it from his hand and places it on her forehead. She stands with eyes closed and head tilted slightly upward for a moment. "It's Erin's." She opens her eyes, looking at the girl for confirmation.

"Yes, you're right. It's mine." Erin is lying. Zelda guessed wrong, but Erin wants possession of it, so she went along with the charade.

"See, Sheriff, you call me when you can't find a body or need help with one of those cold cases. I can help…for a nominal fee, of course."

"Well Erin, you can have it," Knox says. "We're not able to get any fingerprints off it. But you won't be able to reattach it to your car. It's destroyed. You'll have to get a new one."

"Yes, sir. Thank you." She receives Brad's antenna from Zelda, who is sporting an undeserved smug expression of paranormal accomplishment.

BRAD PULLS UP TO THE OLD ABANDONED FACTORY in his Vette with Big John riding shotgun. Just thirty minutes earlier, both guys had received word of the threats against Brad and Erin via John's father, the sheriff, who called immediately after Rose and her family left the cemetery. In light of recent events, the two knew exactly who was behind the written curse and decided to pay a little visit to Lucus without informing their parents or Erin.

Brad is going to confront him with one final warning to keep away from Erin. Big John has his own plans involving physical persuasion, something he has wanted to do for a long time.

They get out and make their way past a lot full of cars toward the front entrance. Loud music can be heard, and felt, booming from inside, with sporadic flickering multicolored light beams racing out of a few breaches in the corrugated metal exterior of the large building. There is only one window, up high on the second story. Lucus has decided to throw another one of his famous rave parties, but this time in the middle of the week—unusual timing, even for him. Big John got wind of it earlier in the day at school.

The two approach a rather large older man, more massive than even Big John, barring entrance to the facility. His slightly cocked fedora, salt-and-pepper goatee and gold loop earring, along with the dark pinstripe three-piece business suit, make him look like a mafia hit man. Brad addresses him.

"We need to see Lucus."

"Who are you?"

"Brad Ross."

The well-dressed bouncer slips a cell phone out of his coat

pocket and hits a button. Plugging the opposite ear with a finger, he informs the person on the other end about the uninvited visitors. After nodding a couple of times, accompanied with a few muffled grunts, he hangs up. "You can go in. He's waiting for you upstairs, but your little buddy here is not welcome."

Brad looks up at the window just in time to see a silhouetted figure disappearing from view.

Taking offense to being called "little buddy" and fearing for his best friend's safety, Big John pushes his way past Brad and blows up in front of the man who seems unimpressed at the cocky punk's display. "Look here old man, you may be bigger than me, but I can take you down and snap your brittle bones! I *am* going in there, and you ain't stopping me! Got it?"

The husky door guard slowly peels back his unbuttoned suit jacket to reveal a shoulder holster bearing his rather large silver-plated pistol.

"Whoa, whoa, guys." Brad grabs his friend and pulls him backward. "Let's not get carried away here."

The fact that Brad can pull Big John back shows how his friend is not really resisting and all too happy to have some distance placed between himself and the armed thug.

"Look, John, I'll go in by myself. It's okay, nothing's going to happen, especially since you're here as a witness."

"Don't do it, man. I've got a bad feeling about this."

"I've got to."

Reluctantly, Big John silently nods, avoiding eye contact with the bouncer. Brad pats him on the shoulder and heads for the entrance. The guard turns, retrieves keys from his pocket, and unlocks the heavy metal door. For the first time, Brad notices the black sports car parked next to the bouncer. He recognizes it as the one that tried to run him and Erin off the road. It must belong to Lucus.

Stepping through the doorway, Brad trips on the unusually high threshold and stumbles, as if some unseen force has made a last-ditch effort to keep him from entering. Luckily, Brad catches his balance without falling. The door slams behind him, and the distinctive click of the lock announces there is no turning back.

This is really going on in my town? he thinks.

The narrow black corridor stretches beyond him about thirty feet. A thick fog of swirling dust particles is illuminated by an ambient glow of pulsating light emanating from the end of the hallway. Fast-paced music in sync with the rainbow lightshow grows louder with every cautious step he takes forward.

At the end of his march, Brad finds himself facing a wall of thick hanging strips of translucent plastic, each about twelve inches across. All he can see through them are faint silhouettes of people, some not so human looking, moving about frantically, yet somewhat in unison. There must be hundreds of them. This divided curtain of man-made polymers is all that separates Brad from a whole other world—a world of pure darkness. He looks back but cannot see the door at the other end any longer. There is no illuminated exit sign.

Brad turns back around, takes a deep breath, and slowly pushes his way through one of the slits. Just as he breaks through to the other side, a bright beam from an oscillating spotlight swipes across his eyes, temporarily blinding him. He places his hand over his face and lets out a loud moan, but the music is so deafening he cannot hear even his own voice. A few moments of recovery return part of his vision. He slowly moves his hand away and blinks violently, trying to open his eyes fully again.

Though still squinting, he can now see everything...and everyone. There are people dressed in all manner of costumes, none of which are the least bit conservative. Many are dressed in black, some in all leather. Others are adorned with bright-colored clothes, glow-stick accessories, and fluorescent body paint that comes to life under the many black lights. A few wear grotesque Halloween masks and costumes to appear as creepy as possible, yet some girls are dressed as little school girls with pigtails, holding baby dolls and sucking on pacifiers.

The young man is startled by the fact that there are not as many here as it appeared on the other side of the plastic. A couple of girls dressed as red devils saunter past him holding hands, both looking at the handsome young man and giggling. Their bodies are thinly covered in tight-fitting costumes that accentuate every curve, which is meant to arouse, and he immediately diverts his eyes. In this process Brad discovers the stairs that lead up to the second-story room where Lucus is. He starts making his way toward them.

At the foot of the stairs stands another giant guard. This one, however, is much younger than the one outside. His completely bald head is punctuated with a row of surgically implanted metal Mohawk spikes each about two inches in height. The modern-day sentry, with massive tattoo-covered arms crossed over his chest, stands in front of the stairs, blocking access. Brad just stares up at him, not exactly knowing what to do.

The lights go dark.

A deep synthesized murmur penetrates the room, and the crowd starts cheering fanatically. Brad turns around to see everyone, actually just their glow-stick jewelry and devices of illumination, shifting toward the same direction in the large room.

Spotlights burst forth, revealing an elevated stage about four feet high. A shallow stream of rolling chilled fog radiates across the stage floor and cascades over the front ledge, creeping into the audience.

Standing front and center is Scarlet, Lucus's number-one girlfriend. She is outfitted in what can only be described as a blasphemous mock hybrid mutation of a Victorian-style wedding gown crossed with a Catholic priest's outfit. The leather costume is lavishly adorned with lace and is all black except for the white priest's collar, starkly glowing beneath the black lights, that tops off her plunging V-shaped neckline. Four other band members, all female and dressed similarly, but not as ornately as the lead singer, stand poised in the background ready to start the worship service.

Above them is large hanging banner with the band's name: *Our Lady of Endor.*

Brad's gaze keeps moving upward and he notices above the banner what appears to be a network of metal tree-like branches almost as high as the ceiling, some with pulleys that have cables dangling from them. He does not notice the large pentagram painted on the stage floor, on the end points of which each band member stands. And anchored to the floor in the middle of the pentagram are not one but two lambs. They are young, very young; practically newborn. Their necks encompassed with thick leather collars linked to large, heavy chains that tether them to the floor. Scarlet belts out a verse, a cappella, in her strong, resonant voice:

"Welcome to my lair, won't you come in."

The crowd goes wild and the band kicks in. This music, dark and foreboding, is different than the upbeat, techno party dance music that had been playing. Scarlet stands perfectly still, and Brad realizes she is staring straight at him while she sings with an intense, concentrated passion. He is mesmerized.

The lambs' cries are smothered by all the noise.

"Snuggle up against me, be my boyfriend."

At a few forceful taps on his shoulder, Brad spins. The husky guard, without saying a word, motions up the stairs behind him with his thumb. Brad squeezes himself past and starts the climb. All of the young man's senses are dulled except for his hearing. Scarlet's voice seems much louder now, and her words forcefully enter his mind. It is all he can concentrate on.

"Find comfort in my arms, find pleasure in my bed."

Toward the top, taking up most of the office wall facing the spectacle below, is a large window covered in two-way mirrored film. Deep vibrations from the booming bass distort the mirror reflections of the frenzied crowd. Brad pauses outside the door and looks back down. Scarlet, like a predator, is still fixated on him.

"Now shut your eyes and go to sleep, you'll wake up being dead."

Brad turns away, slowly twists the knob, and cautiously walks in. The room with black-painted walls is dark, except for a few black lights and a red lava lamp. Situated behind a desk is Lucus, with his back to the room. Above him hangs a mounted goat's head with asymmetrical gnarled horns spiraling outward—dark pits where eyes should be. Underneath, violently scratched out so white Sheetrock bleeds through, are the words WAKAN TANKA.

A girl on the floor in the far corner slumps over a small glass-top table. She springs up, wiping under her nose, and notices Brad. As she realizes who he is, her eyes widen. Then she sinks back down, head lowered in shame. He recognizes her from school—and from the church youth group.

The door behind Brad has quietly been shut, and another minion stands in front of it, barring any attempt at an emergency exit. Lucus swivels around, ending his cell phone call. "Brad!" He springs up and makes his way around the desk with arms open wide. Brad instinctively backs up, bumping into the guy behind him. This startles the out-of-place teen, which brings Lucus to raucous laughter. "Why so jumpy, Brad? All of this is for you."

"Excuse me?"

"This is your birthday bash. Since I wasn't invited to the one out in Potter's field the other night, I decided to throw you a bigger, badder one. Of course, there are no screaming pigs coming back to life over roasting flames to startle anyone, mind you, but it looks quite interesting out there nonetheless. Don't ya think?"

"There's no way all this is for me."

"Well, you are a sharp one, aren't ya? Okay, you got me. It's actually *my* birthday bash. But since we were born on the same day in the same hospital, I'm willing to share it with you."

Brad's expression changes to that of astonishment.

"Oh, you didn't know we shared the same birthday? We're practically brothers."

Brad does not respond.

"Wow, wouldn't that make my old man's day?" The semihumorous thought of the two being switched at birth races through his mind. "To find out *you* were his son instead of *me!*"

Lucus gets caught up in the moment thinking through that scenario. Looking through the office window vibrating with the deep, pulsating bass that distorts his view of the small sea of humanity below writhing in sync with the music, he becomes angered deep within. The only response he knows to such feelings is to attack.

"You know, Brad, before this building was a manufacturing plant it was a slaughterhouse. Mostly hogs, really. But I'm sure the occasional lamb or two found themselves here, oblivious to their doomed fate." Lucus makes this last statement while caressing the head of the young girl kneeling on the floor, who looks up smiling with eyes closed. He can scarcely hide his disdain for her ignorance and weakness.

"It's dark in here," Brad finally says.

"What's that?" asks Lucus.

"It's too dark in here. Turn on the lights."

"These are the only lights we have, that are on. Besides, I love the darkness. I find comfort in it. I feel…at home in it."

"I came here for a reason, Lucus."

"I suppose it wasn't to party." He responds with an overly-exaggerated sad face then makes his way back behind the desk.

"It's about Erin." Brad's tone turns more forceful.

Lucus stands with his back to Brad, looking out the other office window, which faces the parking lot outside. He notices Brad's Corvette. "I see you have an affinity for my…trash."

Brad instantly realizes the statement is a passive-aggressive stab at Erin.

Lucus continues. "My dad got your Vette on one of his used car lots, and yours truly took it for a test spin. I found it didn't respond the way I wanted, so I opted for a newer, faster, more responsive model. Isn't that right, Elizabeth?" He turns to the girl still hunched on the floor in the corner. She lifts her head and grins from ear to ear with heavy eyes, more relaxed now.

Brad sequesters his anger at the insults to Erin. "Lucus, I was hoping we could talk in private."

"We are alone. Chuck over there can't hear a word we're saying, can you Chuck?"

Chuck shakes his head.

"And Elizabeth, well, she's not quite here, if you know what I mean."

"What's the matter, Lucus, are you afraid?"

Lucus's grin dissolves into a bitter scowl. He looks over at Chuck and nods, indicating they can leave. The bodyguard crosses the room and yanks on Elizabeth's arm. She springs to her feet and dances out the door, shouting, "Let's go parrr-tayyyyy!"

While Brad watches the two leave and the door shut, Lucus stealthily grabs his umbrella, right hand firmly clutching the handle and left hand wrapped around the collapsed canopy.

Brad spins and walks up to the desk, leaning forward. "Look here." His expression is deadly serious. "Do what you want with your voodoo mumbo jumbo, but any more threats against Erin, veiled or otherwise, will be dealt with harshly."

"Oh, my dear child, it's a bit more complicated than voodoo. Besides, I haven't the foggiest idea of what you're trying to dig up here."

Lucus's play on words goes past Brad.

"Emily's grave, you had it dug into and a curse placed inside the coffin."

"Enough already, Mr. Ross, with the baseless accusations. Now I know why you wanted to talk to me alone."

"Who else could it be? I'm warning you. Any more hints at harm coming to Erin, and I will go to the police."

"With what?"

"For starters, the debauchery going on in this place. And the drugs, the drugs you gave Elizabeth here."

"As for the 'debauchery' going on here, as you put it, as far as I know is not against the law, except for maybe your God's law. You might be able to get me on some building code violations, but my lawyer's connections with the mayor, thanks to my so-called dad who is at least good for something in my life, would make it all just go away. And as for these alleged drugs, did you see any? Did you see me give her anything, for that matter?"

Brad can only stare without responding.

"Look here, frat boy." Lucus leans in toward Brad. "You're way out of your element here. I can understand that. But I will meet you on your own battleground and you still won't have a chance."

"What do you mean? A spiritual battleground?"

"That…and otherwise."

"Look, Lucus, I have no idea what you're talking about. Just know this, if any harm comes to Erin whatsoever, you will pay and pay dearly."

"We'll see about that." He presses a button underneath his desk, and the bodyguard immediately walks in. "Escort Mr. Ross outside. He needs to go home and get plenty of rest. He has a busy couple of days ahead of him."

"Just exactly what do you mean by that?" Brad snaps.

"All in due time, my friend. All in due time."

The goon places his hand on Brad's shoulder. He immediately shrugs it off. "You've been warned." Brad jabs his finger at Lucus.

"Go home and say your prayers, Brad. You're going to need them."

The guard places his hand on Brad's shoulder a second time, and he responds as before, shrugging it off forcefully. "All right.

I'm leaving."

He makes his way out the door and down the stairs with Chuck shadowing him all the way out of the building.

NOT LONG AFTER THE WITCHING HOUR later that same night, Erin lies in bed, having just finally fallen asleep. But the girl's rest is interrupted by a hand that slowly reaches out and squeezes her ankle. Erin subconsciously kicks and rolls over on her side with a slight moan of disapproval. The hand again violates her peaceful slumber but this time with an accompanying beckon in a soft, sweet voice, "Erin."

The unconscious girl begins waking up and directs her squinting eyes toward the vicinity of the somewhat familiar sound. There, the ghostly image of a young female stands. Her eyes blurry from having just been opened from a deep slumber, Erin rubs them and mumbles, "Queenie?"

"No Erin, it's me."

This time she focuses more clearly on the face. Upon realization of who it appears to be, Erin loses her breath and scampers back up against the headboard with knees tucked into her chest.

"It's me, Emily."

Very awake now, Erin's eyes dart back and forth across the room, returning to the vision of her deceased sister looking just as she remembered before the accident.

"Please don't be afraid, Rin."

Rin was Emily's nickname for her twin.

The apparition makes its way around the bed and sits next to Erin, who squeezes in tighter. "I've come to tell you something very important, and to ask you something. About that night, when you left me stranded and I was killed on the side of the road—I want you to know that I forgive you. The guilt and shame you've been carrying ever since is not warranted. I now know that everything happens for a reason. Truly, I have forgiven you, found peace, and want you to have peace too. You have to believe me."

Erin cannot believe it, what is actually happening right now. Her eyes begin to well up. "You forgive me? *You* forgive *me*, even though it was *my* fault you were killed?"

"That's right," Emily replies with a warm smile, gently rubbing Erin's cheek.

Erin buries her face in her hands and begins sobbing.

Emily pauses a few moments to let it sink in then speaks again. "I need you to do something for me, though."

Erin looks up with glassy eyes. "What is it?"

"Mother is going to host another meeting Friday night. I need you to be there."

Erin's countenance changes. "Will mother ever forgive me?"

"That's why I need you there; the both of you together."

"I…don't know…"

"Rin, listen to me. If you want all this cleared up, and if you truly cherish my forgiveness, then you must be there. You must."

"Well I—"

"Doppelganger! Doppelganger!"

The words shriek in a high-pitched voice from the doorway. Emily turns immediately and Erin looks as well to see Queenie, with eyes tightly shut, standing and pointing at the vision sitting on the bed. She yells again even louder, "DOPPELGANGER! DOP-PELGANGER!"

Erin glances back only to see that Emily has vanished.

"YOU'RE GOING TO DIE! DIE, ERIN, DIE!"

It is apparent that Queenie is pointing at Erin, who springs out of bed and rushes to her little sister. She places her hand over Queenie's mouth and gently begins to shush her, at which point the girl's body becomes completely limp. Erin latches on, preventing her from falling onto the floor. She swoops Queenie up and confirms the unconscious girl is still breathing. In fact, Queenie is in a very deep sleep.

Erin carries her little sister out and heads into the other bedroom, looking up at the moth still pinned above the doorframe. She places the girl back in her bed and covers her with a sheet and blanket before heading back out into the hallway. At her own bedroom doorway she hears a voice.

"Erin?" It is her dad. "Erin, what's all the commotion out there?"

She tiptoes to his door. "It's nothing, Daddy. Go back to sleep."

THURSDAY EVENING FINDS BRAD at the desk in his room trying to study for the following day's tests, but all he can focus on is Erin. Sure, nothing happened today to warrant such reflection, but last night's meeting with Lucus sticks with him and ominously warns that something bad is going to happen at some point in the near future.

His cell phone buzzes with a call. It is from Erin.

Brad answers immediately. "I was just thinking about you."

"Oh, isn't that sweet. It just warms the cockles of my heart, it does."

The voice on the other end is not Erin's.

"Lucus?"

"Meet me at the football field in ten minutes. It concerns what's-her-face."

"Where is Erin?" Brad demands.

"I don't know."

"What do you mean, you don't know? You're calling on her phone."

"I haven't seen her. Really. Ten minutes. Oh, make that nine, now."

Brad jumps from his chair. "I swear I will kill you!"

"I don't know what you're talking about. I haven't touched her. Oh, did I fail to mention that this call may be monitored for training and quality purposes?"

"Where is she?"

"You will find out in nine—eight minutes, if you get here in time."

Click.

"Hello? Hello!"

There is no response.

Panicked, Brad grabs his jacket on his way out the door and bolts out of the house and into his car. As his Corvette screams down the highway, Brad prays. "Dear God, please don't let anything happen to Erin. Please place a hedge of protection around her. Send your angels. Anything. Please!"

He reaches for his phone to call Big John for backup, but pauses. Brad can feel his panic turning to anger, a seething rage and contempt for this evil that has invaded his and Erin's lives. No, he will not call John. He is going to take care of Lucus once and for all, no holds barred, and does not want John to try and talk him out of decimating this soulless freak of an animal. It would probably be better not to have any witnesses.

As Brad approaches the stadium he notices something unusual: the field lights are all on. There is nothing happening there tonight that he is aware of. The JV team is playing away, so it can't be them.

His Corvette rumbles to a stop in the parking lot, kicking up dust that floats in the headlights' beams. Brad jumps out and runs through an unlocked gate to the brightly lit field, where he pulls up short. Placed right in the center of the field on the fifty-yard line are two facing chairs with a football resting on a small wooden table between them. Planted on one of those chairs is Lucus, sitting erect with his gaze focused forward. His hands rest on the handle of his umbrella, which is wedged between his two thin legs. He just sits motionless, like a statue, patiently waiting. The sight of him turns Brad's stomach. Anger overtakes and he explodes toward Lucus.

"I'm going to kill you!" he yells, sprinting at full speed. "Where is she?"

Lucus calmly looks at the approaching danger without flinching. As Brad gets closer, he leisurely stands up, then dislodges the umbrella handle, exposing a narrow, two-foot-long, razor-sharp dagger pointing directly at his foe. Attempting an abrupt halt to avoid impaling himself, Brad slips on the grass, slick from watering, and lands flat on his back. He finds himself looking up at the dagger hovering just above his heart. The knife appears old, having a rusty blade speckled with what appears to be dried blood.

"Well," Lucus says, "that was too easy. I expected much more from you, Bradley."

Brad remains focused on the pointed blade mere inches from his chest.

"Oh, like my dagger? I obtained it from a Haitian voodoo priest who used it for sacrifices—some human, I'm told. I've also been warned not to touch the blade, as it harbors bacteria collected from its many victims. So I wouldn't think about grabbing it if I were you."

"You know I'll tell the authorities about it. You're not worried about that?"

Lucus bursts out laughing. "Oh Bradford, you are forever the consummate good guy, aren't you?" He gazes down to see Brad looking up in all seriousness. "Okay, fine. Go ahead and tell. But it won't do any good. Only I know how to draw the dagger. You can have whoever you want examine it, but that won't do any good. And if you're thinking it could be x-rayed, think again. If this can make it through airport security, it can fool any other scanner, too."

Brad remains speechless.

"So, Mr. Goody Two-Shoes, what shall I do with you?" Lucus lowers the dagger's tip, almost touching Brad's expanding chest at each deep inhale. "I know. I shall let you go—an extension of grace. But…only if you promise to be good." Lucus calmly turns his back to Brad. "If you'll look up in the bleachers—visitors' side, of course—you'll see two of my protégés up at the top recording everything that happens down here."

Brad looks up and sees two guys standing behind a video camera on a tripod. One raises his hand to wave and the other immediately pulls it back down.

This does not go unnoticed by Lucus, who sighs at the stupidity of the two nimrods. "So I wouldn't try anything foolish. And besides, if you want to see Erin again, you had better do exactly as I say. Why don't you have a seat?"

Brad slowly gets up and sits in the other chair, eyes fixed on Lucus, who continues to ramble.

"You know, Bradbury, I was impressed with your willingness to confront me on my turf. So I thought it fitting to meet you on yours. You know…under the *big lights!*" He holds up his hands and slowly turns, looking at imaginary cheering fans in the stands. Lucus continues. "I thought it important to show you that I'm not afraid of you anytime, anywhere. You and I, we're not so different, really."

"Oh yeah." Brad can't keep silent any longer. "Put on some pads and we'll see who can last on this field. Don't you dare try to compare us. We are nothing alike."

Lucus, with his back still to Brad, pauses a moment then gives a faint chuckle. "Worship."

"Excuse me?" Brad is not sure he heard Lucus's mumble correctly.

"Worship, I said. We both just want to be worshipped."

"You know nothing about me."

"Oh, don't I? Dreams of earning a football scholarship where you can be the big man on campus, win the Heisman, play in the NFL, be interviewed by *Sports Illustrated*, and maybe win the most coveted prize in all of sports…your picture on the Wheaties box."

Lucus spins, smiling widely and points at Brad. "You thought I was going to say Super Bowl, didn't you?"

Brad sits stone-faced.

"Oh come on, Bradster. You know that was funny."

"Why are you doing all this, Lucus? Why?"

"You want to know why?"

"Yes. Seriously, what do you get out of it?"

"Oh, it's not so much pragmatism, really. It's a reaction, I suppose."

"Reaction?" asks Brad. "Reaction to what? Me and Erin?"

"No. It's not that."

"Then, what?"

The question triggers a memory for Lucus, a memory that is as fresh and vivid as the day it happened. In fact, it is a memory that hauntingly repeats itself every day in Lucus's troubled mind.

A BRIGHT WEEKDAY AFTERNOON SUN lit the first day of a pee-wee league football practice taking place on a nondescript field at the city park. Youngsters went through the paces of learning the game while parents watched from the sidelines, some with high hopes of their sons making it big someday. But none more so than the head coach, who had been evaluating each kid for his ability, especially focusing on one, his own son, who missed yet another tackle and fell down again.

The coach blew his whistle and stormed over to the scrawny boy lying on his back, reached down, pulled the lad up vertically by his facemask, which had a chunk of sod stuck to it, and dragged him off a short distance for semiprivacy. "You are embarrassing the living daylights out of me, boy! Why are you not trying?"

"I…I am trying."

"No, you're not! If you were trying you wouldn't be making a fool out of yourself—and out of me for that matter!"

"But Daddy, I—"

Furious, Earl grabbed the boy's facemask, shook it, and forcefully pulled it forward. "Listen here, Leslie," he barked right in his face, "do NOT call me Daddy. Out here on the football field you call me Coach, *not* Daddy! Out here, I am the law! Out here, I AM GOD! You got it?"

The boy's eyes started to well up.

"Oh, for heaven's sake! Why are you crying?" The man had convinced himself that he was just administering "tough love," but what he was doing was far beyond tough and nowhere near love. In actuality, he was just getting more irate out of embarrassment because he had produced a no-good, untalented son.

"I AM trying! Honest!"

"Well then, I guess you're just weak. A weak little boy with a weak girly name."

The boy's mom had named him at the hospital, after her grandmother, while the father was out of town on one of his many business trips, something he never forgave his wife for. The coach looked up to see the players and assistant coach watching.

"What are you all doing? Keep going with the drills!"

The boys lined up across from each other and practiced tackling two at a time.

"Now watch this, boy, and see how it's done."

The other coach yelled, "go!" and one boy tried to run past the other, who tackled him to the ground perfectly.

"Now that's how you do it!" the coach yelled. "What's your

name, son?" he asked the one who made the tackle.

"Brad, sir. Brad Ross."

"Very good, Brad! Excellent! People are going to remember your name."

"Thank you, sir."

Then Earl shifted his fiery gaze down and said, "Now why can't you be like him? Like Brad Ross? He's trying."

Unable to hold it in any longer, the boy burst out crying, bawling his eyes out.

Coach rolled his eyes and sighed. "Oh, good grief. That's it. I have had it with your frail personality. You think you're going to get anywhere in this world being weak and crying all the time? Huh? The world is going to chew you up and spit you out, boy. I didn't become an all-American at the university and build up three successful car dealerships by being a quitter like you. I had to fight and scratch for everything I've achieved—an attitude you obviously don't have. I swear sometimes I think your mother cheated on me. There's no way you and I share the same DNA. No way. That's it. You have disappointed me and embarrassed my name for the last time. Go to the car. Go right now. We can't have crybabies out here."

The boy looked up and raised his hands, "But Daddy—"

"Go!" The man swiftly turned the boy in the direction of the car and gave him a push.

As Leslie walked away, barely able to see through his water-filled eyes, he heard the coach yell, "And take your pads and cleats off before you get in the car. It's a loaner from the dealership and very valuable—worth more than you'll ever be!"

As the young Lucus made his way off the field he mumbled to himself, "Hate you."

BRAD, WAITING FOR AN ANSWER as to why all of this is happening, watches Lucus stand silently stiff, fists clenched as the memory replays itself from the beginning. It is an incident that Brad certainly does not recall. Lucus turns toward the star quarterback with glassy, bloodshot eyes. The look of pain and rage etched onto Lucus's transformed face catches Brad off guard. Lucus stands on the other chair, elevating himself. He raises his umbrella toward the heavens with a tight fist and screams at the top of his lungs, "*I will ascend into heaven! I will exalt my throne above the stars of God! I will become the most powerful being! I will ascend above the heights of the clouds! I will be the Most High God! I will be the Most High God! I will be the Most High God!*"

"Oh dear Lord, Lucus. You need help. Serious professional help."

"No." He steps down. "You're the one who's going to need help."

"We have counseling at the church. I will help you—get the help you need."

"What I'll be getting is Erin back, you can be sure of that."

"I will never give her up."

"You won't be able to keep her if you're not around anymore."

"Is that a threat?"

"It is."

"That's it." Brad stands up. "I'm going to the cops."

As he walks away, Lucus calls out, "Hey, Brat!"

Brad turns to find an object flying at him. He catches it before it strikes his chest.

"It's Erin's cell phone," Lucus announces. "I had it swiped from her…I mean, I found it on the sidewalk. She probably doesn't even know it's missing."

"She had better be at her house unharmed, or you *will* be sorry!"

"What I am sorry about is that I had to spend this much time with you, but I accomplished everything I needed to. You are free to go now. Goodbye, Brad Ross."

Brad spins and runs off the field. As he approaches the sideline, a loud pop resembling a gunshot echoes in the stadium. He spins to see, in a small, faint cloud of powder, Lucus's hand gripping the handle of the dagger, which has just punctured the pigskin and become lodged in the table.

ERIN LIES CURLED UP ON TOP OF HER BED in a fetal position, lost deep in thought, obsessed with retracing every place she went during the day. There is no music playing, no background noise whatsoever, just a thick heavy silence that fills the room. Curtains are drawn together to—maybe subconsciously—offer a buffer of protection from outside forces intending to enter and do harm.

The girl's eyelids are closed as well, but her eyes, in concert with her mind's eye, frantically scan back and forth through time and space within the past twelve hours or so. An empty purse and its regurgitated contents lay sprawled at the foot of her bed, randomly organized so no one item touches another. Outside, Shep peers from the shadows as someone, or some thing, stealthily but quickly invades the premises.

Tap.

An unexpected sharp noise from the window violently yanks Erin out of the school hallway that is buried deep within the recesses of her mind and forcefully slams the girl down onto her bed in this present reality. With eyes now open but not turning her head, she peeks toward the window, unable to see it.

TAP!

Another louder noise forces Erin to quickly sit up and face possible danger. The closed curtains now serve as a disadvantage, concealing what is on the other side. Slipping off the bed and tip-toeing over to the window, she slowly reaches up and takes hold of each curtain. Intending to pull them apart slightly and peek through a small sliver, she involuntarily opens them up in a quick burst. "You?"

Below is Brad, cocked back ready to hurl one last stone at her window. Erin raises the sash.

"You're home." He drops the rock.

"Yes," Erin replies, puzzled. "I'm home."

"Are you all right?"

"Sure. Are you?"

"Are you sure you're all right?" Brad asks again.

"Yes, I'm fine. What are you doing here?"

"You don't want me here?"

"Well, of course I do. But it's Thursday night. You're usually hunkered down in your man cave studying for tests and mentally prepping for your Neanderthal game of real estate."

"Oh…well…I was just thinking of you and wanted to come by."

"Okaayy," she responds, still puzzled. "Why didn't you just come to the front door?"

"I didn't want to alarm anyone."

"Alarm?"

"I mean, disturb. I didn't want to disturb anyone."

"Hmmm," she ponders. "I get the sense you're keeping something from me."

Brad's body flashes a jolt of adrenaline out to every nerve. How can she tell? He does not want to mention anything about what happened earlier with Lucus, especially now that he knows she is okay and unaware of the altercation. "I've got something for you." He reaches into his coat pocket and pulls out the object.

"My cell phone!" she blurts joyously. "I was just racking my brain trying to figure out where I left it. How did you get it?"

Not wanting to lie, but not wanting to tell her exactly how it came into his possession, he offers a vague answer. "Someone handed it to me to give to you."

"I must have dropped it somewhere. It was awful nice of them to give it to you for me."

Brad does not respond. Then Erin holds out her hands. "Toss it up."

"Are you crazy? It might break."

"Oh come on, a stud quarterback like you can't get it up this high?"

"It's not *my* ability I'm worried about."

"Are you saying I can't catch?"

Brad gives a smirk.

"Oh, now it's on," she replies to his unmistakable expression. "Let's make a bet."

"A bet? That you catch it?"

"Yes."

"Whoever wins, what do they get?" he asks.

"Let's just say she can call in a favor when she needs it."

"Or *he* can call in the favor," Brad retorts.

"Whatever. Toss it up. Come on."

"Okay, are you ready?"

"Yes."

Brad slowly bends at the knees and gently tosses it up underhand, but way out beyond her reach.

"I win!" a declaration comes below as he catches it.

"Brad Ross! You cheater! You know there's no way I could catch that!"

He laughs. "I know, I know. I was just messing with you."

In fun, she decides to mess with him back in a stern tone.

"I could have fallen out this window!"

"I would have caught you."

Erin was hoping he would say that. She smiles. "Okay, toss it up again."

Brad again lobs it up, but much closer, so it stops right at her hands. She grasps it almost effortlessly. "I did it!" Pointing down to him she adds, "In your face!"

"All right, all right." He raises his hands, chuckling. "You proved me wrong."

"Now I have something for you." With a smile and twirl of her body followed by a swoosh of her hair, she disappears from view.

Erin grabs something from the top of her dresser and bolts downstairs, out the door, and around the corner. Brad is down on one knee, rubbing behind the ears of Shep, who wandered up after determining the boy was not a threat.

"So I see you've met Shep."

"I love this dog," Brad looks up, still petting him. "And he's so soft."

"Yeah, he hates the water but I bathe him regularly anyway, since about the only thing he's good for is petting. But that's good enough for me."

It's not that Shep hates the water—he is deathly afraid of it as he nearly drowned in a pond as a puppy, an incident of which Erin is unaware. Fortunately, at the last second a ranch hand passing by pulled him out of the watery grave. The hands of the man who rescued and revived him were wearing a pair of leather work gloves.

"Well, if you ever want to get rid of him, I'll take him off your hands."

"Oh no, Shep and I are going to grow old together. Even though he's along in years, I've determined he's going to live as long as I do."

Brad is only half listening, as his attention has turned back to tail-wagging Shep, who is still the happy recipient of a comforting head massage. Erin watches them for a moment with a warm feeling of joy deep down inside, a rare emotion for that tormented girl.

"Well boy," Brad says to the dog, "I've got to get going. Got a big day tomorrow." He gives the dog one last rub on the head then stands up to face Erin. "You said you got something for me?"

She pulls the object from behind her back.

"Is this the antenna off my car?" He examines it closely.

"Yes it is."

"How did you get it?"

"Someone handed it to me to give to you."

"Oh, um. Okay."

"I don't know if it can be fixed, but maybe you can try."

Brad knows it cannot be fixed. "Well, thank you very much." He holds it up with a nod of gratitude.

For some unexplainable reason, Erin does something totally spontaneous. "I want to play the game."

"What, you mean the game where you tell me something about you that I don't know?"

"Uh-huh," she answers with a wide smile.

"Okay, I'm all ears."

"Well, I don't know how you feel about ghosts, but I've seen one."

"Really?"

"And not just any ghost. It's Emily!"

"Emily? Your sister Emily?"

"Yep, and not just one. I've seen her at different ages at the same time."

"Wait…different ages…same time…"

"Yes. There must be multiple dimensions on the other side or time is different there or whatever. There are multiple spirits of Emily.

"Really?" Brad is totally floored.

"Anyway, that's not the big news!"

"It's not?"

"No. Emily visited with me the other night in my bedroom."

"Um, which…Emily?"

"The current one. I mean, the one our age. Anyway, she looked just as she did before the accident—beautiful. She said she forgives me, Brad. Can you believe it? She said she forgives me!"

No, he can't believe it. This is way too much info too fast to take in. Brad has trouble collecting his thoughts. Erin leaps forward and hugs him.

"It has to be of God. He's all about forgiveness, right? God sent her to me, I just know it. This *must* be a sign. Oh Brad, I'm so happy!"

"I'm…I'm happy for you, too."

Erin squeezes tighter.

"Well…I have to get back home. Studying to do, and all."

"Sure, I understand. There's more I can tell you, but it can wait. We can talk some more this weekend, after your game. I know you need to focus on that now. I just wanted you to know how happy I am. Tomorrow's going to be a great day—for both of us!"

"Sure it will, Erin. Sure it will."

The two exchange a few more words of departure, and then Brad heads off, escorted by Erin and his new best friend. When they reach the front of the house, Shep meanders up the steps onto the porch and Erin goes inside while Brad walks to his car and gets in. A turn of the key awakens the sleeping giant of an engine. While his Vette purrs, the exhausted boy leans his head back, eyes closed, and exhales a big sigh. His mind is spinning.

After a minute or so he sits forward and turns on the headlights. At that moment, an enormous hog rustles across in front of the car from right to left, squealing intensely. As Brad tracks it to the far left, he is startled by the sight of Queenie standing by his door. She is draped in a long nightgown, hands hanging straight down. She faces him with eyes closed. Brad rolls down his window to see what she wants. The girl slowly opens her mouth.

"Do not ever come back here again or you will die."

Stunned, Brad does not know how to respond.

Queenie turns and dashes off into the shadows toward where the pig went. Her dissipating voice can be heard beckoning, "Sissie! Wait up! I'm coming!"

Twenty-Four

ON FRIDAY AT NOON ROSE IS SPIED UPON as she nibbles on lunch at the unpainted wooden table in their tiny kitchen. Queenie stayed home today, claiming to be sick, but her absence from school is due to something much worse than a physical ailment. She stands in the doorway of their kitchen clutching a piece of paper down by her side, staring intently at the woman who birthed her. She coughs.

Rose looks up. "What's wrong with you?" She notices Queenie's intense scowl.

Without saying a word the girl walks over and plops the paper on the table, then backs up, arms folded. It only takes a quick scan for Rose to realize what it is. Expressionless, she places her hand on her chest where a scar hides underneath the loose-fitting night-gown. A few years back she needed surgery to repair a defect. The solution—a transplanted heart valve. "Where did you get this?"

"Does it matter?" answers Queenie in a short tone.

"Yes! Tell me, girl! Where did you get it?"

"It crawled out of the grave, Mommy dearest," the bitter girl retorts sarcastically. "Or should I say…out of a trash can?"

The paper is a printout of an old article from the local newspaper of a nearby town. It is about Queenie's birth…and her twin sister.

The girl coughs again, this one rougher than the last. "So, I'm the survivor of an attempted abortion?"

Rose releases the paper, then looks down at her food and starts picking at it without answering. She is not sure how much should be divulged.

Before the birth of Emily and Erin, Rose lived a somewhat se-cluded life, somewhat self-imposed, somewhat just the way life turned out. She had always desired to not only fit in with the right people, but to be special in some way. Then one day God finally blessed her.

The birth of twins in these parts is almost nonexistent, and with the delivery of her first two girls came immediate notoriety. And those eyes, those green eyes. For the first time in her life, she felt like she was somebody. The local news coverage during those initial weeks was almost suffocating, but Rose breathed it in ever so deeply. After their arrival into this world she was noticed in town, especially when parading the large, brightly colored double stroller. People knew her name and smiled warmly while they initiated friendly conversation regarding her little miracles.

But as with all hot news stories, this one cooled—as did the attention. There was an article in the paper when the girls turned one and another when they entered first grade, but that was it. Rose longed desperately for the attention again, so eventually she took herself off of birth control without telling her husband, who insisted they could not afford any more mouths to feed. Years went by and she did not conceive again—until Queenie surprised them.

When Rose became pregnant, she kept it secret from everyone until she could confirm what she was hoping and praying for. With her first two she carried them well and didn't start really showing until further along than usual for a woman her small size. When she finally felt she couldn't hide it any longer with lame excuses, the hopeful mother snuck off to another town for an ultrasound.

The result was not good—here was only one fetus. Healthy, but alone.

Rose was severely disappointed, and that disappointment quickly exploded into bitterness and anger. How cruel it was of God to give her the false hope of having twins again and the adoration that would come of it. Yes, it was God's fault. He is the one who prevented the second child in a cruel, sick joke. Well if the Almighty would prevent one from coming into this world, Rose had determined she would likewise prevent the other as a returning blow in this war of the wills.

And she was not interested at all in giving birth to only one kid and then having the responsibility and burden of rearing it, especially with an angry husband. So she left the doctor's office and immediately made her way to the nearby clinic. It was the middle of the day, and Rose was the only patient at the time. There, she was whisked though the obligatory paperwork and in no time lay on a metal table they called a "bed" in a secluded room down the hallway.

"HELLO, MRS. GARY," the fifty-something physician said, briskly entering the room, looking down at the paperwork in his hands.

"That's Gray," Rose responded.

"What's that?" He looked up at her.

"My name is Gray, not Gary."

"Oh, yeah. Sure, sure." He gave a few nods of his head. "My name's Dr. Guylord and I'll be performing the procedure this afternoon. And this is my nurse, Joan."

Rose wasted no time with salutations and just murmured a low grunt of acknowledgement. The doctor continued.

"I want to tell you, Mrs. Gray, that—"

"Get it out," Rose interrupted.

"Yes, we're going to take care of you. But I just want to assure you that—"

"Get. It. Out. Of. Me. Now."

Guylord and Joan made eye contact. He shrugged. "All right, let's get it over with."

The abortion went as planned. With the fetus discarded, Joan wrapped things up with Rose while Guylord was down the hall at the front desk taking a smoke break and filling out paperwork.

"Adam!"

He cut his eyes toward the room where the scream came from. It was Joan.

"Something's wrong! Get in here now!"

He raced down the corridor and burst into the room to find Joan in position.

"There's another one!" she yelled. "It's crowning!"

It took a moment for the good doctor to collect his thoughts. "Don't let it out, you hear me?" he commanded. "Don't let it out!" The physician made a dash for his instruments. With his back to the commotion, he suddenly heard the unmistakable cry of a new-born baby. He stopped scrambling, then slowly pivoted to find Joan holding the bloody infant in her cupped hands.

"I...I couldn't stop it," Joan said.

All was deathly quiet except the weak, high-pitched wailing of a preemie. No one moved a muscle. Joan looked at the deflated doctor, wanting to know what to do next, while he stared at the floor. After a moment, Rose spoke up, breaking the awkward silence. "There's just us. I won't tell no one."

Guylord looked deeply into Joan's eyes, searching for her opinion. They both knew exactly what Rose meant.

Either because he had some shred of conscience left, or he was too afraid of losing his license and business should the deed ever become public knowledge, Guylord decided to not do it. "You take care of the baby," he instructed the nurse in a defeated tone. "I'll call an ambulance. We need to get these two to the hospital."

ROSE WAS TOLD that due to complications she would never be able to have children again. Through secret negotiations via the clinic's lawyer, Rose agreed on a modest settlement with both the doctor and the clinic, and all agreed that nobody would ever mention any details of the incident. A local reporter heard rumors about the miracle baby who survived an abortion, and did indeed confirm it with his hospital contacts, but couldn't pry any details out of them, so he wrote the best article he could on the matter devoid of specifics.

Thinking of how close she was to having another set of twins churned Rose's stomach, but she didn't blame herself. God either hid Queenie during the ultrasound, or supernaturally created her during the abortion just for the sake of pure spite against the woman. Instead of the incident humbling her and encouraging self-reflection, it strengthened her resolve against the deity that rained down so much pain and misery upon her. She was prepared to battle to the end.

Rose looks down at the article which has no names in it, but has the word *woman* circled in red with a line drawn out to the margin, where is written *your mother*. In the same sentence, the word *baby* is circled and its line points to *you*. Further down the article is circled *fetus* which is labeled as *your murdered twin*.

"I'm waiting," Queenie says.

"How do you know you can trust the person who scribbled this nonsense?" asks Rose.

"So you're denying it."

"I am," answers the stone-faced woman who has still not looked up at her daughter.

Queenie pauses, studying her mother's body language. "I can tell you're lying. I know this article is about us. What is my sister's name? Is she even buried somewhere?"

Rose does not answer. Queenie waits a few moments then continues as if she did.

"And I guess this is why I'm sick and feel horrible all the time."

Again, no response.

The incident ends with Rose alone once more in the kitchen rearranging the peas on her plate with a bent-pronged fork while the loud ticking of a wall clock marks time slowly drifting off into oblivion.

A HUGE BATTLE WILL BE FOUGHT TONIGHT, as today is game day. Like everyone else, Erin knows Brad's Friday routine. He is basically a zombie either preoccupied in his mind with tests for the day, or running football scenarios in preparation for tonight. She knows that it is all but impossible to carry on any meaningful dialogue at length, so earlier at school she just gave him his space, and they only made small talk during lunch.

But today was different in that he was not absorbed with academics or sports, but rather recounting last night's altercation with Lucus as well as his conversation with Erin. He is thinking about the girl's belief that she is being visited by her dead sister. For the first time since they became a couple, doubts are creeping into his mind as to whether or not it is possible to ever have a normal relationship with her—and it scares him.

Throughout the day, Erin had no clue as to what Brad was really struggling with internally. To her all was normal at school, except for assuring him that she would definitely be at tonight's game— that was a first. So while he is home killing time before heading up to the field house pre-game, Erin paces around in her room either trying on clothes to determine what she will wear or thinking about where to sit—certainly not the student section. Rose has driven into town to acquire more occult supplies, and Queenie has sequestered herself in the barn yet again.

The front door creaks open. Footsteps ascend the stairs, becoming more prominent until they abruptly halt.

"Mom? Queenie? Is that you?"

No response.

"Hello?"

Still nothing.

"Brad?" She steps into the hall to investigate. "is this another one of your impromptu visits?"

Lucus is standing at the top of the stairs, umbrella in hand, to greet her. "Hello, my sweet."

"What are you doing here?" She gazes at the umbrella, knowing its deadly secret.

"I came to pay you a visit."

She glares resolutely at him and points. "Get out. Get out of my house now!"

"I'm afraid I can't do that," he responds in a soft tone. "Besides, I'm here on a mission."

Her eyes dart once again to the umbrella and she takes a step back. "A mission?"

"I'm here to give you something."

Erin reaches up and grasps the cross dangling from her neck. "I neither need nor want anything you have to offer. Now leave."

"I'm here to give you a message. Two, actually."

"Nothing you have to say will carry any weight with me, because I've finally come to the realization that you are pregnant with deceit and give birth only to lies."

"Ooh, spoken like a true poet...and a plagiarist. You stole that 'pregnant' line from me."

"If you recall, I first used the expression on that game warden who surprised us in Miller's Landing that night. So you are the word thief."

Lucus pauses a moment, then remembers the incident. He chooses to move on. "Your words may be elegant, but mine are laced with the sweet fragrance of reality."

"Your words are foul, like the stench from an open grave."

"Funny you should mention grave."

"What do you mean?"

"It's about your father."

"What about him?"

"Come on Erin, you know. Deep down, you know."

"I have no idea what you're talking about."

"Really? When was the last time you saw him?"

"I saw him just the other day, as a matter of fact."

"No you didn't. Maybe you talked to him, but you didn't see him now, did you?"

"Well, I…um…"

"Dig deep, Erin. I know you can do it," he urges in a sarcastic fashion.

"Just tell me. What are you trying to get at?"

"Your father…he's dead, Erin."

"What?"

Lucus looks up while raising his hands heavenward. "That's right, he's departed this plane and gone on to the next. Been gone for a year now."

"No…no, that's not true. You're lying."

"Oh, am I?"

"Yes." Her voice rises, and she points down the hallway. "He's in *that* room, *right* there, *right* now."

"No, he's not. He hasn't been in this house since he was buried a week after Em was."

"Listen, my daddy's been in that room ever since he got sick, but he's getting better."

"Oh yeah, then tell me, what's his illness?"

She contemplates for a moment but cannot remember. "I…I don't know. I seem to have forgotten at the moment. It's you. You've wormed your way into my head again and I can't think straight. But that doesn't matter. I know he's alive because we converse often."

"No, Erin, all of that is happening in that pretty little wacked-out head of yours, and, oddly enough, this time it has nothing to do with me."

"You're lying. You're lying like you always do."

"My sweet little naïve Erin, what is this obsession you have with lies? Don't you know by now that lies, truths, and half-truths are merely tools to be used toward an end? I only lie when it suits my purpose. It just so happens that right now telling the truth does so quite nicely."

"Your head games will not work on me, not this time."

"Don't believe me?" Lucus asks with an air of certainty. "Then by all means go ahead and check for yourself."

Somewhat overcome by events perceived to be unfolding in slow motion, Erin gazes at her dad's room down the hallway that, at the moment, appears to be a mile long and growing. She turns back to Lucus and, at that very instant, he purposefully releases his umbrella and it crashes to the hardwood floor. A smirk slithers across his face. This is no random act, no accident. She recognizes what this means. It is a warning, his second message. They both are aware of deep-rooted folklore that warns when an umbrella is dropped in a house, someone will soon be killed.

While she stares at the prostrate omen on the floor and contemplates its ramifications, her locked gaze is interrupted by the rushing sound of wings violently flapping. As she looks up, a grackle bursts over Lucus with a shriek and heads straight for the startled girl. Erin squeals and ducks. Kneeling on the floor, she tracks the airborne intruder as it heads past her and for Queenie's room. It works to hover in position above the doorway, then, once in place, rips away the pinned angel moth with its beak. The bird swoops once again at Erin, who drops to the floor completely, covering her head for protection.

After the bird's beating wings disappear down the stairwell, all is silent. Erin lies on the floor shrouded in self-imposed darkness, wanting to just camp there forever, but she knows Lucus will not relent. There is no rest for the wicked.

Some time passes, then a waft of cool air tingles her arms. She cautiously looks up and the first thing that catches her eye, from floor perspective, is her father's door at the end of the hallway. A check behind reveals that Lucus has vanished. Strange, she did not hear him leave. Erin begins to wonder if all that actually happened or if it was just in her mind. The uncertain girl glances above Queenie's door and sure enough, the moth and the pin are gone.

The happening, indeed, was not cerebral fiction.

Erin's attention is drawn back down the hallway to her father's room. The silence is beckoning, calling her to uncover the truth once and for all. She stands up and reluctantly tiptoes barefoot down the hallway, then, stopping at his door, softly knocks.

"Daddy?"

No response. She taps again.

"Daddy? Say something, anything."

Dead silence.

"Please, I need you to be here for me." Her voice cracks. "You're all I've got."

Her pleas go unanswered. The girl timidly places her hand on the handle and twists. It rotates fully with a click. A gentle nudge forward opens the door with ease, and a cold wisp of stale air escapes. The room is lit only by the afternoon sunlight leaking around the lowered window shades. Obviously unoccupied for quite some time, the bed is meticulously made, and a layer of dust liberally coats the wood floor and furniture.

Erin steps in and gradually makes her way around the other side of the bed to the closet, leaving a trail of dark footprints behind. She opens the closet door and discovers it has been gutted—devoid of any clothes, artifacts, and even hangers. A picture frame rests on the bedside table. She picks it up. A quick swipe of her hand clears the veil of particles, and Erin sees her dad clearly once again. The image triggers an avalanche of memories: the phone call, the morgue, the funeral. But it does not stop there.

The missing pieces of the gruesome puzzle, the facts, come together in almost an instant. Erin is horrified and starts hyperventilating, because the truth that she has been subconsciously suppressing all this time has finally, thanks to Lucus, mercilessly been forced to the surface.

That night...Emily's accident...the drunk driver...it was her father.

He had been at a dance hall in the neighboring town, without Rose who never went with him, partying the night away and getting plastered as was his custom on weekends, holidays, paydays, and most any other day that seemed fitting for one reason or another. Due to his drunken stupor that night, and the fact that the girl was unrecognizable after impact, he had no idea that it was his own daughter whom he had run over and then dragged off into the woods.

Once Erin's father sobered up and learned what he had done, the grief was too much to bear. One week after the accident, on the day of Emily's funeral, the grief-stricken man was found hanging in his jail cell, a belt cinched tightly around his neck.

Six days later, without ceremony, he was buried next to Emily.

The picture slips through Erin's hands and crashes onto the floor, glass shattering. But she does not hear the explosion. Enclosing walls of the spinning room force her to start moving. One step at a time she makes her way out of the bedroom, down the hallway, and into her own room. Without thinking, she grabs her keys and heads for the car. At some point the dazed girl realizes she is behind the steering wheel and halfway to Brad's house.

THE ENTIRE ROSS FAMILY IS DEAD quiet on Friday afternoons when there is a home game. One part strategy and one part superstition, they keep the house free of noise and distractions so Brad can prepare mentally for the night's battle. It is such a reverent time that one might deem the only thing absent the saturating aroma of Sunday's after-church meal stewing in a Crock Pot.

However, today is different. Brad's father, Jack, has summoned his son into the office for a serious discussion that cannot wait, even if it means throwing Brad off his game. Some things are more important than sports.

"You wanted to see me, Dad?"

"Yes, I've got some news about Erin's pigs."

"And?"

"According to John, the Feds have determined who is behind them. It's an outfit that has been in trouble with the FDA before, but they aren't spilling the beans as to who it is. Off the record, John was told these guys are conducting research into harvesting pig organs for the purposes of transplanting them into people."

"You can't be serious."

"As a matter of fact, valves from pig hearts have been used to repair cardiovascular defects in humans for years. But the next big thing will be to use pig lungs, then the holy grail of transplants, hearts. The potential for profit is astronomical. That's why millions of dollars are pouring into projects like what's happening at Erin's."

"Whoa."

"That's not all. This organization has been busted several times for illegal and immoral practices involving the splicing of human

DNA to that of pigs through the use of embryonic stem cells, as well as other means which, not divulged due to top-secret classification, were violating the laws of nature, man, and God. What they produced were both human and pig, yet not really either; unnatural hybrids. Well, they were stripped of their licenses for medical research, but apparently are still moving forward undercover using small locations like Erin's. There's no telling how many other farms there are across the U.S., or even the world, where this is going on."

His son stares at the floor. Jack continues. "Your girlfriend and her family have gotten involved with some very dangerous people whose power is almost unlimited, and their reach global. But we're supposed to keep quiet and let the authorities handle it. You can't even tell Erin."

Brad looks at his dad.

"I mean it, son. John pulled a lot of strings to get this information, and he told me in the strictest of confidence for your protection. You will not betray his trust and our honor now, will you?"

"No sir. I won't say anything."

"Good. Now, grab that chair and pull it around the desk here so you can see the monitor."

Brad does as asked and waits for his dad, who lets out a deep sigh then begrudgingly begins another undesirable task.

"I…received a letter in the mail today; actually an envelope with just a disk in it. There was no name or return address label, but that doesn't matter. What matters is what's on the disk."

"Okay." Brad has no clue where this is going.

"On it are some videos. I know this is going to hurt you, son, but I need to show you this. The ramifications for you, and for our family, are far too great to not address immediately. I'm not going to add any commentary. I'm just going to pull these up and play them so you can see the truth with your own eyes. But I want you to know that I love you and will help you get through this."

Now Brad is really anxious, and, not knowing what to expect, just nods his head to indicate that he is ready. In actuality, Brad will not be ready for what is about to hit him; nothing could prepare him for this.

Jack double-clicks the first video, titled *Just Hanging Around*, then presses the play button.

A close-up focuses on two black dots about three inches apart on an indistinguishable area of someone's body. Then a couple of fingers come into the frame and start pinching and massaging the skin, rolling it up between the marks, to prepare it. After a few times, another hand enters from the opposite side grasping a large metal hook. In an instant flesh is pierced in on one side and out the other causing a trickle of blood that is immediately dabbed with a cotton swab then treated with a coating of salve.

As the camera slowly zooms out, another hook is already punctured in place above the other shoulder blade, but that is not all that is exposed. Down a little further is a black tattoo of an inverted pentagram encompassing a Pisces icon at its center. Continuing footage reveals a girl's whole back with a black bikini strap stretched across. She turns, facing the camera, flashing the devil sign with split fingers while sticking her tongue out as far as possible.

Brad's countenance transforms from revolted bewilderment to sheer horror.

"No. No. That can't be her. That has to be her sister Emily."

Jack says nothing as the video relentlessly continues its barrage of revelation.

Panning left, the camera focuses on an identical girl who just went through the same procedure. Then the video immediately cuts to footage showing the twins hoisted about two feet above the floor with a series of pulleys and cables attached to the hooks in their backs. Another edit shows the girls, on opposite sides of a suspension rod of this macabre carnival ride, being swung in circles as the weight of their bodies pulls down stretching the flesh on their backs to what almost looks like the point of ripping.

"Wheeeee!" shouts one girl exuberantly as she zooms past the camera.

"Yeah! Rock-N-Roll!" screams the other as she comes around.

Another cut reveals one of the girls being interviewed after she had been lowered and bandaged up.

"So how was it?" asks the person holding the camera in a deep tone that Brad immediately recognizes.

"Religious!" she responds. "Absolutely religious!"

"That's my girl. I love you, Rin."

"I love you too," she responds with a big smile and leaning forward past the camera for what is obviously an affectionate kiss.

The video abruptly stops after that, showing just a dead black screen. Brad sits stunned, not knowing how to digest this, but unfortunately for him it is only the beginning. Without saying a word, Jack closes out that window and opens another file titled *Worship.*

This video shows people adorned in dark robes and occult ornamental jewelry performing various rituals deep in the woods at night with some clips revealing, without a doubt, Erin and her sister both participating at the same time. However, skillful editing deceitfully portrays Erin sacrificing a small animal—something she never did.

Now hunched over in the chair, Brad rests his elbows on his knees and clasps his hands over his mouth, eyes still glued to the screen. Jack places his hand on Brad's shoulder as a show of support then launches the third video titled *Secret Rendezvous.* This one will be the back-breaker.

"You'll notice on this one, son, that the time stamp in the corner indicates this particular incident happened last Friday while you were out of the town at the game."

The blurry image takes a moment to focus. When it does, two figures are seen facing each other in front of a store. As the camera slowly zooms in, it becomes clear that the store is Madame Zelda's and the two people are Erin and Lucus. They are too far away to hear, but it is clear that they are having a conversation.

Then Brad's eyes are filled with a shocking image. Erin steps toward Lucus and hugs him. As they embrace, the umbrella swings down shielding their bodies from view. The time they are behind it seems to last forever, and their body movement paints a horrific picture in Brad's mind of a long passionate kiss. The clip stops, freezing on its last frame showing a passing box truck for the local salvage yard whose name is painted largely across—*SCRAP IT!*

Brad's entire face is now buried completely in his hands.

BEAUTIFUL HARMONIC TONES CHIME throughout the stately residence. Granna happens to be passing by in the foyer lugging a half-filled bucket of fresh warm water and rags. She finds that cleaning something, anything, is the only way to keep her restless self occupied and quiet during these grueling Friday afternoons of audible suppression. She opens the front door.

"May I help you?"

Before her stands Erin, who is doing all she can to keep it together.

"Um, hi. My name is Erin. I'm a friend of Brad's. Is he here?"

"Oh, you must be his special lady friend that I've heard about. My, you *are* pretty. Let me give you a hug!"

Granna steps out and reaches up with one hand while the other struggles to lift the weight of her cleaning supplies. Erin leans down and reciprocates, lightly hugging the sweet elderly woman. Their embrace is both comforting and awkward for Erin, as the socially distant girl can only remember ever hugging Brad and Lucus.

"Come on into our house, beloved. You are welcome here."

Erin gingerly follows Granna onto the shiny marble-tiled floor of the foyer, where it seems a certain someone has already forgotten a part of the conversation that just transpired.

"So why are you here, sweetie?"

"Brad. I was hoping to see Brad."

"Oh yes, you said that before, didn't you?"

"Brad said you have to use a cane to walk," Erin replies noticing there is not one.

"Why yes, I normally do. But for some reason today I'm feeling spry. Yes, quite spry. In fact, feel as though I could smack a demon right in its choppers—give it the ol' one-two." Granna then glances down and a sharp breath passes her lips. My heavens, child, you're not wearing any shoes!"

Erin looks down to discover the woman is correct. Her feet are only covered in dust from the dirt driveway of their farmhouse.

"I'm so sorry! I didn't mean to get your nice floor dirty! I guess I just didn't realize I didn't have them on. I'll step back outside and wait for Brad."

"Nonsense! You'll catch your death of cold out in that chilly weather. Besides, a little dirt is easily dealt with. Now don't you be at all embarrassed, some days when she first gets up this old woman forgets to put in her teeth. Here, sit right down on this."

Erin eases onto the wooden bench and to her surprise Granna reaches down and gently pulls her foot up then positions the bucket underneath. The kindly woman plunges her rag deep down into the warm, clean water and begins to softly wipe her feet with it.

"Oh no, ma'am. I can't have you cleaning my dirty feet! Here, I can do it!"

"Hogwash!" Granna replies in a more authoritative tone. "You just sit there and be still. Besides, I consider it a privilege. Our Lord washed the feet of His friends, and it blesses me to follow in his footsteps."

Inexplicably, this experience is not at all awkward to Erin like the hug. Her feet unreservedly absorb all the love and energy Granna pours into them and feel as though they are being healed in some way. Newly resurrected. Thoroughly alive. The humbled girl looks on with astonishment, as she believes it is the dignified and gracious elderly woman who has earned the right to receive this sort of loving care—certainly not herself. Granna joyfully hums a tune, a hymn, unbeknownst to the unchurched girl, while drying Erin's cleansed soles.

"You see those French doors at the end of the hall, Erin?" Granna points, a small damp towel dangling in her hand.

"Yes."

"Brad is in his father's office there. Just knock on the door, and he'll come out to greet you. I know he'll be happy you're here."

"Thank you. You've been very kind."

"You're welcome my child, and call me Granna. Now give me another hug. I need to go clean some areas that the weekly cleaning lady missed."

After their second embrace, Erin watches Granna shuffle off to another part of the house. Then she turns her attention down the hallway to the office where Brad and his father are meeting. She begins to make her way down.

STORM CLOUDS GATHER in the sky above—celestial powers organizing into a massive system that will unleash dangerous forces culminating in the loss of life prior to dawn's rising sun.

Brad feels as though all the life has been sucked right out of him. He sits doubled over in emotional agony as those horrific images loop through his mind, stirring up feelings he has never experienced before. Rocking back and forth fails to ease a queasy stomach. Betrayal is a bitter pill that, once swallowed, eats away at the core of an individual—and Brad is no exception.

He is reminded of Big John's warnings and how they were repeatedly shunned, wondering how he could have been so naïve, so blind, so manipulated. What were her motives? Many options arise that his imagination seizes and manufactures into answers, all of which are twisted and toxic—but none more so than what hits him next.

Instantly his mind reverses in a blur back to when his dad told him about the high school fiasco with Erin's mom at the dance. The conclusion is quick and decisive. It was definitely revenge; an elaborate deception coordinated by the vengeful mother in conjunction with her daughter and Lucus. It is the same cruel act his dad's friend did to Rose—the bogus breakup, the newfound duplicitous romance, and coming humiliation at the hands of those involved—only on a much larger, maybe even more dangerous scale. To be just, vengeance cannot be equal—it must be paid back with interest: A jaw for a tooth. A head for an eye. A pound of flesh weighed on a scale secretly rigged to misreport and obtain perverse profits.

It was all so clear now, whispers the voice in his ear. Mentally he kicks himself for not heeding earlier advice against becoming emotionally involved with a girl at this stage of his life, and vows never again to turn a deaf ear to his father's voice.

"Son, I need you to look me in the eye."

Brad struggles to lift his shoulders from their wilted position. It is as though crouched upon them with hooves digging in is a five-hundred-pound beast—one that is extremely intelligent, immensely powerful, has a name, personality, and will—yet takes orders from its commander in another realm. It is barred by an even higher power from entering the young man but is allowed to whisper into his ear, covertly planting seeds of destruction.

Facing his father at this point is one of the hardest things Brad has ever had to do, because he knows what is probably coming. His father's countenance confirms the suspicion. He will have to finally divulge concealed secrets, like a little boy who has just been told to empty out his pockets to reveal their contents for inspection.

"I'm pretty sure there are some…instances, some…red flags you need to share with me about this girl. I need you to tell me everything you've experienced with her that would be clearly seen as disturbing…unbiblical…ungodly."

The defeated young man recounts what he can to his father—in abridged form, and omitting his encounters with Lucus—what has transpired over the last week, finishing with his and Erin's conversation the previous night. It is this last revelation that has Jack scrambling for clarification and details.

"She's being visited by ghosts? Of her deceased sister?"

"According to her, yes."

"You know what that means, don't you?"

"I'm…not sure what you're getting at."

"The Bible clearly teaches that to be absent from the body is to be in the presence of the Lord."

Brad still has not made the connection, and his father can tell by the look on his face.

"Son, if when people die they directly go to be with God, then there is no way that the ghosts visiting Erin, or any other ghosts for that matter, can be human spirits. They are angels…fallen angels."

"Are you saying—"

"Yes. Demons."

To Brad, this just went to a whole other level—not one he ever imagined. The young man, even though his sacred book teaches of them quite extensively, never really put much stock in Lucifer's demonic dominion. His secularly influenced, engineering-based mind just never took seriously such things in the midst of this enlightened scientific age.

Now he has to face it head on, as well as what to do with Erin—who has just now quietly approached and stands next to Brad's shoes, which are parked outside one of the office doors which has inadvertently been left cracked open. Their conversation seeps out like the putrid stench from roadkill gradually falling apart in the middle of a sun-scorched desert highway. No, worse than that. Toxic. Like the pungent aroma of mustard gas. Deadly.

"And you know," his father continues, "Erin still hasn't come to grips with what happened with her dad. She still believes he's alive. She has serious problems, delusions, problems far beyond your ability to fix. Son, you've done your part. You've reached out to her like Pastor Mike asked you to. You've made a valiant effort, but I'm afraid it's time to sever the relationship. And I think you know that, too."

Erin, gently gnawing a fingernail, waits for her soul mate's response. Lungs frozen still with anticipation, Erin feels she could go forever without inhaling again until hearing the answer. She is confident in what he will say.

It would have been merciful had the verdict never been pronounced.

"You're right, Dad. I'll...end it tomorrow."

That is it. No more talk comes from the room. Erin keeps waiting for a qualifier from Brad—something about a cooling off period with a second chance or something like that. But it never comes. She still has not inhaled and begins to drown in anxiousness, like an infidel nearly discovered snooping around in a holy place—as one who is absolutely forbidden to be there. She must slip out from her dark recess and make a daring escape before the priests of this sacred shrine discover the trespasser and enact punishment fit for sinners guilty of the most heinous of crimes.

Erin makes her way back down the hallway as quietly as she came but at twice the pace—a brisk walk interspersed with hops forward on feet that are numb. Not the pleasant walking-on-clouds kind of feeling, more of a your-feet-have-been-hacked-off-and-the-nubs-injected-full-of-Novacaine type of sensation.

Erin still has not inhaled upon reaching the door, as if keeping air from entering her lungs will keep reality from setting in. But both oxygen and truth are essential for life, and suppressing either brings about certain death.

Slipping outside seems to grant her permission to breathe again. Permission to think. To leave. To vanish.

HIGHLY PRESSURIZED SILENCE IS GOING TO EXPLODE into a million razor-sharp fragments bouncing off corrugated metal walls once Scarlet stretches up and delivers the bad news, with a reluctant hushed tone, into Lucus's ear.

"WHAT?" he shouts with all the force his powerful lungs can blast out.

Scarlet does not reiterate, knowing full well that the angry outburst was only a rhetorical reaction—and that repeating it would just make the situation double-worse.

"It's missing? How?"

The curly-haired beauty just looks up at him and makes a facial expression of ignorance, with pouty lips and innocent-looking eyes to buttress her credibility.

"Well it just didn't get up and walk out of here on its own! We've been virtually starving the thing for nearly a week now!"

The other participants in attendance, four females and two males, all in thick robes, hang their heads low in hopes that the oversized hoods will cloak them from the boogey man. A shirtless Lucus shrugs off the heavily-tattooed bald guy dabbing his hook-pierced back with blood-stained cotton swabs.

"That's enough. I'm good! Leave us! Now!"

The bod-mod technician picks up his tackle box and bottle of rubbing alcohol, then makes a hasty exit as ordered. A nearby door thumps loudly into place, informing Lucus they are now all sufficiently sequestered.

"Everyone! In front of me! Now!"

The seven quickly assemble before him, like Marine cadets

scrambling for their drill sergeant's surprise inspection. Going down the line, Lucus places his hand under each one's chin and raises it to read their eyes—a quite reliable lie-detecting technique. All of the followers, including Scarlet, appear to have nothing to do with the disappearance.

"We'll just have to make do with what we have. For all of your sakes, it had better be good enough. Go get the other one. There's not much time."

Scarlet quickly shuffles off to another part of the building. Upon her return, Lucus has already been tethered with the four hooks pierced in his back to the lifting apparatus affectionately referred to as "the crucifix." He stands in the center of the stage floor's painted pentagram waiting for his offering. Scarlet approaches and makes the delivery—a lamb.

The baby is extremely weak, having been nearly starved to death, but still manages to wheeze out another cry for help—a pitiful-sounding request that falls on deaf ears and stone-cold hearts.

"Everyone in position," Lucus orders in business-mode tone.

The five girls kneel at each point of the pentagram, facing its center, with Scarlet directly in front of their master. Standing on either side of him about six feet out, the two others cling to vertical chains and wait for the go-ahead signal.

"Now."

Chains clanking, they hoist him up. As he ascends, Lucus cradles the emaciated lamb in his arms, clutching a dagger in his right fist. Another bleat from the emaciated suckling, this one weaker than the last.

Once he is in position up high, the chains are secured, and the two step back a few paces with heads bowed reverently. Scarlet leads the other kneeling practitioners in chants of Latin phrases as before, with the book spread open on the floor in front of her. A large lit candle sits in the middle of the pentagram directly under Lucus. After a few moments the chants of Latin taper off and there is silence. Then, up above, more mantras begin—but these are Native American ramblings, littered with repeated requests for the assistance of his spirit guide Wakan Tanka. He starts off quietly and somberly but eventually increases in both volume and intensity.

Lucus has incorporated into his ceremony elements of the sun dance, a Native American ceremony that features piercing of skin as a personal sacrifice offering to bolster one's prayer requests to the Great Spirit. At what appears to be the climax of the ritual, blood begins splattering on the floor—drops that eventually extinguish the candle's flame. Then the chants stop. A moment of silence.

Then the body of the sacrificed lamb plummets to the floor with a distinctive thud. Afterward, a small piece of paper descends and lands on the carcass. It is the photo of Brad and Erin taken by the giggling freshmen girls at school.

ERIN SITS ON THE GROUND with her back up against Emily's roadside memorial cross. Knees bent up to her chest and head buried into her arms resting on them, the weary girl runs through thoughts of Brad, Emily, nothing, then back to Brad again in a loop of despair. Occupying the most amount of time is her dwelling in the emptiness. She is all out of tears. All out of energy. All out of hope.

A nudge. On her leg.

The soft bump brings her back to the here and now, but she does not lift her head. Not out of fear, out of apathy. If she is in mortal danger again, so be it. She is ready to go.

Another one. It is as gentle as the first.

Erin slowly lifts up to discover a boar standing in front of her—the same one that knocked her into the pit, as well as the dead one in the road. From this angle it looks to be the size of a young bull, but does not appear aggressive. It is docile. Tamed.

"Don't be afraid."

The voice is Emily's.

Erin feels the comforting soft touch of a hand from behind on her left shoulder and, instinctively knowing whose it is, places hers on top of it. "I'm not. Not anymore."

The apparition, appearing fresh, young, vibrant, and dressed in a soft white cotton summer dress that gently flows in the steady breeze as she walks past, sits on the ground facing Erin, beside the boar that lies down, eyes closed, breathing deeply—its massive frame expanding and contracting with every inhale and exhale as it slumbers. The rhythmic motion brings a peace to Erin, as did the undulating wings of the angel moth on her chest a few days ago. Emily warmly smiles at the creature as she tenderly rubs its gigantic head, petting it affectionately as if it were a beloved lifelong pet.

"Tell me what you're thinking," she asks.

"Oh, nothing. Everything," answers Erin.

"Care to talk about it?"

"Not really."

"Okay. That's fine."

Emily leans on what would be considered the boar's neck, if you could call it that, and hugs the creature while she too closes her eyes—patiently waiting like someone who has all the time in the world.

Erin fixates on the two for who knows how long, eyes panning back and forth on occasion to see if anyone is around—and to try and determine if all of this is real or just another dream or vision concocted in her mind. No vehicles pass on the highway. More time lazily flows down the deep river of infinity.

"Are you real?" Erin asks finally.

Emily smiles first, then opens her eyes without adjusting her position on the beast. "It depends on what you mean by 'real.'"

"Are you here? Really here, right now?"

"Yes."

"Why?"

"Because I love you. You're my sister. My family."

The somewhat vague reply leaves Erin waiting for more details. Emily simply shuts her eyes again. More time drifts away.

"What do you hope to accomplish?"

Emily separates from the boar and stares at Erin. "To bring us back together as a family."

"A family? Were we really ever one?"

"We can be now."

Erin rests her chin atop the crossed arms perched on her knees, gaze cast downward in contemplation. Another lingering pause of silence.

"I don't know. What would that do, really?"

"Daddy."

Erin's head pops up. Emily's right hand has moved up the shaft of the boar's tusk with index finger leisurely rubbing circles on its tip.

"Daddy? What about Daddy?"

"He's with me on the other side. Wants us all to be back together again."

The look on Erin's face is unmistakable. Emily addresses her concern.

"You think that since Daddy committed suicide, that he is forever in the awful place of torture as taught by some factions of the so-called Christian religion."

That is exactly where Erin's mind is parked.

"Think about it. Would an all-loving God really send people to torment in a fiery hell for eternity for maybe once having a bad thought? For making mistakes from time to time? For wanting to end the pain and anguish? It's not true."

"So he's still around?"

"In a manner of speaking, yes. And he wants to be with you again."

"Why doesn't he just appear to me like you do?"

"It's more complicated than that. Because the way he, you know, died, he is barred from certain access to the other realms."

"Then how can we possibly be back together?"

"Tonight. At our house. In my room. Mom is going to have another connection and, with everything in place, including you, *especially* including you, he will be allowed to manifest."

"What about Queenie? Should she be there?"

"No," comes a quick and short burst of a response. "Oh, no."

"Why not?"

"Because it would be too much too soon. Neither Queenie, nor anyone else, can be there. Except Madame Zelda."

"Zelda? That fraud?"

Emily laughs. "Oh, Erin. Don't be so hard on the old gal. She's more useful than you might think."

"So me, Mom, and Zelda. That's it."

"Yes."

"I don't know," replies Erin with a tone of reluctance. "I swore off of all that stuff after you died."

Emily pauses for a moment. "I want you to look behind that cross, Erin. On the ground."

"What?"

"Just do it."

Erin leans around then reaches over, returning with something in her hand. It is a joint and lighter apparently dropped by a hitch-hiker or visitor to the area.

"You know it helps you think straight when you're frazzled. Go on. Light up."

She looks at the joint, then at Emily, then back at the joint. A flick of the lighter. A deep inhale. An extended sigh of relief.

"Hello, old friend," she says out loud, head tilted back, eyes shut. A few more drags bring Erin to a level of ease and comfort she has not felt in a very long time. Eventually, singeing of her fingers indicates that the break is over. She flicks what is left off to the side where it lays on the ground smoldering.

"Erin, there is mercy on the other side. I've forgiven Daddy for what he did to me that night. I've forgiven you. On our side we can't help but forgive, and love, because we are free of all the lies and demands that your side binds you in—a side ruled by nothing but hateful judgment. The town has judged you. The school has judged you. Sheriff Knox labels you as just another habitual offender. And Lucus. I don't need to remind you of what misery he has brought into your life. Then there's that so-called Christian who has thrown you to the curb like a piece of filthy trash. Really? Your lips are not good enough to touch his? Like you are some sort of leper? You heard his father say the only reason he spends time with you is because the youth pastor told him to. To Brad you are nothing more than a ministry project. Another notch on his spiritual belt to earn reward. Merely a rung to be stepped on in his climb to heaven."

Emily continues without skipping a beat or taking a breath. "You are not trash, Erin, but a jewel to be treasured. Neither he nor anyone else is better than you. You are a good person, and don't ever let anyone else try to convince you otherwise. Most everyone is good in their own way. There *is* a hell, an outer darkness of torment, but is reserved for only a few who really deserve it. Murderers.

Rapists. Child molesters."

"Politicians," Erin adds in her own sarcastically humorous way.

Emily laughs. "That's my Erin. Always the quick wit, yet with profundity. Yes, some politicians as well as some so-called religious leaders."

"Pagans?"

"Look, Emily, there are only a few who are really bad enough to be cast down below with Hitler and his ilk. *That* is the world's best-kept secret. And because of the light we have in my realm, this truth is apparent. But sadistic people in your world invent impossible-to-follow rules and horrible-sounding punishments in order to control others. You haven't realized it yet, but that is the darkness you refer to so often in your writings. But on my side, it is as if the sun has risen, causing the darkness to fall. And it is this light of truth, love, and forgiveness we want to share with you tonight. So what do you say, Rin, will you come?"

It is now dark outside, and the discarded butt is completely burned out.

"Yes."

AN EERIE DISHARMONIC NOISE radiates from the student band section of the bleachers as Reagan High's amateur musicians, almost in sync, blare out "Eye Of The Tiger" with an excess contribution from the hard-core dudes, plus one chick, all wearing dark sunglasses, in the drum section. Underneath beaming stadium lights, money and nachos change hands at the concession stand while Mr. Thompson, the balding still-a-bachelor band teacher, conducts the teen orchestra and, at the same time, spies out of the corner of his eye cheerleaders prepping for "their" game by checking mirrors, straightening hair bows, and applying another all-important layer of body glitter. Except for the two who actually took gymnastics—they show off their skills, end-over-end and backward, in an informal competition of talent and endurance near the hash marks between the fifty- and thirty-yard lines.

The stands are almost full, and after warm-ups both teams are back in the field house waiting for show time. The Ross family members, including Granna, have taken up residence in their usual place, as has the team's biggest fan, Earl—Lucus's so-called father.

"Hey Jack!" comes a yell from a few spaces across.

"Here it comes," Jack mutters to his wife.

"I got a fever!" Earl continues. "And the only prescription is…"

In unison, Jack chimes in but with barely more than a whisper.

"…more cowbell!"

The joke was sort of funny the first time he did it—Brad's freshman year. But. Not. Every. Home. Game. Since.

Jack gives a forced mandatory smile and waves back at a now standing Earl, who flails the aforementioned cowbell high in the air, screaming, "Let's go, Eagles! Woo Hoo!" Earl's wife sits stoically next to him immersed in a romance novel, ignoring her husband while waiting for the game to begin.

Jack pours, for his huddled family, hot chocolate from a thermos into waiting Styrofoam cups. A hand slaps down on Jack's shoulder, causing a jostle, a splash.

"I tell you what, Jack. How 'bout we trade sons? I'll even throw in a new car to sweeten the deal. Whataya say?"

Another joke that has worn out its welcome.

"No thanks, Earl. I think I'll pass this time. Again."

"Oh, all right. But you let me know if you change your mind."

"Would you like some hot chocolate?"

"Oh no. Got the good stuff." Earl pats his coat pocket where the flask hides. "Put a fire in your belly."

No use in telling him again that it is illegal to have alcohol on school property.

"Say, what's with Brad tonight anyway?"

"What do you mean, Earl?"

"During warm-ups. He was a bit sluggish. Passes off target. Seemed mentally preoccupied."

"Sorry. They had already gone into the field house by the time we got here. Didn't see."

Jack has not mentioned the conversation with Brad to his wife.

Earl puts on his serious face. "Now, we need him to be on top of his game tonight. This is Rawlings. They're tough. Real tough. We gotta win this one for home field advantage throughout the playoffs."

"He'll do just fine, Earl."

The concerned fan pauses a moment then relaxes with a big smile. "You're right, Jack."

Another vigorous pat on the shoulder. Another spill.

"If there's one thing we know about Brad, it's that he is indeed reliable."

The young man they speak of is inside the field house sitting on a bench in front of his equipment locker. He slouches over, elbows on knees, dangling his helmet between spread legs. Most everyone else has made their way out to the side of the building, waiting to burst onto the field of battle once coach says go. Usually Brad is the first one out there rallying troops and giving a pep talk, but not tonight. He is a million miles away.

"Hey!" comes a familiar yet agitated voice from the side.

Brad sits up and is met with a forceful blow to his midsection. His hands feel a football in their grasp, the helmet now wobbling on the cement floor.

"*That* is your girlfriend tonight!"

Brad looks up to see Big John pointing at the football. Then he points in the general direction of Erin's house and continues lecturing.

"Not that girl, that…witch. Whatever spell she has over you, you had better shake it off. You were horrible in warm-ups, and I know it's because of her. You can go back to dancing with the Devil tomorrow, but tonight, tonight you need to break up with her. Put her out of your life and mind until after the game. This one is too important. I…we have scouts out there, and I am not going to let you blow it. You got me?"

Brad is stunned. No witty comebacks to Big John's nuggets of miswisdom come to mind, as is usually the case. But tonight is no ordinary night, and his friend has no idea how close to home he has come with his little diatribe. He continues.

"It's out of respect for you and our friendship that I waited till we were alone before mentioning this. But next time I won't be so thoughtful. Now come on, it's time for war. Don't let us down."

With that, Big John turns and limps out through the open doorway. Two junior-highers and a coach round the corner. They are the last to leave besides Brad.

"Now you two get out there and make sure the water bottles are full," barks the coach. "And if I catch you distracted by the cheerleaders again I'm gonna stuff you into the water jug and screw the lid on tight; you got me?"

"Yes, sir," the two respond in unison.

As the trio are exiting, a bird swoops in from outside just above their heads.

"*Whoa, cool!*" The two boys stop and turn to marvel at the unusual incident, which irritates the large man.

"You two act like you've never seen a bird before! Now get moving!" He pushes the boys out, and then they are gone.

On the floor in front of Brad stands the grackle with something in its mouth. The bird twitches its head back and forth looking at the boy with each eye on either side of its head. First the left, then the right, then the left again. A bob of its head, then what was in its mouth now lies on the floor. Brad stares, thinking he has seen it before. But he hasn't. Then it dawns on him; it was actually described—verbally. By Erin. This bird has delivered the angel moth that was pinned above Queenie's door.

A flutter of wings past Brad's head, and the creature now clings to the metal crisscrossing weave that makes up the door of his equipment locker. The bird screeches, then is gone as quickly as it arrived. But Brad's eyes do not follow it out. They are fixated on his phone, which shows a voice message has been left by Erin. He opens the locker, pulls it out, taps a few times, and then listens.

"B—Brad...this is me." Her voice cracks with weakness. She made the call after leaving his house, but he was too preoccupied to notice it. "I know what you're planning on doing. I know you're breaking up with me. Let's spare the awkwardness and consider it done now. We knew it couldn't last. We're too different. You are rising; I'm falling. Don't call or come by. I'm not going to the game. We'll just pretend this whole thing never happened. That's what everybody wants anyway. It's over. We're fini—"

Click.

The crowd outside roars as both teams enter the playing field. It's go time.

ERIN WALKS PAST MADAME ZELDA'S CAR and encounters something quite bizarre for this time of year. Standing at the foot of her front steps, she notices an unusual number of geckos. Dozens of them clinging to the porch walls, posts, and ceiling; none moving, though, as if waiting for some sort of signal. All eyes are on the hesitant girl as she clutches a purse close to her chest and timidly makes it to the front door.

After nervously fidgeting with the handle a moment, Erin makes her way inside—and not a moment too soon as far as she is concerned—then goes upstairs. Upon cracking open the door of Emily's room, she faces an all-too-familiar sight: darkness sporadically interrupted by flickerings of candlelight. A table littered with occult paraphernalia. And the presence of sentient beings from the other realm. Three of them, to be exact. All appearing to be Erin's age. All appearing to be Emily.

"Come," the trio beckon with a single voice. "We've been expecting you."

Erin nudges the door open wider, revealing her mother and Madame Zelda sitting at the table, both looking at her and smiling. The nearest chair is empty. Rose pats the seat. "Come, baby. They said you would be here."

Erin looks back at the apparitions who smile as well and nod, appearing to indicate that all is okay. Everything within the girl is screaming at her to leave immediately, that something dreadful is going to happen, but she finds herself sitting down next to her mother anyway.

There are no cameras, recorders, or electronic devices of any kind this time. That was the stipulation given to Zelda by her spirit guide in a dream if she was going to be allowed to witness tonight's miraculous event. And nothing was going to keep her from taking it all in this time. That excitable woman determined she was not going to pass out again, like those silly goats that stiffen up and topple over when frightened.

"So what happens now?" inquires Erin.

"We're going to show you something wonderful," the Emilies respond, again singularly.

"Daddy?"

"Patience, my sister. In due time. But first, we need you to relax. All three of you. To open yourselves up."

"To what?" Erin presses.

"The possibilities."

"Do as she—they say," Zelda chimes in. "You must be fully cooperative."

The standing three hold hands, each staring at the seated mortals before them. Then their eyes close and heads tilt back. A feeling of immense power invades the room. They open their mouths, and deep vibrations of otherworldly sounds emanate from them. The reverberations penetrate everything, and everyone, in the room.

It is a feeling like no other.

Then the resonances take on a physical appearance in the form of small lights, flowing from the visitors' mouths, that swirl about the room like lightning bugs dancing in a starry-skied midnight meadow.

Rose gasps. "They're...they're beautiful!"

"They tickle my ears." Zelda giggles.

A cautious Erin studies them carefully as the other two wonder in amazement at the tiny orbs slowly swarming around them. Soon darkness begins to dissipate, and the partially lit room brightens substantially.

"Look!" Zelda points. "They're glowing!"

Indeed, the three now have an aura of white light not only shining out from them, but also an inner luminosity radiating from their chests.

"Angels!" Rose cries out. "My baby has become an angel!"

Their beams become even brighter. Blindingly bright. The three sitting down raise hands to shield their squinting eyes, which soon they aren't even able to keep open at all. Even with their eyelids tightly shut, the light is unavoidable and painful.

Then, as if a switch was flicked off, the light disappears instantaneously. All that illuminates the room are the candles. Rapidly blinking their eyes to adjust, Zelda, Rose, and Erin struggle to see what has become of the angelic hosts. They are now as before, holding hands but this time with heads bowed down. Dangling hair shields their faces. A few minutes pass with no sound or movement.

"Emily?" Rose calls out.

Still nothing. More time awkwardly passes. Again, Rose softly enquires.

"Emily?"

The middle one jerks its head up, which is met with gasps. Her face is horrifically distorted. Crushed, with skin peeled away and fragmented bone showing—as if she had been struck by a car on the highway and dragged a hundred feet down the pavement. The other two begin speaking in unrecognizable tongues—loud echoing whispers that invade the room, mind, and soul. Erin instinctively adjusts her position in the chair and readies herself. Rose is frozen with fear. And Madame Zelda's forehead lands on the table, arms dangling by her side.

A loud shriek from the middle one triggers a reflex in Erin to burst out the door, and her mother is left a sitting target. Out in the hallway more danger is lurking.

Grrrrrrrrrrr!

"Shep?" Bewildered, Erin looks down at him.

The dog curls his lips more, baring sharp teeth and taking a step toward her. Rose screams. Erin turns to see more specters resembling Emily, five in total. Three of them hold her struggling mother down and another stretches the woman's mouth open wide while the last leans in to enter it head-first.

Shep comes closer and growls with more intensity. Eyes raging.

Erin turns back around to the dog. "Oh baby, not you too."

As Rose violently gurgles in the bedroom, Erin slides her back and palms along the wall toward the staircase. Shep tracks her for a moment, then bolts into the bedroom, barking insanely. At the bottom of the stairs, Erin hears a shrieking yelp then a thud. In her haste, Erin bumped the Lincoln portrait, which now hangs cockeyed. She whisks the front door open to leave, but is stopped dead in her tracks.

The porch is moving. No, not the porch. What is *on* the porch. It is covered in a blanket of geckos. No surface showing, just a sea of the flat fleshy lizards forming waves as they crawl over and around one another. Sporadically, one or more lose their grip and drop from the ceiling.

Another hellish squeal from upstairs shoves Erin out the door. She steps on a fallen gecko, left foot sliding across the deck on its streaking slick body parts, but she keeps from falling. Another lands in her hair. She screams and jumps off the porch and into the night. Blindly running into the darkness, grabbing wildly at her hair, she catches the gecko in her fingers and flings it. Still barreling across the yard, the frightened girl bumps into something, something big, which brings her to a crashing halt. It grabs hold of her arms and squeezes. Hard. She struggles at pulling away but the grip is too strong.

"Let go of me!" She kicks frantically.

"Erin! I won't let you go!"

The voice. It is familiar. She looks up.

"Brad? What are you doing here?"

"I finally heard your voice mail. You said you were falling, and I told you I would catch you if you did. I'm keeping my promise."

"You came back…for me?"

"What's happening? What's going on?"

"Upstairs. My mother. She's in danger."

He looks at the house then back at her.

"I'm calling in that favor. We need your help, please."

"You stay here." He points at her, then turns and runs toward the porch.

"And Shep! Get Shep, too! I think he's hurt!"

Brad stops at the steps and surveys the situation. The geckos—all those geckos. He steps up and skillfully maneuvers around the ones scurrying about on the floor boards. After entering the front door, he bounds up the stairway. At the top he eyes Shep's body

strung out on the floor, a large dent in the wall just above the lifeless dog.

The athlete clenches his fists and tenses for what may happen
next. He stealthily peers into the room. Nobody here except Zelda
still in hunched-over limbo. A barely open closet door creaks slightly, drawing Brad's attention. He tiptoes over and reaches up, then
quickly swings it wide. Someone, or some thing, lunges at him and
they both fall to the floor. He immediately shoves whatever it is off
and scoots backward.

Lying on the floor is the body of a teenage girl resembling
Erin. Or Emily. It lays motionless not because she is dead, but
because it is not real. What lies before a confused Brad is Pretend
Emily—a human-size doll special ordered to look as similar to
Emily as possible. Rose slept with it every night, cuddling the syn-
thetic twin and stroking its hair while singing lullabies until they
"both" fell asleep.

OUTSIDE, ERIN YELLS a single word that changes the course
of tonight's events—and her life. "Queenie!"

Ignoring Brad's order to stay put, she rushes around the side
of the house to the barn. Winds have picked up intensely, changing
direction every few seconds as clouds high above spin, forming an
ominous pattern. Erin approaches the open barn door and walks in,
swiping hair from in front of her eyes. Queenie's back is to the door.
She is wearing a pig mask with a tiara perched on top, and the hogs
have encircled her. Watching. Waiting.

Swung wide open is the trap door leading to the secret room
below. Straining under the force of ever-increasing wind gusts, the
wood-slat walls moan eerie creaks like a wooden ship in the old
days being tossed about in a raging tempest.

"Queenie?" Erin squeaks out.

The girl turns, revealing that she has a syringe pointed at the
crook of her arm, the needle indenting the soft skin.

"They say it will make me not sick anymore." Queenie's tone is
desperate—despairing eyes are visible through holes cut out in the
mask. "They say it will even give me special powers."

A HOWL FROM DOWNSTAIRS breaks the lock Brad's gaze has on the humanoid doll. He cannot tell who yelled, but immediately gets up and rushes out the door, past Shep, and down the stairs. Another sound, the clanking of metal pots crashing onto the floor, comes from the kitchen. Brad enters and sees a wild-eyed Rose mumbling incoherently and cutting her arm with a large butcher knife, blood flowing profusely.

"Oh my—"

Rose hears Brad, shrieks, and throws the knife at him. As it tumbles toward the boy, he ducks. It bounces off the wall, landing on the floor spinning on its side.

"Kill you!" Rose growls, walking toward Brad with hands stretched out as if to strangle him. Every tendon in the possessed woman's neck is stretched tight like piano wire, while the crooks of her mouth point downward as if pierced with fishing hooks and being pulled on from below. Her eyeballs spasm uncontrollably, rapidly vibrating back and forth.

"I don't wanna hurt you, Mrs. Gray. Please stop!"

She lunges at Brad with another screech, and he grabs her wrists. The tiny woman easily breaks free of his hold and hurls him across the room. Like a rag doll, Brad ricochets off the top of the table, crashing into the counter, his head knocking against the white porcelain sink. Rose picks up the knife, lumbers over to him and raises it. "Kill you!"

Brad, lying on the floor, sees a double vision of the attacker standing over him with kitchen dagger held high and poised to strike. All he can do is hold up his hands in a last-ditch effort for protection and cry out.

"Jesus!"

Immediately Rose shrieks and drops the knife, her eyes wide and filled terror. She plummets to the floor then begins gurgling and convulsing uncontrollably—as if a bolt of high-current electricity is surging through her jerking body—arms and legs flailing, knocking against furniture and floor. Brad retreats into a corner of the cabinets, doing his best to return to complete awareness and make sense of what is happening.

Suddenly, the tremors stop. Rose's back arches high. She lets out a loud extended exhale and her body lowers to the floor like an air mattress being deflated. A blast of wind howls through the house from the open front door all the way through the kitchen and out the back, toward the barn.

ALONG WITH A GUST OF WIND, Shep rushes past Erin, the barn door slamming shut behind him. The revived dog violently lunges toward Queenie, barking and snarling at her. The frightened girl drops her syringe and stiffens with fear. In reaction, the large sow stands up on its back two legs and squeals out one barely distinguishable, but certainly recognizable, word: *"Queee-nieee!"*

The other hogs all converge on Shep, ferociously thrashing and biting him. He valiantly fights them off, causing a diversion for Erin to make her move. She runs to Queenie, grabs the frozen girl, and backs up to the hayloft ladder. Turning to lead her sister up to safety, Erin hears the ripping of her shirt, snagged on a protruding nail.

Barks, growls, and squeals fill their ears while Erin and Queenie hastily climb to the top. As they both look over the edge of the loft to see what is going on, the pig mask slips off Queenie's head and falls to the ground below where it is trampled underfoot, the tiara mangled beyond recognition.

Erin feels a tug. A crying Queenie places her hands over her ears and desperately pleads, "The strange music. The voices. I can't get them out of my head! Make them stop. Help me, please!"

Outside, a fully-formed twister, barely visible through the darkness in a nearby field, approaches, etching a jagged path to and fro as it draws nearer.

Erin pulls her little sister in, hugging her, rocking back and forth. She is out of options. Not knowing what to do, and wanting to drown out the violence going on below, she sings in a broken voice, eyes closed.

> *Rock-a-bye baby, on the treetop.*
> *When the wind blows, the cradle will rock,*
> *When the bough breaks, the cradle will fall,*
> *And down will come baby, cradle and all.*

"Is that a train?" Queenie shouts over the rushing sound of what sounds like one nearby.

"I don't know, baby. Just shut your eyes." She hugs Queenie tighter.

The barn walls begin to breathe in and out, accompanied by the sound of metal straining, like a submarine plunged fathoms into the deep and about to implode from crushing pressure. Down below, Shep suffers a fatal blow. The large sow rears up again and comes down on his back with the full force of its bone-crushing weight. His back legs instantly go limp. The partially paralyzed dog can no longer defend himself, and the other pigs pounce on him to finish the job.

Then the unthinkable.

The sound of an explosion, then a portion of the ceiling violently rips open. A flood of water pours in. The large cistern outside has toppled and partially crashed through the roof, spilling its contents. The small room fills quickly. A strong current swirls the struggling animals in a circular motion. Shep fights to keep his head above the surface, but only having his front legs to paddle makes this nearly impossible.

Water that was rising in the room now lowers as it follows the path of least resistance and drains into the subterranean room. Erin helplessly looks on as a swirling whirlpool sucks everything below down through the trap door opening and into a watery grave.

Shep is the last to be drawn under; his yelp prematurely cut off by water flooding his lungs as the trap door slams shut.

"Shep! Shep!"

Then all goes quiet, and the only thing heard is the muffled clacking of pigs' hooves on the underside of the floor as they kick about, upside-down, in feverish desperation to find an opening through which to escape. These soon taper off in frequency until they are no more.

ROSE LIES ON THE COUCH FACING ITS BACK as Erin pulls a blanket over her, covering her bandaged arm. Brad kneels beside the sofa with her. Queenie is upstairs.

"At least the cuts on her arm weren't deep. They should heal without too much scarring," says Brad.

"Thank you for not calling the police or paramedics."

"It looks like everyone is fine here. I'm sorry about Shep."

Erin does not acknowledge this last statement. After a pause, she begins the difficult and awkward task of facing reality. "I want you to know…I overheard you and your father talking about me in his office. You shouldn't feel obligated to stay with me, seeing how your family thinks of me. Especially since what happened here. I want to be with you. If I'm honest, I want it more than anything in the world. But I'm messed up. My family is messed up. None of which is your problem. So really, I understand if you decide otherwise." She gently takes hold of his hand, but does not look into his eyes.

No response from Brad. As time silently goes by, she believes he is weighing the options in his head, the pros and cons. Then she glances back at him. The look in his eyes does not go unnoticed. He is staring at her back. A faint breeze brushing bare skin reveals that the pentagram tattoo is now visible through the hole in her shirt.

Without saying a word, he stands, pulling his hand from hers, and somberly walks out the door.

Exhaustion finally overtaking her, Erin slumps over onto the couch and falls asleep.

Tap-Tap-Tap.

Knocking on the front door awakens Erin from a deep slumber. Lifting her head, she wipes some drool from the corner of her mouth, having no idea how much time has passed.

TAP-TAP-TAP.

More, louder rapping motivates the groggy girl to finally get up and crack open the door. Standing on her porch is the youth pastor, framed by the darkness of night.

"Hi, I'm Mike from the church."

Little does she know that he is here to deliver a heart-crushing, life-altering message.

"I remember you."

"May I come in?"

"Sure. Why not." Erin turns, leaving the door still barely open.

Mike enters and softly closes the door behind him.

"I'd offer you a drink of some holy water, but we're all out at the moment."

"That's pretty funny. I heard you have a sharp wit. How are you all doing?"

"As well as can be expected, I guess. What brings you here?"

"First, to offer any help you may need."

"Well, you're about a year late on that offer, Padre."

"I want you to know, Erin, that several of us at the church reached out to your mother back then, but she spurned every attempt. I truly am sorry for all you've been through."

Rose is awake, staring at the back of the sofa, pretending to still be asleep. Queenie sits atop the stairs listening, lightly scratching a red rash that encircles the needle prick in her arm.

"Well, we don't need any help. So you can leave now."

"I still wanted to have a talk with you, if that's okay."

"About?"

"God."

"So, you've come to save the poor soul of the wicked witch of the Midwest, have you? Or am I to be burned at the stake?"

"I'm not here to judge you, Erin."

"Funny, everyone else sure seems to be."

"Let me ask—do you think you will make it to heaven some day?"

"Sorry to burst your bubble, but I don't think I believe in heaven."

"But *if* there is one, do you think you will go there?"

"I don't know. I suppose. Don't see why not."

"So, you consider yourself to be a good person?"

"I'm thinking you don't?"

"I'm asking you what *you* think."

"Yes, I'm basically a good person. Especially compared to many people out there. Sure."

"Let me ask you this, do you think you deserve to go to hell?"

"Why, because I've been a Wiccan before? Participated in pagan rituals?"

"Let's put that on the back burner for now, not consider any of that at all, pretend it never happened. Without that, do you think you have lived such a life that God would send you to hell?"

"To burn a fiery torment forever? Absolutely not."

"Can I ask you a few questions to see if that's true? To see if you're a good person?"

"Okay, I guess."

"How many lies do you think you've told in your life?"

"How many lies? I don't know; too many to count, I guess."

"What does that make you?"

"A sinner."

"No, more specifically."

"You mean, a liar?"

"Yes. How many things do you think you've stolen in your life, if any?"

Erin's mind quickly recalls all of the overpriced cheaply-made imported junk she swiped from Madame Zelda's store.

"My fair share."

"What does that make you?"

"A thief."

"I appreciate your honesty. Last one. Have you ever taken the Lord's name in vain?"

"Yes. Habitually. Well, until the last year or so."

"So Erin, by your own admission, you are a liar, a thief, and a blasphemer."

"Hey, I thought you said you weren't here to judge me. You're just another religious hypocrite who thinks he's perfect."

"I'm not judging you, I'm showing you God's standards. I've

broken those commandments too. I'm just asking you to judge yourself in the light of God's law. You admitted those things out of your own mouth."

"Well you're sure not doing much for my self-esteem. Isn't that your job?"

"No. My job, as is any Christian's, is to share the truth in love. I'm no better than you, just better off. I'm trying to help you see who you are in light of who God is. You see, I took you through just three of God's Ten Commandments. These commandments are his laws. So when we sin, we are breaking God's laws. Does that make sense?"

"Well, I guess. But I've never done anything terrible, like kill anyone—or any other living creature, for that matter."

"Have you ever hated anyone?"

"I can think of several." Lucus. Her mother. Emily. And possibly the man who sits across from her at this very moment.

"Scripture says that anyone who hates is a murderer in their heart, which is breaking the sixth commandment. All sin is, as you put it, 'terrible' to a just and holy God. That's how high His standards are."

"I…I still don't—"

"If you just average three sins a day, that's about one thousand a year. At your age that means you have already committed seventeen thousand crimes against almighty God in your short life." Mike can see she is still not fully convinced, so he shares another thought. "What if we could record all of your thoughts for a week, then play them on a movie screen for all to see? Would you be okay with that, or would it make you cringe?"

"I don't think that would be such a good idea."

"You see, what I'm doing is holding up the mirror of God's law so you can see yourself for who you truly are, how God, who is holy, sees you."

Erin looks at her hands, like in the bathroom with the old man—all of the pieces begin to fall into place. She is not a good person. She has been lying to herself. Living a lie. She has been the lie.

Mike asks, "So, would you be innocent or guilty on the day of judgment?"

"It sounds like guilty, with a whole long list of other offenses,

I'm sure."

"So if you're guilty before God, would you go to heaven or hell?"

"Sometimes I think I'm already suffering the horror of hell, if you want to know the truth."

"I know you've had a rough life and been through some major ordeals. But do you know what Jesus taught about hell?"

"Eternal separation from God, I think. Honestly doesn't sound all that bad."

"Well, it's more than that. Scripture describes it as a lake of fire where the torment never ceases. It is the place where God's righteousness meets His justice. Nobody there will be able to shake their fist at God and say they are not getting exactly what they deserve, because crimes against an infinite, eternal authority deserve an infinite, eternal punishment. I promise you, anything you've experienced here in this life will be nothing compared to that. The real horror, Erin, is that people think they're good enough to go to heaven when they're not."

"So you're saying I'm headed for hell?"

"I'm not. Listen to your conscience and Scripture. It says all liars will have their part in the lake of fire, and that no thief or murderer will enter the kingdom of heaven."

For once, Erin's quick wit has been stopped. Her mouth silenced. She sits and stares at the floor while Mike prays silently. Outside, a group of about a dozen or so secretly gather in the front yard, forming a circle and holding hands to summon their deity to possess Erin. Mike checks his vibrating phone, reading a text. Placing it back, he asks her two vitally important questions.

"Does any of that make sense to you? Does it concern you?"

With one word she answers both, "Yes."

Mike says authoritatively yet tenderly, "Erin, I want you to look at me."

She raises her head.

"You need to know that God loves you. The Bible says He is not willing that any should perish. But because He is a good and just judge, He cannot just let guilty sinners, lawbreakers, walk free without their crimes being punished."

"So you're saying it's hopeless."

"No, there's good news. Amazing news. Two thousand years ago, God became a man in Jesus Christ and walked on this earth, under that Law that you and I have broken so often. He never once broke God's commandments—was perfectly sinless. Later He suffered and died on the cross, then arose three days later. You broke God's laws, but Jesus paid your fine in His life's blood. And if you'll repent, turn from your sin once and for all, and place your faith in Him and his work, surrendering your whole life to Him, He will forgive your sins and grant you the gift of eternal life."

"He did that for me?" A tear drops from her cheek. The window shades glow with light from the morning sun rising just above the treetops—darkness falling.

"Yes, and for me too. When I was in college, alone in my dorm room after hearing this message, I got on my knees, then repented of my sins and placed my faith in Jesus and He saved me. He gave me a new heart with new desires. I began to love what God loves and hate what He hates. It was an internal change that had nothing to do with me but rather an indwelling of the Holy Spirit. Jesus called it being born again. And He wants to do the same for you. Erin, are you ready for God to change you?"

Mike stops there to give some time for all of this to soak in. He waits patiently while she sits silently pondering the message within the quietness of her heart. Prompted by the Holy Spirit, Mike makes his final plea.

"Erin, I want you to know that scripture says instead of crushing you for your sins against Him, God is the good father who laid down his life for you. And that He will also be a father to the fatherless. If you will let Him in, He will be the kind, wise, loving daddy you need and long for."

She breaks down, face in her hands, crying. "I'm sorry," she muffles out.

"It's okay, I understand. I've been where you are now."

Erin gathers herself and wipes the tears with her sleeve. "You know, over the last year I think I see now how God has been reaching out to me—through circumstances both good and bad. Brad has been a big part of that, but now he's..."

"He's what?"

"He's—" She can't bring herself to say it.

Then Mike makes an unexpected statement. "I think you need to take a look outside."

"Outside?"

He just nods his head and motions toward the front entrance.

Erin gets up, walks over to the door, and opens it. The morning light floods her eyes, and after they readjust she sees a group of people standing in a circle out in her yard holding hands with heads bowed. Some she does not know, but others she recognizes instantly. Brad's parents with Granna. And even Sheriff Knox! No Big John, though. And in the center of them, humbly on his knees in fervent prayer, is Brad.

"He came to me and insisted we do this, that I talk to you. Said this situation was far above his ability to handle alone." Mike says from the den. "He cares for you more than you know."

"Brad!" Erin screams.

The group unlocks hands and turns to face her. She jumps off the porch and races toward him at full speed.

"Erin!"

As she approaches, the group spreads apart to make room for her while Brad comes to his feet. Erin leaps into his waiting arms and they twirl, her feet swinging above the ground.

"I love you, Erin. I don't care what you've done or whatever anyone else thinks. I love you."

"Thank you for loving me. I love you too. Thank you, God. Thank you."

Some worlds should never come into contact. But theirs are colliding—polar forces converging, meshing, head-on in a steady, irreversible impact with life-altering consequences. Up until one year after the tragic death of her sister and daddy, Erin and Jesus were two lives co-existing yet never connecting—like parallel universes running side by side with one having no clue as to the other's existence. Until now.

Then a sound, a familiar sound. Everyone's attention is drawn to the neighboring field. There is the one that escaped the clutches of death. It stands there calling out in its own voice. It is revived, healthy, and strong. It is a miracle. It is the lamb.

The End

CPSIA information can be obtained at www.ICGtesting.com
Printed in the USA
LVOW10s1053130914

403935LV00001B/9/P